THE FIRES OF BELTANE

"Ah, Scahta, but I want you to love me," Anlon said softly. Slowly, gently, he moved to hold her again, bending down so that his lips brushed her eyes and cheeks as he spoke. "You have had my love for so very long. Come to me and let us love each other . . . tonight, on Beltane Eve."

Once more, she started to melt against him—but then braced hard and shoved him away. She looked up into his eyes, spoke: "There is something you must understand, if ever you are to return to Caher Idir."

He took hold of her wrist. She made no move to break away. Instead, she threw her head back to look up at him. "No man touches me unless he is my husband," she said, with some difficulty. "And I have never had a husband."

"Never . . . " He whispered the word and allowed her wrist to fall away.

They stared at each other in the moonlight, both breathing deep of the night air, the tension between them threatening to snap. Finally, Anlon looked away, and Scahta too lowered her gaze.

"Let me walk with you back to Caher Idir, Queen Scahta," he said. "I will see you safely home. But be warned—I do not give up so easily. I will find a way to make you want to be with me, and only with me. I will find a way to make you want me for your king—and for your lover—and for your husband."

JANEEN O'KERRY

SISTER OF THE MOON

LOVE SPELL   NEW YORK CITY

. . . for all those who live between the worlds.

A LOVE SPELL BOOK®

December 2001

Published by

Dorchester Publishing Co., Inc.
276 Fifth Avenue
New York, NY 10001

ISBN 0-505-52466-X

The name "Love Spell" and its logo are trademarks of Dorchester Publishing Co., Inc.

Printed in the United States of America.

Visit us on the web at www.dorchesterpub.com.

Sister of the Moon

PRONUNCIATION GUIDE

Caher Idir—*KYE-er ee-DEER*

Cian—*KEE-an*

Fehin—*FAY-in*

Fianna—*fee-AH-na*

Geal—*gyall*

Greine—*GRAYN-ya*

Liath—*LEE-ath*

Mactire—*mac-TEER*

Maidin—*my-DEEN*

Samhain—*SOW-ehn*

Sidhe—*shee*

Chapter One

It was the end of autumn, just a few days before the Samhain fires would be lit. Into the bare and quiet forest came a shouting and a jangling and a pounding of hoofbeats as the men of the Fianna rode home through the golden afternoon.

They had spent the summer riding and hunting and training to be warriors in the service of their king, their youthful energies safely directed away from the confines of Dun Mor. But now the winter was fast approaching, and it was time for them to return to their fortress home.

They did not know they were being watched. Scahta had hidden herself too well.

Of the twenty-seven, each was young and strong and fair. Each wore fine clothes and heavy gold and carried a painted wooden shield and a cold iron sword. Each was no less than a king in his own mind—except for the very last of them, the one who struggled to keep up on an aged grey pony, further slowed by the two plodding pack animals he led.

That man, bringing up the rear like a servant, was plainly different from the others. He rode upon a tattered fleece instead of a saddle. His clothes were of coarse undyed wool and worn, stained linen. His dark and ragged cloak was held at his shoulder by his only fine possession, a bronze pin beautifully made in the shape of a curving willow leaf. All the other men had their colorful, rectangular cloaks pinned with heavy circular brooches of shining gold. Strangest of all, he had no sword; his only weapons were a sling, a dagger made of bone, and a stout blackthorn club.

He was rough and unfinished compared to the rest. He could only be a man from a poor background, the son of a common farmer—or worse. Except for his young and handsome face, there was no outward sign of nobility about him. Why did the proud Fianna allow this shaggy commoner among them? They did not normally take servants, tolerating nothing that might slow them down.

At the clearing, just up the hill from a lovely small lake, the men turned off the road. They dismounted, unsaddled their horses, rubbed the animals' backs briefly with rough woolen rags, and hobbled them so they could graze and make their way down to the lake to drink. As the horses moved off, the men began shouting.

"Anlon! Anlon! Get those fires going! Where is the food? We are starving, ravenous! And we will need some shelter; it will surely rain tonight! Hurry, now, Anlon! Hurry! How long do you expect the men of the Fianna to wait for you?"

The rough young man called Anlon threw his leg over the grey mare's neck and leaped to the ground. There were stacks of armor, saddles, and clothes scattered everywhere across the grass, and he quickly added his own horse's fleece and the pack animals' burdens to the lot. The others pulled off their clothes and armor and walked casually down to the lake for a refreshing swim, but Anlon's work had just begun.

Using a small axe of cold iron, he cut the sod from a spot near the center of the clearing and ringed it with a few flat stones from the water's edge. Catching up wood and kindling from the bare autumn forest, he soon had a fire started in the pit within the stones, and alternated skinning the wild pig the men had taken in that morning's hunt with hauling up lake water in the bronze cauldron and preparing dough for flatbread.

The rest of the men, having finished their bathing, threw on breeches and cloaks and began combing the clearing, the lake shore, and the entire surrounding woods for clover, watercress, wild onions, mushrooms, hazelnuts, and blackberries. They worked busily and thoroughly, like some sort of insects, going back and forth and cleaning out every bit of edible material their surroundings had to offer. Soon there were great heaps of fresh food in the grass at Anlon's feet. A few men managed to spear some trout in the lake and tossed them flapping beside the firepit.

At last, as the sun began to approach the horizon, Anlon put away his bone dagger and sat back for a moment to catch his breath. The pig was sprinkled with salt and roasting on the spit; the cauldron sat in the glowing coals at one side of the fire, filled with simmering sweetbreads and mushrooms and greens; the cleaned fish were wrapped in leather, pinned closed with a fire-sharpened twig, and buried beneath the hot coals; and the flat oat-bread sat baking on flat stones beside the fire.

He did not have long to survey the bounty. The rest

11

of the men, now clean and dressed, pulled their gold plates from their packs and made short work of Anlon's labors. They grabbed the bread, pulled the fish from the coals with their bare hands, hacked off the outer layers of cooked pig with their cold iron daggers, and stabbed out bits from the cauldron. Using long sticks, they twirled up the greens and threw them on their plates, too.

"Anlon, you will make an excellent wife for a good man someday!" called out one of the men, and all the others laughed.

Anlon barely glanced at him. "Will I still be able to ride with the Fianna?" he asked, turning the half-raw meat on the spit.

"Why should you? You'll be of much greater use hearthside in some *man's* house!"

Anlon remained crouching beside the fire. He made a small move for something at his belt—and, in an instant, the man who had insulted him jerked back as a flying stone glanced off the center of his plate and splashed grease and greens all over his face.

The rest turned and laughed uproariously at the splattered warrior. Anlon slowly got to his feet and tucked his sling back into his belt. "No insult intended," he said pleasantly, "and I am honored to serve all the men of the Fianna—so long as it is plain that I do so by choice because I want to earn my place as one of you."

"And so you will," laughed another of the men, as his companion wiped the last of the greasy watercress from his face. "Should you learn to use a sword as well as you can use that sling, your place is assured!"

With that, Anlon went back to turning the meat, a small smile of satisfaction on his face. The men went back to eating, hacking off chunks of pig as soon they were cooked, exposing the pink raw meat as they did. One of them even tossed a nicely cooked bit to Anlon.

With the others so occupied, Anlon snatched up one of the last pieces of the bread and wrapped it around his bit of meat, eating it quickly while he worked to put up a lean-to. Again using his small iron axe, he cut down a few saplings, propped them against some large trees at the edge of the forest, and covered them with a pair of rolled-up hides.

It would make a passable shelter, at least enough to keep the rain off. While the others sopped up the last of the meat juices with their bread, he carried all their belongings into the shelter—saddles, packs, food, shields, everything.

As the shadows lengthened, Anlon returned to the smoldering campfire and served himself the last of the scraps. He found one piece of oatbread, half-covered with ashes from where it had fallen into the fire pit. Brushing it off as well as he could, he used it to clean out the last of the greens and meat from the cauldron. All that remained of the pig on the spit was the head. A couple of leg bones, stripped clean, lay where they had fallen on the coals.

He sat on the ground where the blackberries and hazelnuts had been heaped and ran his fingers through the grass, but not one nut or berry was left. With a sigh, he began to eat what he had.

The other men gathered together with their gold cups and their leather skins of beer. "It's good that we'll be back at Dun Mor by tomorrow!" one of them called out. "This is the last of the ale!"

"There'll be plenty at Dun Mor, and the whole of the winter to enjoy it," answered another.

"That's not all I plan to enjoy!" shouted a third, and

the rest laughed, immediately adding their own bragging and boasting until the forest was filled with noise.

His meal finished, Anlon got up in the glowing golden twilight and began the cleanup. Soon—for he had clearly done this many times before—the spit was cleaned, the fire built up, the scraps tossed in the flames, and the cauldron rinsed in the lake and left upside down in the grass to dry.

His companions fed, the horses grazing, the packs safely sheltered, the camp clean, and the fire burning, Anlon's fatigue at last began to show. He pulled off his worn leather boots and started slowly toward the edge of the lake. As he walked, he unfastened the bronze leaf pin from his cloak and allowed the ragged shreds of dark brown wool to fall to the grass. A few steps later he wrestled off his old linen tunic and stripped away his rough woolen breeches. He waded into the cold clear water and dove beneath the surface just as the sun disappeared.

Now began the most magical time of the day. Now began the time when it was truly neither day nor night. It was not day, for the sun was gone from the sky; yet neither was it night, for light remained.

Now was the time for Scahta to show herself, to make her presence known to the man she'd chosen.

From the edge of the forest where she had watched the party of men, she moved through the trees to the place where their roots met the lake. Again she turned toward the campsite, where the Fianna talked and drank and laughed, where the fire leaped and crackled. The flames, she knew, would reflect off the pair of polished bronze sun-disc pins that held her white wool cloak at her shoulder.

For a time, the object of her attention merely swam in the cool lake's water and breathed deep of the sweet evening air, no doubt quite happy for a chance to relax and refresh himself; he had spent endless hours working in the service of the others.

Scahta took another step toward the shore, turning slightly. She spoke his name, so quietly that even she could not hear it, allowing only the wind to catch her words and carry them out to where he swam.

Anlon.

He stopped. Something had clearly caught his attention. He looked quickly around, then gazed straight into the forest, straight at her.

She moved forward, toward him, knowing that he would see little more than the gleam of her bronze pins. "Hello, Anlon," she called, louder this time, moving a little closer so he could glimpse her shadowed outline against the trees.

His hazel eyes were large and searching. "Hello, beautiful lady," he answered. His voice was gentle but nonetheless taut with excitement.

"You do not fear me?" she asked.

"I do not." His strong arms moved beneath the water, keeping his place before her against the current of the lake. "You are a woman of the Sidhe."

"So you know of the Sidhe-folk."

"I do. They are the ancient people, the ones who live in the hills and the caves and the deep forests—the ones who lived here long before the coming of Men." He smiled and raised his palms out of the water. "I regret that I have nothing to offer you. When I return to the camp, though, I will share what I have with you by leaving it at the edge of the forest."

"The other men share nothing with the Sidhe, Anlon. Why should you?"

He allowed himself to drift a bit closer. "I am no nobleman's son," he said. "My father was a herdsman. I grew up in the thick of the forest and on the heights of the hills. I learned as a boy that the Sidhe wanted only to share a bit of our food from time to time. And that they, too, can be generous."

"Generous?"

"Once, when I placed milk and bread beneath the trees for them, they left me a beautiful bronze pin—a leaf-shaped pin made in the old way. It is the only fine thing I own."

"I am not so sure that it is the only thing." Scahta smiled down at him. "Come to me."

He hesitated, so again she used the wind-voice. *Come to me . . .*

He swam to the rocky shoreline and climbed out of the lake, walking slowly to Scahta until he was almost close enough to touch her. Instead of rough clothes and grime, he was garbed in nothing but night wind and twilight.

Now there was naught to set him apart from the other men, nothing to say whether he was noble or servant or king. He was not ashamed, not uncomfortable before her; he did not even seem to feel the cold evening air on his wet skin. There was a gentleness about him, an innocence, something she had never seen in any Man. It was the first thing that had brought her to him.

The second she had noted was his great height. The top of her head would just come to his shoulder. His body was hard and muscled from heavy work and training, yet long-limbed and graceful at the same time. There was more than a little of that almost supernatural grace which was usually seen only in her own people. His face, smooth and clean-shaven, had fine young features with deep hazel eyes and dark shining hair.

"The other men work you like an animal," Scahta remarked. "Why do you allow it?"

His lips twitched in good humor, and she noted the fullness of his tender, curving mouth. "One who is not born to the ranks of the Fianna must work his way into them. It is rare that a chance is even given." He shook his head. "A herdsman's life can be a good one, but I cannot help but believe that I am meant for something more. And I want very much to find it."

"Perhaps you are meant for something more . . . something *much* more." She walked around him, still in the deep shadows of the trees, studying the long lines of him and gazing calmly at his fair skin glistening in the light of the half-moon. "You say you are a herdsman's son. It is not often that any herdsman is possessed of such beauty."

He smiled again, almost shyly—yet she could see the pride and strength shining in his eyes. "I know little of my father's family. I know only the story his mother tells, that he was sired by a man of 'exceptional beauty' who came to her at the Beltane fires."

Scahta smiled, nodding gently. He had confirmed her belief. "So, Anlon, your father was a child of the spring rites. Do you not know that he, and therefore you, must both be sons of the Sidhe?"

"I always believed it might be true. I know the Sidhe do sometimes approach the Beltane fires, to find mates just as we—just as Men do on that night."

"That they do. Our women seek strong children, strong enough to survive in the world of Men. The men of the Sidhe have no wish to see their blood vanished from the world, and know that the women of your people often find them quite beautiful." As she spoke, Scahta gazed at him, stirred by thoughts of the spring mating ritual around the flaring bonfires, drawn by the human's strange beauty—as she knew he was to hers.

"*Anlon!*" came a distant shout, drifting across the water on the breeze. "Anlon, the fire is dying down! *Anlon!*"

His eyes flicked toward the sound, then back to her. "I must go now," he admitted. "But, as I said, I will leave a gift for you at the edge of the forest."

"That is kind of you," she answered. A thousand images flashed through her mind. "Perhaps I will leave a gift for you as well."

He started to raise one hand, as though to reach for her, but she cut him off. "Go now, Anlon," she said. "Go."

He paused and smiled, then walked back into the water. Without another glance, he was soon swimming quickly back to his camp.

Scahta watched as he cut smoothly through the dark water, and she smiled to herself. He was exactly what she was looking for.

Chapter Two

The stars were appearing as Scahta headed back into the forest. After walking a little way down the moss-lined path into the thickest part of the wood, she paused. Coming toward her, catching the moonlight filtering through the bare branches of the trees, were a pair of shining yellow eyes.

Scahta crouched and held out her hand. In a moment, an enormous grey wolf had trotted up and pressed its head against her hand.

"Hello, Wolf," she said, stroking its thick coat. "Have you brought the others to me?"

"He has, Queen Scahta," said a male voice close by. Moving out of the shadows was the graceful form of another of the Sidhe—and then another and another, until five figures surrounded her in the darkness, sitting on moss-covered rocks and logs and standing beside the trees.

Like her, they wore rectangular cloaks of the lightest, most delicate wool, though Scahta's cloak was white and all the others were dyed in soft colors. The precious wool had been combed from the shrub trees where Men's herds of sheep passed by or collected from those rare animals that could be taken by the hunters of her people.

Beneath the cloaks, the Sidhe men wore leather tunics and breeches; the women, long deerskin gowns edged with fur from wild animals caught in traps. Soft leather boots allowed them all to move silently in the forests.

Yet the Sidhe-folk fairly sparkled like stars in the airy darkness, for all wore bracelets and cloak pins and neck pieces of gleaming gold and shining bronze and beautifully polished stone. The last of the damp and colorful leaves of autumn clung here and there to their soft wool cloaks and dark flowing hair.

Scahta, too, was dressed as they were, though there were some things that set her apart. She was nearly half a head taller than the rest, even the men. Her skin was a touch fairer, her long hair a lighter golden brown. Yet there was no mistaking her for anything but one of the Sidhe.

"We waited for you, as you asked."

"We saw you speaking to the man who walked out of the water."

"Will you tell us why he has your interest?"

"Did he offer you a gift?"

"Did you try to frighten him, to keep the rest of them from our home?"

Scahta laughed and raised one hand. "Patience, patience. I came here only to observe."

"And to talk," said Cian, the first who had spoken.

"Always to talk, when talking is worthwhile." She

moved toward Cian until she stood very near to him, beckoned the others to draw closer.

"Tell me, Cian," she began, as they gathered around, "how many children have been born to our people since last the leaves fell?"

Cian gazed at her and then looked away. "Only one. And she is weak; she hardly grows at all. . . ."

"She may not live even long enough to walk," Scahta agreed. She looked steadily at all the others, then folded her hands together in front of her. "Two children were born the year before," she said. "How do they fare?"

"Quite well, my lady," answered Ean, one of the women. "They are a wonder, those two."

"And what is different about those children?"

There was a silence touched only by the wind stirring high in the shadowy branches of the trees. Ean finally spoke: "All of us know what is different about them. They are children of the Beltane fires."

"As am I." Scahta reached down to stroke the wolf's back. "Our mothers are of the Sidhe, and our fathers were Men—Men whom our mothers sought during the rites of Beltane."

"Bah. Since the invading men came to our lands, both Sidhe children and parents fall ill far more often than they ever have before," spat Liath, another of the men. "Many of them will die. The invaders sometimes suffer illness the same way, but they recover. It is only the Sidhe who die."

"We have long known that those children of both Sidhe and Men are the strongest," argued the second woman, Geal. "They have survived the best."

"As I do." Scahta looked among them and smiled gently. "As I said, I too am a child of both Man and Sidhe—a child of Beltane."

"So you are, my lady." Cian paused and threw his green-and-white cloak back over one shoulder. "Are you telling us, then, that you too will go to the Beltane fires when next they are lit?"

She looked away and began to pace slowly over the soft wet leaves of the forest floor. "Any of our folk who wish to go to the fires would do well to do so. The more strength we can give to our children, the longer our people will survive." She stopped and looked at Cian. "Yet, I know that there is another way. A better way."

Ean's eyes widened. "Do you speak of taking the infant children of Men for our own?"

"It has been done in the past," agreed the third man, Mactire. "A Sidhe child with no chance to live is exchanged for a child of Men."

"It seems no more than they deserve. It is they who bring the illnesses that destroy us—"

"It is they who steal our cattle and our sheep and our horses—"

"It is they who strip the forests bare of the wild harvest—"

"It is they who destroy our homes whenever they find them—"

"It is they who kill the Sidhe with cold iron swords—"

Scahta stopped the commotion with a wave of her hand. "I know the custom of the changeling. But I am not one who will follow it." She gave Mactire a sharp glance. "There are *other* ways to bring strong children into the Sidhe."

"And will you tell us how this led you to the campsite of Men?" Cian asked. He looked uncomfortable.

She spared a brief moment of sadness for him. He had been a good friend for a long time, and she knew he wanted more. "I will tell you," she said at last. She folded her hands again. "I wish to take a husband. A husband from among the Men."

Her people stared at her, and then immediately turned to one another.

"The Men!"

"How can this be?"

"One of the Men here?"

"Men wish only to destroy us!"

"A Man, as our king!"

"Scahta—you know that I speak to you as your servant and as one who loves you," said Cian, moving closer. "It is one thing for our mothers to go to the Beltane fires and come away with children who carry the blood of both Sidhe and Man, children who will grow up only amongst us and know only our ways. But to bring one of those men here—as your husband . . . You would want us to accept him as our king!"

"My mother was not a queen," replied Scahta. "It was enough for her to bring strong children back from the fires. I have different burdens to carry, and I require more than just a handsome child.

"I need a king—a strong warrior who will help me to protect the people of the Sidhe and help us not only to survive, but to grow. And the greatest strength I know is to be found among the kingdoms of Men."

Cian raised his chin and stood tall so that his height nearly equaled hers. "There is strength among the Sidhe as well, Queen Scahta. I would ask that you do not overlook it."

She met his gaze. "Never have I overlooked it. It is all around me, just as all of you are."

"Then this is a strange and frightening choice you make."

"How could our people wish for a Man to rule over us?" another of the Sidhe joined in.

"What Man could turn his back on his own world and come here to serve us?" a third asked.

Cian nodded as the others spoke, then inquired: "What measure of loyalty could ever be expected from such a one? What Man would accept such an offer, save as a better way to destroy us?"

Scahta listened carefully. "I agree that most of those men would laugh at the thought of serving the Sidhe. They would have no loyalty to our clan. They barely have loyalty to their own."

She took a few steps into the moonlit forest, then turned to face her people again. "Yet I will ask you this: Around your neck, Cian, you wear a stone of great beauty. It shines; it gleams; it is like a star upon your chest. You were fortunate indeed to wake up one fine morning and find it hanging there."

He smiled. "I did not 'find it there,' my lady. I spent many days searching it out, discarding all the others, before bringing this one home and spending many nights polishing it to bring out its beauty."

Scahta gazed at him pointedly. "A king is no different. A king is rare, whether Man or Sidhe, and that is as it should be: a rare thing to be carefully sought and even more carefully—and harshly—tested."

"Tested." Mactire jumped down from the rock where he had been standing. "And how shall such a man be tested?"

"For one year, he shall live as a servant among us— and he shall be subjected to every test of character I can set for him. His choice will be clear."

"I can think of a way to make it clearer, my queen," said Cian.

Scahta merely raised her head and waited.

"Allow one Man and one Sidhe to take your tests. Allow each to test the other."

She considered. "Would you be one who is tested, Cian?"

"I will serve my queen and my people in whatever way I can, be it as a slave or as a king."

"Perhaps you wish only to be a king. Perhaps you believe that now you have found a way, by standing against the idea of a Man as our king." She waited for his response.

"I will tell you this, my queen: I would be happy to see any other man of the Sidhe stand beside you as our king, if it means that no man of the invaders will cast his shadow over us."

Scahta gazed at him and saw the intensity in his eyes. She had expected this. Did part of her welcome his pursuit? She was not certain. "No one could be stronger or more loyal than you, Cian. And I do not doubt there are others among us who feel as you do.

"This is what I will do: If I find a Man to test, I shall test you right alongside him."

The Sidhe warrior began to smile, but she held up a hand. "Do not misunderstand me, Cian. Let *no one* misunderstand me. I do what must be done. It is not for me to simply do as I wish. You and I will always come second. The people of the Sidhe come first."

As it always did, the first grey light of dawn brought Anlon out of a peaceful sleep and back into the real world of work. Quickly, silently, he rolled out of his ragged cloak, damp with mist from the lake, and got to his feet.

Like he did every morning, Anlon immediately set about building up the campfire and preparing oatbread.

As it baked, a few of the men snoring around him began to stir beneath their heavy wool cloaks, roused by the brightening sun and by the smell of wood smoke and cooking bread.

Yet one thing was different about this particular morning. As Anlon began packing up, his excitement grew. Today was the last day he would spend with the Fianna— at least until next summer. They would all pass the winter at Dun Mor, the king's great fortress, serving as guardians for the people and enjoying the very best hospitality as befit the warriors of their sovereign.

Though he knew he would miss the freedom and adventure of riding out with these men each day, he did not regret leaving behind the enormous amounts of work he was forced to do. He could only hope when next they rode out, his status would have been raised enough that he was no longer made to do the worst of the party's labor.

But well before that, there would be several months spent at the fortress. Anlon was himself a child of fields and flocks; though he had seen the great *dun* from a distance, he had never set foot inside it. All his life he had wondered about that place with all its warriors and druids and nobles, to say nothing of its king. He could only imagine the excitement and adventures that awaited him there. . . .

"Anlon!"

As it always was, his pleasant daydream was shattered by a shout from one of the men gathered around the campfire. "Anlon! Where is the honey for the bread? Where is the honey?"

For a moment he froze. The honey. Had he forgotten something? There was a faint memory, misty and half-remembered, of a mysterious encounter the night before:

He had gone out swimming in the lake ... there had been a woman ... a strange and beautiful woman ... a woman of the Sidhe.

Quickly he got up and ran to the edge of the forest. There, propped neatly against a tree trunk, was the leather bag that had held their supply of honey.

It was empty.

He picked up the sack, folded it over, and walked back to the fire. "I am sorry, Fehin. There is no more left."

"No more honey? But yesterday there was enough for at least one more meal! Did you get hungry last night, Anlon?"

"I did not. I gave the honey as a gift."

"A gift?" Fehin paused. "And just who would you be giving gifts to out in the forest late at night? A woman, perhaps, looking for a man like you?" The large warrior laughed.

"It was a woman, as you say. A woman of the Sidhe."

"The Sidhe!" His companions looked at each other. "A woman of the Sidhe came to you last night?"

"She did."

"What did she want?"

"She wanted ... she wanted ..." Why was it so difficult for him to remember? He could hardly recall anything that had happened. "She wanted me to leave her a gift."

Anlon was sure the rest of the warriors would laugh heartily at him, make a stream of crude jokes, and go off to catch their horses. But they stayed where they were, silent and frowning, glancing at one another.

"The Sidhe will not be tolerated around Dun Mor, I can tell you that," said Donn.

Anlon stared at him. "Not tolerated? Why not? They would come near my father's home from time to time.

They only wanted a bit of food to share. Never have I known them to do any harm."

"No harm, you say." Fehin glared at him, his heavy brows drawing together. "They steal milk from the cows in the dark of night. They take horses and cattle and sheep if they get half a chance. They ravage our stores of grain and fruit. And worst of all, they leave their hideous children in our houses and take our healthy infants in their place!"

A chill ran up Anlon's spine. "I have never known them to do any harm," he repeated.

Fehin caught up a pebble and flung it hard into the forest. "You are a boy of the herds and hills," he snapped. "The king's men are the ones who must defend the riches of the *dun* against the predations of the Sidhe. Do not tempt them here again."

They were getting close to Dun Mor. Though Anlon could not yet see the walls of the fortress, the sight of open land, cleared and plowed and separated into small fields by low stone walls, told him they were very near a large settlement. Even old Nealta managed to trot a little faster, seeming to sense that she was nearing the end of her long journey.

He could see men and women combing through the crushed and broken stalks in the fields to get every grain they could find. Children moved in and out of the forest at the edges of the fields, carrying small sacks of berries and apples and nuts—the last bits of food that could be stripped from the woods.

"They've done a good job of the harvest," said Fehin. "There's not a single grain of wheat in the fields or a blackberry left in the woods."

"Neither frost nor Sidhe will get any of Dun Mor's

harvest," crowed a second man. "It's all safely brought in for us!"

"Food is not all that waits for us at Dun Mor," called another, and the others immediately joined in the raucous shouting and boasting.

"I've got my own harvesting to do, and it's not out in the fields!"

"I hope the winter is a long one!"

"I'll need all the summer to rest!"

Anlon smiled, but kept his silence. Finally Donn turned to him and said, "Anlon! You've said nothing so far. Have you no plans for how you will spend the winter?"

"He'll spend it with his strong right arm!" shouted another man, and the rest of them laughed uproariously. "Who else would have him?"

Anlon merely gazed out over the fields. He knew there was no malice behind his companions' words, that they were just enjoying yet another joke at his expense. They all teased and insulted each other in the same way, and he had learned long ago that it was usually best to simply let the insults run their course.

They rode on, and as he had expected the conversation quickly turned back to the women of Dun Mor. The riders started around a bend in the road—one that took them close beside the forest again—when suddenly they halted in their tracks.

Anlon tried to see what had happened, but the lead riders were beyond the bend and out of sight. "What is it?" he called, but the others would not answer. They only glanced over their shoulders at him and murmured among themselves.

Finally he dropped the lead lines of the pack ponies

and guided Nealta past the others, around the bend in the road.

There, some distance away, suspended by a braided leather cord from the bare and crooked branches of a blackthorn tree, was a weapon—a sword like none that Anlon had ever seen.

He was well accustomed to the long, straight iron blades the men of the Fianna all carried, even though he did not own one himself. But this sword was made of softly shining bronze, narrower near the smooth bone hilt and widening slightly until it tapered to a sharply pointed tip like a beautiful metal leaf.

Anlon slid down to stand beside his horse. He gazed up at the bronze weapon, admiring the soft gleam as it turned slightly in the wind. Then he became aware that all the rest of the men were staring at him.

"It is a weapon of the Sidhe," growled Fehin. "Do not think of touching it." He drew his own sword, one made of iron, rode up to the hanging weapon, and slashed through the leather cord that held it.

The bronze blade dropped to the muddy forest floor. Fehin wheeled his horse around and started off at a gallop down the road. "Come on! Come on! Will you stay here and stare at some child's toy all day long? Dun Mor is waiting! Come along!"

The rest of them followed, all thoughts of the bronze sword forgotten.

Anlon watched them go, catching hold of the ropes of the pack ponies as the two beasts trotted past. When the galloping hoofbeats of his compatriots died away, he left the animals, reached down into the mud, and slowly, carefully, lifted the shining sword from where it had fallen.

A silence descended as he raised the weapon into the

air. The cool wind touched his face and caressed the shiny bronze blade, and it seemed that just below the level of his hearing the wind on the sword whispered to him, calling his name.

"Anlon . . ."

He could not have moved if he had wished to.

"Anlon . . ."

The sound was clearer now.

"Anlon . . ."

He looked up and over toward the forest. There was a slight movement deep within the underbrush—a soft gleam once, then again.

Chapter Three

A woman of the Sidhe stood watching him. Small and slender, with long golden-brown hair and large brown eyes, she wore a gown of fine buttery leather and fur held closed by slender, curving rings of gold. A cloak of milk-white wool was fastened over her shoulder by two discs of bronze, decorated with concentric circles so that they looked like strange eyes staring at him. Deep within the shadows, she fairly gleamed with shining metal and mystery.

She seemed so fragile, so delicate, like some sort of wild elusive creature of the forest that on an ordinary day would turn and run from him.

But this was no ordinary day.

Now he remembered all of what had occurred last evening. He had been swimming in the lake when this same woman had called to him, and they had spoken most pleasantly together for a time until she had sent him back to the campsite. Now she was here before him again, as if she had walked out of thin air.

He placed the sword across both his palms and held it out to her. "Is this yours, lady of the Sidhe?"

"It is. Yet I may offer it to you, Anlon."

"To me?"

She stepped nearer. "I thank you for the gift of honey you left for us last night. I have come to tell you that this sword is meant as a gift for you, though I require more than honey in return."

"More . . ." He looked down at the gleaming bronze that rested across his hands. "What more can *I* do for you?"

"You can live with me as my husband for one year."

He could not possibly have heard her correctly. "Your . . . husband?"

She shrugged. "I seek a worthy man. If that man is you, and if you wish it, you will be my husband for one year."

He felt hardly able to breathe. "Why do you believe that I am worthy of you?"

The lady smiled. "I began my search by looking for kindness, for that is the measure of a worthwhile man. Anyone can show brutality and strength. And among your people, few demonstrate even a simple kindness to one of their own, let alone to one of the Sidhe. Those who do are special indeed."

"A year," Anlon breathed, lowering the sword and looking away. "One year . . ."

"If you stay with me for twelve months, at the end of that time you may return to the world of Men—your world—and you may keep the sword."

He hardly dared to breathe. He could not possibly believe what she was offering. This beautiful, ethereal

33

woman, this magnificent sword—he could return to the Fianna as a man with a shining blade instead of as a boy with a crude blackthorn club.

He looked up at her again. But before he could speak, there was the sound of hootbeats racing toward them on the road. Fehin and Donn swung around the trees and pulled their horses up short right in front of him.

"Anlon!" cried Fehin, looking both baffled and frustrated. "What are you doing? Why did you stay behind? You've got the pack ponies and all our equipment! Do you plan to stay out in the forest all winter long?"

Anlon took the sword in one hand. "I may at that," he said.

"What are you talking about? Get on your horse, get those pack ponies, and come with us! And drop that cursed sword back into the mud where it belongs!"

Anlon's finger tightened on the bone hilt. "I have received another offer."

"Another offer?"

"The woman of the Sidhe has come to me again." He turned to the lady, intending to show Fehin what he meant, but there was no one among the bare trees.

Fehin looked at him as if he had gone mad; then both he and Donn glanced at each other and howled with laughter. "So, at last you have found a suitable mate—a woman of the Sidhe who shows herself only to you! Certainly no other man of the Fianna would bother with such a creature!"

Anlon squarely faced the large warrior. "Perhaps if you do not want her, it is because you fear her." It seemed to him that he saw a slight gleam in the forest, just out of the corner of his eye.

Fehin sat back on his horse and glared down at Anlon. "A woman of the Sidhe!"

"She has offered me ... offered me a place with her for one year."

"I do not doubt that she has! Trying to lure you into her realm with shiny gifts and empty promises! Do you intend to go?"

"I ... *I will.* I will go." For a long time he gazed deep into the forest, holding the fairy sword close to him, before glancing back at Fehin.

"Surely you know that those who go with the Sidhe are not seen again in the world of Men. Surely you know that!"

Anlon started to respond, then turned and looked into the forest again.

Fehin jerked his head at Donn, and the other warrior rode up and grabbed the lead ropes of the pack ponies. Fehin looked at Anlon one last time, his expression cold. "You are already lost, Anlon. They already have you." And, with that, the two rode away, leaving Anlon standing alone with his horse on the windy road.

He stood very still for a long moment; then he peered back into the forest. Before him stood the lady of the Sidhe, posed beneath the trees exactly as she had been before.

This time, though, she held across her chest a long and beautiful scabbard. It was made of smooth dark wood and tipped with polished metal. "Those were fine words, Anlon. Perhaps I have made a good choice."

"I can only hope to serve you as is your due," he whispered in response. She smiled, her expression as mysterious as the shadowed forest where she stood, and slowly extended both her arms so that she held the scabbard out to him.

Anlon approached her slowly, still feeling that perhaps she would turn and flee as if she were a wild doe; but she remained unmoving even when he lifted the heavy scabbard from her hands.

The lady watched as he worked the tip of the sword into the finely crafted sheath and pushed it home. The fit was perfect. With shaking, awkward hands he untied his old leather belt and slid the scabbard onto it. Refastening the belt, he stood up tall and proud before the lady. Her eyes flicked over him, and her expression grew serious.

Anlon stood even straighter, acutely aware of his ragged old cloak and work-stained tunic and boots, so thin they were nearly worn through. His arms and wrists and neck were bare of any of the fine gold bands or torques other men of higher birth wore. And his dagger was a herdsman's knife, made of bone instead of the iron that a warrior should have.

He could not possibly look like anyone a Sidhe beauty might want for her husband. Perhaps she was reconsidering her choice. Perhaps she would want the sword back. . . .

She held her hand out to him.

Anlon went to her and she placed her hand on his arm, light as air; then together they walked into the deepest shadows of the forest. Nealta followed closely.

They walked in silence, but Anlon soon became aware that they were not alone. Here and there he would see a suddenly swaying fern, or a little fall of leaves, or even the occasional flash of something that looked like the glint of sunlight on gold. They were being followed, he was sure, but the lady seemed not to notice.

When at least half the day had been passed in foot travel, they began climbing, for the path turned uphill. All around, the world began to change. The light became soft and then almost disappeared; their surroundings shadowy, almost like twilight, so deep were they in the forest. Anlon had no idea where they were or where they might be going. At last, they came to a place where the brush and shrubs and small sapling trees had all been cleared away.

Here only the largest, oldest trees remained to spread their great bare interlocking branches like a canopy above the mossy earth. And within this lovely, airy clearing were curving stone walls, grey-white beneath the shadows, set with solid gates of wood on glittering bronze hinges.

As Anlon walked to those gates with the lady of the Sidhe on his arm and the magnificent bronze sword at his belt, small shadowed figures began moving out of the forest to join them. In a moment he and the lady and Nealta were at the closed gates of the circular stone fortress, surrounded by the silent folk of the Sidhe.

Anlon drew a deep breath and turned to the lady. "This can only be your home."

She smiled. "This is Caher Idir, and it is home to all of us." She glanced at the silent, curious group that stood around them. "And these are my people."

Anlon stared at her. "*Your* people," he whispered. "Then you are a queen. A queen of the Sidhe . . ." He turned and nodded to the group. "My name is Anlon, and I am honored to be among you."

They made no response. He could feel their heavy gazes upon him. Well, that was as it would be. Anlon nodded again and turned back to the lady. "I realize that I do not know your name. Will you tell it to me?"

She looked up at him with luminous dark eyes. "Scahta," she answered, and as she spoke the gates slowly swung open.

Anlon's eyes widened as he walked inside with her. The interlocking branches of the great oaks and willows bent so low to the tops of the stone walls that it seemed, even in their bare state, that they formed a roof over the fortress. Scattered throughout were several more enormous trees, dropping acorns and dry golden leaves onto the fortress grounds and adding their branches to the rooflike structure. He could only imagine how it would look in the summer, with green leaves sprouting everywhere.

Among the trees were nine round houses, some larger, some smaller, with stone foundations and smooth clay walls and steep conical roofs thatched with fresh rushes. Anlon stopped, nearly forgetting about Scahta's hand on his arm. "It is so beautiful," he breathed. "And so big! Nine great houses, all ringed with stone and sheltered by trees!"

"You have lived only in a single house all your life, Anlon. Caher Idir is not nearly so big as Dun Mor . . . and there are far fewer of us who live here."

They continued, walking along the curving wall, and Anlon saw that there was a second, single gate on the opposite side of the circle. "So large it requires two gates," he marveled.

"That gate, I am sorry to tell you, has little use now." When he glanced at her, a question on his face, she went to the gate and stood back as one of the men pulled it open. Anlon went to look and saw more walls of grey-white stone, like a half-circle placed against the main fortress. But this area was empty and bare with only a damp dirt floor.

"It was for our cattle and sheep and horses. As you can see, we have no more animals. Men have taken them all, taken them from the fields and hills."

"Then—my horse Nealta now belongs to you, Queen Scahta. To you and all the people of Caher Idir. She will be only the first of more to come, I promise you."

38

She glanced at him. "We thank you. But beware of promises easily made." She took his arm again and they continued.

"No one would ever find this place!" Anlon marveled. "I know that I would not."

"We keep it well hidden. It is rare that any outsider finds our home. Any who do either stay with us for the rest of their lives, or simply cannot remember how to find their way back once we lead them home."

Anlon sighed, looking up at the overhanging trees. "I thank you, Queen Scahta, for bringing me here. Already it seems to me that I have known no other world."

She stopped and turned to him. "Then stay in this one for a time, Anlon. But do not forget—what is beautiful may also be fierce. Dangerous."

He gazed at her fragile beauty, at her large eyes staring straight back at him. "I promise you I will not forget."

She gave him that mysterious smile he was beginning to know quite well. "Then go now with Liath and ready yourself for the evening meal. We will share it together in my house. I will be waiting for you."

Almost before he realized what was happening, Anlon found himself within one of the round houses in the company of the small Sidhe man called Liath.

The house was not so very different from the home he had left to ride with the Fianna. This one, too, had a high thatched roof, a deep bed of rushes on the floor, a stone-ringed hearth in the center, sleeping ledges along the perimeter, and tools and equipment hanging from wooden pegs driven into the smooth clay walls.

Yet he was struck by the way that everything in this house seemed both very old and perfectly new at the same time. The rushes on the floor were green and fresh, as though cut and strewn that very day. The hearthstones were clean, hardly touched by smoke or soot, though a fire burned brightly in the pit. The sleeping ledges were covered with furs, beautiful and soft and perfect, as though the living creatures still wore them and had merely lay down to sleep inside the house. But perhaps most striking of all, the tools hanging on the walls and resting beside the hearth—the cauldrons, the knives, the cups—were made of finely crafted, polished bronze.

Soft leather, marvelous furs, glittering precious metals . . . this was the world of the Sidhe. Not for them the rough wool and cold iron of Men.

His dark-haired companion, who did not come up to Anlon's shoulder, reached up to remove the leaf-shaped bronze pin holding Anlon's ragged, nearly rotted brown woolen cloak. He placed the pin on the edge of the hearth, then dragged the heavy fabric off Anlon and over his arm.

Anlon did not object to this, but when Liath began lifting Anlon's tunic to pull it off, he stopped him with quick hands on the small wrists. "Ah, I can take care of this. But thank you."

It seemed they wanted him to change clothes. Well, that was fine with him; he had not failed to notice how clean and well kept all the Sidhe folk appeared. It was something that added to their beauty and made him more conscious than ever of his stained and faded shirt and the dark woolen pants nearly worn through from long days of riding.

If they wanted him to wear something else, he would be quite happy to do so.

He pulled his tunic off and threw it aside—and to his surprise Liath caught the wad of linen before it could touch the rushes. The Sidhe tossed it into the fire, followed quickly by the old cloak Anlon had worn.

"Why—" But Liath only looked at him, and his gaze flicked down to Anlon's threadbare wool pants and mud-crusted, weather-beaten boots before meeting Anlon's eyes again. Clearly he expected the rest of it, too.

Anlon sighed. "It probably is for the best." He took off the old boots, then unfastened his equally worn leather belt, which looked so very unworthy of the fine sword and scabbard that hung from it.

Even as Anlon held the scabbard, Liath pulled the belt from it and caught up the boots. All the old leather instantly joined the cloak and tunic in the fire.

Before anything else could vanish in the flames, Anlon placed his bronze sword safely in a corner beneath the rushes. Then, knowing it was futile to protest, he stripped off the remains of his heavy woolen pants and threw them into the hearthfire himself.

He was left standing in the short linen pants he wore beneath the wool. "That's as far as it goes, I must tell you," he said to Liath with a smile. "Now . . . I am assuming you don't want me to go about like this. What would you have me wear?"

To his surprise Liath took him by the arm and led him outside, out to the fortress grounds.

Anlon was very much aware of many hidden eyes peering out at him from behind the trees and houses. He drew himself up to his greatest height and walked boldly across the grounds, following as he was taken out through the great wooden gates.

Being in the forest was like an extension of being inside Caher Idir. There was the same interlaced rooftop of branches with massive, solitary trees scattered across the open ground. The birds called and echoed throughout the wood. The earth was cool and mossy underfoot. And still he was aware that, here and there, small figures moved in the shadows.

In a moment, Liath had brought him to a wide stream where clear water tumbled over rocks to form shallow pools. "Here," said Liath, gesturing toward an especially inviting pool; then he quickly turned and ran back to the fortress. He made no noise as he disappeared into the trees.

Anlon had little doubt about what they intended him to do. He waded into the cold water and began scrubbing as best he could, as he always did each evening after a long day's work. He, too, liked to be clean, and this was as beautiful a place to wash as he had ever known.

It was not long before Liath returned. Anlon was quite happy—and relieved—to see that he had brought clothes with him. He carried an armload of fine leather, new wool, and soft fur, with pieces of bright gold sitting atop it all.

Liath placed the stack of garments on a grassy spot beside the stream, then left as quickly as he had come. Anlon wasted no time getting out of the water and reaching for the fine new apparel.

Scahta awaited him.

Chapter Four

The world outside had quietly disappeared into darkness. The only light came from the glowing hearthfire in the center of Scahta's house, and from the flickering flame burning in the hollow of a small stone lamp that rested on the sleeping ledge just above Anlon's head.

He sat on a pile of the softest grey and white furs atop the floor's thick cover of rushes. Warmth rolled over him, from the fire and from the presence of Scahta, who was seated on her own furs in the shadows a little ways from the hearth.

He knew she could see him better than he could see her. But he understood that even though she had invited him, he was still quite a mystery to Scahta and to all her people. He was someone who would normally be perceived by the Sidhe as one of the enemy, and he did not mind allowing them to scrutinize him until they felt satisfied that he posed no danger—not if it meant he would be allowed to stay here for a year, to stay with Scahta.

He felt with some pride that he now presented a better figure for her to see. The cold, pure stream had washed away the dirt and fatigue of long weeks spent on the road and left his skin clean and glowing like that of the Sidhe. His hair fell smoothly past his shoulders, now that he had carefully picked out the knots and tangles with a long wooden pin.

He felt, too, as if the cold waters of Caher Idir had washed away all the derision—however good-natured— he had been forced to endure for the last months. No longer was he an overworked servant. Now *he* was the honored one, not a slave to the Fianna but an equal to a queen!

His deerskin clothes, newly made and no doubt sewn for him while he bathed, were wonderfully soft and light. The breeches were long enough to fit into the high soft boots. The tunic, sleeveless like his old linen one, fit long over his hips and was held closed at the throat by a curving half-ring of gold pressed through small holes in the leather. A pair of wide gold bands covered his wrists.

Perhaps the most beautiful of all was the woolen cloak. Surely it could not have been woven for him this very day! Yet the wool was light and clean, as though it had never been worn, and was dyed in beautiful soft shades of blue and grey.

The rectangular cloak was held at his shoulder by his bronze leaf pin, the only thing he wore from his old life. He could not resist reaching up to touch the beautiful gold ornaments at his wrists and throat once again. Like so much else in this place, they seemed at once inscrutably old and pristinely new.

"They are mine," Scahta said.

Anlon blinked, and looked into the moving shadows. "Yours?"

"The wool cloak. The gold half-rings. The wristbands. They are mine. I have been keeping them for—for a time when I might have a guest who would have need of them. The rest were made for you this day, as soon as you arrived."

"I guessed as much. It seemed unlikely that anyone here would have clothes to fit someone like me." He smiled into the shadows. "Never have I worn such fine garments. And never any colors, save for the natural shades of wool straight from the sheep. It seems this cloak has had the blue of the sky and the grey of the clouds spun down into its wool."

"A lovely way to describe it. Perhaps you should be a poet, Anlon, rather than a servant."

Her praise warmed him even further. "If anyone ever had need of decent clothes—much less clothes fit for royalty—I am that one. It is all so beautiful, so much more than I deserve. I thank you."

Scahta rose from her place in the shadows, stepping out so that her face could be seen in the flickering hearth-fire. "You are welcome, Anlon. But this may be the last time you thank me for anything." She looked him over carefully. "You do not wear your sword."

Anlon felt his face reddening. He got quickly to his feet. "I—I am not familiar with the proprieties of wearing a weapon, my lady. I was not sure if I should wear it here. It is in a safe place, I assure you. If you wish, I will go and—"

"Never mind, Anlon." There was a trace of amusement in her quiet voice. "You will have no need of it tonight."

She glanced over her shoulder, and Anlon saw a small movement at the doorway: two women bringing in wooden plates and bronze cups. They set the food down on the hearthstones and left as quickly and as silently as they had come.

Scahta sat beside the hearth, and Anlon moved to join her. When she had lifted down her plate, he reached for his own and examined the food on it with increasing wonder.

Bread, dry and light and flat. Green apples, cut in half crosswise. Some type of large roasted brown seeds he did not recognize. Thin slices of meat, still hot in their own juices. And small, delicate joints that could only be from some sort of bird.

He shook his head. "I never thought I would ask to have food explained to me, but I never saw it served in such a way! The only familiar thing is the bread. It is made of barley, is it not?"

"It is, with acorn flour to make the barley last. The apples are sliced to display their five seeds, which make a five-pointed star . . . reminding us all that apples, growing as they do suspended in the air, are a link between earth and sky."

He nodded, fascinated by her explanations. "I never thought of such things before. Please, tell me—what are these?" He touched one of the large seeds with a fingertip.

"The seeds of water lily. Something Men do not care to eat, and so they are left for the Sidhe."

"I see. And the meat? Always I have heard that the Sidhe-folk never eat meat."

Scahta laughed, short and cold. "Another tale told by Men, to justify taking our herds and killing our game. Yet I am told that Men do not eat the flesh of birds. Is that true?"

He considered. "I have heard that some of us do not.

Some believe that birds are the spirits of those traveling between this world and the next—or are perhaps even gods themselves." Anlon grinned. "Though I will admit to sometimes having taken swans or geese when there was nothing else for the cooking spit that night."

Scahta nodded and reached for her cup. "And do you know of this, Anlon?" she asked, raising it in front of her.

He lifted his own cup and took a drink. Instantly the intoxicating sweetness rushed through him. "Honey-wine," he marveled, and took another sip. "It's wonderful."

Scahta placed her finger on the side of his cup and guided it back to the hearthstones. "Then eat now, and save the wine for later. Else it will go straight to your head."

"Too late," he murmured, gazing at her, but then turned his attention back to the food on his plate, as she did.

It was the finest meal he'd had in a very long time. Though the Fianna always had the best food available, he was usually left with whatever remained after the other men had torn through it. Here was choice meat and fresh bread and crisp apples—and even the water lily seeds, roasted hot and dusted with a little salt. He found it all filling and good.

Soon the plates were empty and resting on the hearthstones once again. He and Scahta sat across from each other on the furs with their cups of honey-wine.

Anlon had never felt so good, so cared for, so complete. He had thought that riding and living with the Fianna was the finest way of life anyone could have, but it had been nothing like this . . . and there had been no one like Scahta on the cold nights out in the forest.

Now, suffused with the warmth of the fire and the furs

and the sweet honey-wine, he gazed into Scahta's dark eyes and found that he could think of nothing else.

Scahta returned his gaze, waiting, leaving everything up to him, as though he were already a king, her king, and she was his queen, waiting for him alone. . . .

Anlon reached for her. He wanted nothing more than to touch her soft hair. Yet as his hand moved toward her face, he found he was barely able to feel the difference between the warm air of the house and the cloud that was her hair.

Now his fingers reached her cheek, soft and delicate as a flower. He ran his work-roughened finger down the petal-smooth skin and felt a great sweetness when she closed her eyes in response.

Anlon set his cup down on the rushes, not caring that it fell over and spilled his honey-wine. Scahta too set her cup back on the hearth and reached for him just as he reached for her. Her small hands slid down his arms to his gold-covered wrists and held him there just as he touched the curve of her waist.

"You are not my husband yet, Anlon," she said, releasing him, and her voice was as cool as her hands had been warm.

She sat back and reached calmly for her wine. Anlon could only stare at her, feeling as if a chill winter wind had suddenly found its way into the house.

He picked up his cup. It was empty. "I do not understand, Queen Scahta," he murmured, toying with the bronze vessel. "I thought you said . . . I thought you had chosen me as your husband."

She looked at him over the rim of her cup. "I told you that I searched for a worthy man, and that if that man were you—and if you wished it—you would be my husband for one year."

"And you do not believe that I am worthy? I thought you told me . . ." He paused, thinking. " 'Kindness is the measure of a worthwhile man.' Those were your words. Did I not understand you?"

"I did not mislead you, Anlon. I told you only that kindness was the beginning. I am in need of much more."

He closed his eyes. "Only the beginning . . ."

Scahta stood up and began to pace slowly across the soft rushes. "You must understand me. I do not need merely a handsome man for a night of passion. I do not look for simply a mate. I, or any woman of the Sidhe, need only go to the Beltane fires if that is all we require—and indeed some of us have done so.

"I am a queen. My kingdom is in danger of destruction. I search not just for a mate but for a king, a king who will be loyal to me and to my people and who will help me to guard and preserve them."

She stopped on the other side of the hearth and gazed down at him. "If you stay, I will test you. I may even make you my husband. But I cannot make you a king."

He shook his head, growing ever more confused, ever more uncertain of what was happening. "I don't understand. If you are a queen, and I am your husband, is that not enough to make me a king?"

Scahta smiled, almost laughing, though her eyes were serious. "Only the people can make you a king, Anlon. You will have to prove yourself both to me and to them. I might choose you and commend you to them, but until the people of the Sidhe accept you themselves you are not a king."

"I see," he answered, beginning to understand. "And if they will not accept me?" It seemed a difficult task, to win over those who were so ready to hate him.

"If you prove not to be a king, I will keep my sword

49

and perhaps your child, and send you back to the Fianna . . . and I will go on searching until I find the right man to be my king."

She took a step toward him. The firelight flickered on her face. "Do you still wish to stay?"

He smiled up at her. "I am here, Queen Scahta. And I will be your servant until I can be your king."

She moved around the hearth again, until she stood over him. "Then share this wine with me," she said, offering her cup.

He reached up and took one long sweet sip, and she moved the bronze container away just as he closed his eyes and rested his head on the grey and white furs.

The fire burned low, and Anlon slept.

The night passed slowly, in warmth and peaceful dreams. It seemed a very long time until the light of day finally found him, but when it did Anlon jerked and quickly sat up.

How long had he slept? The men of the Fianna would be shouting for food and fire. There was equipment to pack and horses to catch. How could he have slept through the dawn?

But he was no longer among the Fianna.

He was alone in Scahta's house, within the strange and magical fortress called Caher Idir. Last night he had sat with her in this house and they had eaten the most wonderful meal together. They had shared honey-wine and he had ached with desire for her, but she had told him that he was not her husband yet . . . and he had slept.

The desire remained, and always would, he was certain. It was just as well she had allowed him to wake alone. He forced his mind to turn to other things.

Right now he had an entire new world to discover. It

seemed the best way to become a part of Scahta's life was to learn all he could about her people and her home. He got to his feet, brushing off his fine new clothes and admiring the gleam of gold at his wrists yet again; then he went outside into the grey morning to learn about the Sidhe.

For the rest of the day and on the several that followed, Anlon left his fine new sword hidden in the rushes while he observed the other Sidhe-folk going about their daily work. He tried to help as much as he could but found these small people difficult to follow; they seemed to delight in slipping away the instant he turned his back, leaving him alone in a house or in the forest with simply a little laugh hanging in the air where they had been.

He managed, however, to begin learning the daily routine of life at Caher Idir, and was amazed at how much of the burden had been lifted from him. Here, others did the cooking and clearing away. There were no animals to tend and no farm work to be done; at this time of year, the fields were long bare of the harvest. After the never-ending labor the Fianna had expected of him, simply carrying a few buckets of water from the stream, searching out hazelnuts in the forest, or preparing a snared rabbit for the fire seemed like no work at all.

The nights were spent on the rush-covered floor of the house where he had been taken upon his arrival. He soon learned that it was the home of the man called Cian. Cian had little to say to him, as did did Liath or Mactire or Amhran, the three other men who lived there; but Anlon understood. He was the intruder here, and it was up to him to give the Sidhe whatever time they needed to relax in his company and learn to accept a Man as a friend.

Yet the people of Caher Idir were anything but relaxed. By the morning of the seventh day, Anlon realized that a kind of urgency was spreading among the people with every moment that passed. They went deeper into the forest and stayed away longer, but each time they returned with less and less food and fewer and fewer trapped animals.

"Samhain," whispered Scahta.

Anlon turned to her and nodded. He had been watching as a smallish group of women came back from one last trip into the woods, carrying only a tiny handful of blackened and broken acorns into the fortress.

There was simply nothing more to find.

He and Scahta stood together just inside the great wood-and-bronze gates of Caher Idir. "Even *I* know that tonight the moon is full, and this is Samhain Eve," said Anlon. "This day is the last for any hope of bringing in any of the wild harvest. The cold of winter always arrives just after Samhain, if not on the day itself."

"It is also the time of the third and final harvest among Men." Her voice was cold, and she looked away.

He nodded. "The harvest of hides. Of meat. Of blood. I know that well. I am the son of a herdsman, and the third harvest was ours. The first belonged to the farmers, bringing in the grain from their fields; the second was the wild harvest of fruit from the forests. The third, and last, was ours."

Scahta turned back to face him again. "Yours. We know that very well, Anlon. All of the harvests now belong to Men."

"Oh, but I did not mean that—always we left something out for the Sidhe-folk after the Samhain harvest. . . ."

"I know what you meant. But that does not matter now. Get your sword."

"My sword?"

Cian walked up, along with Liath and Mactire. All wore their bronze swords and daggers and carried slings and small leather bags of stones. They refused to look at Anlon as they stood in silence behind their queen. "Get it," she said again. "We leave at twilight."

The gates closed behind them just as darkness fell. Anlon stayed close to Scahta as she started off into the forest. Following behind him—though he could not see them—were Liath, Mactire, and Cian.

He was not sure what they intended. His apprehension grew with each step they took through the cold and windy night.

Scahta must have sensed the tension in his silence, for she stopped and turned to him. The other three remained hidden somewhere in the forest. "What is wrong, Anlon?"

He paused, holding tight to the hilt of the sword. "Tonight is Samhain Eve," he finally said.

"It is."

The awkward silence fell between them again. "I have been warned since my earliest days that no man—that no one should be out on Samhain Eve."

"And why were you told such a thing?"

Anlon closed his eyes and tried to find the appropriate words. "In some ways, it is like the eve of Beltane. It is another night when the worlds of Sidhe and Men are likely to meet."

He smiled, and tried to search out Scahta's face in the darkness. "Beltane is a joyous time, where all gather in the moonlight to seek mates and spend a night of love around the bonfires. But on the night before Samhain . . ."

"On the night before Samhain, the Sidhe are out for

different reasons." Scahta took a step toward him. "The Samhain ritual marks the last chance that the Sidhe-folk have to gather stores of food for the winter. It is the last chance we have to wrest what little we can from Men, before cold and frost settle over the land and Men lock themselves away in their great fortresses of earth and stone. If we are to have any hope of surviving the coming months of cold and darkness, we must go out this night."

Anlon looked at her, and could only nod silently. She turned away and started on the path into the darkness once more.

He touched the bronze sword as he walked, its unfamiliar weight and swing growing heavier by the moment. He thought of the slings and leather bags filled with small polished stones that he and the three behind all carried. He was almost afraid to think of what they might do, and was not sure whether he would end up helping the Sidhe or defending his people against them.

Chapter Five

The full moon, enormous and yellow-orange, hung just above the hills as Scahta and Anlon and the three men of the Sidhe reached the edge of the forest. Anlon moved a step ahead of the others, going as close to the treeline as he dared, until Liath placed his hand on his shoulder to stop him. Yet Anlon could barely contain himself. There, in a huge and windswept field between the forest where they stood and the black silhouetted hills behind it, was the king's fortress.

Dun Mor.

It was huge, far larger than he remembered—but he had seen it only once, as a young boy. At least three of Caher Idir could sit side by side within its massive inner wall. But Anlon quickly forgot all thoughts of the hidden home of the Sidhe, for as he watched, the huge gates in the outer wall began to move outward. The groan of their heavy iron hinges reached all the way to the forest's edge.

A torchlit procession of about thirty men walked out through the gates. As they passed beneath the walls of the great *dun*, their torches cast flaring light onto the walls—and Anlon froze when he saw what hung there.

Heads. Severed heads, their faces seeming to move in the leaping light of the flames. Some looked as though they'd been alive this very day, while others were little more than skulls.

It seemed breath had left him. In a moment he felt Scahta's light hand on his arm. "Breathe, Anlon," she said, and he closed his eyes and drew a long cool draught of the night air. "They mean to frighten us away."

"They nearly did," he whispered, and shook his head. "We never did such things as this at my home. I have heard that the warriors sometimes keep the heads of vanquished enemies, but this—hanging human heads on their own walls—"

"Those are not the heads of Men. On this night, they display the heads of Sidhe."

"Of Sidhe . . ."

He looked back toward the *dun* and studied the procession. Such people he had never thought to see—all of them, men and women both, were tall, strong, and powerful, with skin white as milk and long hair of red and gold so bright it seemed to be aflame.

Their clothes held colors he'd scarcely imagined. All wore plaid and striped cloaks dyed in deep shades of blue and yellow and red and green. One man, the tall one who walked surrounded by his warriors, wore a huge long cloak of red and blue and deep purple, so wide that it was folded and pinned several times over his chest. There was the shine of thick heavy gold at his throat and shoulder, of pieces even larger and brighter than those of the others.

"The king," he whispered.

This was the king he had thought to serve, the king whose fortress he'd longed to see. For all the long months of drudgery with the Fianna, the dream of Dun Mor and its king and its great numbers of people had maintained him—and now he could only watch it all from a distance, hidden in the shadows like a wild thing.

"It is not too late, Anlon," said Scahta. "You can still be a part of them."

Anlon looked at her shadowed profile, seeing only the gleam of her luminous eyes. He glanced back at the scene in the field and saw the ones who, he had always been told, were his own people.

"They are your kind," Scahta continued. "Look at them. Look at the most powerful warriors in the land. Look at the strong and beautiful women who bow to no man, at their massive impenetrable fortress and the king who rules over it all. The bounty of the land yields itself to them alone. All that grows in the fields and forests is theirs; all the animals, wild and tame, belong entirely to them.

"They are not just Men. Those who are so powerful can only be gods, and they are your people. They will accept you without question. They know you already. You will find your place among them. Why do you not go to them, Anlon? Do you not hear them calling you? Do you not hear them calling?"

Anlon closed his eyes and wished he could close his ears as well against the power of her soft and insistent words. "I am here, Queen Scahta, because I wish to be here. You invited me to your home. You offered me a chance to be your king. I will stay with you for as long as you will allow me to stay."

She merely looked at him, saying nothing, then coolly turned her gaze back to the field.

The procession had stopped. The torch-bearing men surrounded a stack of wood so large it seemed like a mountain. One man, old and round shouldered and grey bearded, walked forward with his wind-whipped torch held high overhead. He stood in silence beside the mountain of wood for a moment, then began a low and fearful chanting. The sound of drumming rose from within the crowd and accompanied him in a powerful, ominous rhythm.

Anlon's heart began to pound, though he could hear nothing of the words. But it was not long before the chanting stopped and the drummers ceased. A heavy silence descended over the people, broken only by the snapping of the torches' flames.

Then the man who had been chanting—the druid, Anlon realized; he would certainly be a druid—tossed his torch high into the air and onto the enormous stack of wood.

That seemed to be the signal for the others to do the same. The torches clattered down on the wood, creating bright spots of flame throughout the pile. And then came a low roar, like a heavy summer windstorm, as the wood caught fire and became a mountain of roaring, billowing flame.

It was blinding, terrifying, and even the men fell back from the wild torrents of flames and flying sparks. The drumming started again, deep and insistent. The people of Dun Mor began moving in a wide circle around the fire, first marching, now dancing, faster, faster, circling around and around. . . .

"Will they ever stop?" whispered Anlon.

"They will circle thirteen times. Once for every moon of the year," Scahta answered.

At last the circling was finished. The dancers stood breathless, their faces serious. They constantly glanced over their shoulders into the night toward their fortress home before again turning back to the blinding light of the fire.

The druid spoke a few short words. The people immediately turned away and started back to the safety of the fortress. They moved hurriedly, it seemed to Anlon, as if they had no wish to remain outside on this night for any longer than necessary.

In no time, all had disappeared within the massive double walls of Dun Mor—but the gates remained open. Anlon could feel the tension rise among the Sidhe who stayed hidden behind him, and even Scahta seemed to hold her breath and force herself to keep very, very still.

Flaring torchlight again appeared at the gate as another group of men ran out. They drove their torches into the earth at intervals, creating two widely separated lines of fire between the bonfire and the *dun*. As soon as the pen of flames was ready, some twenty, thirty, forty head of shaggy brown sheep and red-and-white cattle came bursting out through the gates of Dun Mor.

This was the third harvest.

The frightened animals milled about, bawling, trapped between the fortress and the flames. Suddenly, one old cow fell to her knees as a great iron axe came down on her head, once, twice, three times.

One by one the animals fell, and soon the field ran red with streams of blood. And when the butcher's axe did not strike cleanly enough, a frightened, painful shriek would rend the night.

"Why would they wait until nightfall to do this?" asked

Anlon. "My father, and all my family, did the sacrifices in the daylight. All was finished long before dark."

Scahta shook her head. "They are determined that none of the Sidhe will share in any of the harvests, including this one. The darkness, the fire, the cold iron, the screams, the death heads—all are meant to frighten us away."

She smiled, but her expression was cold. "They have not succeeded. And they will never succeed, not so long as I am queen, not so long as I have fighters such as these around me." She glanced at Cian, who gave her a grim smile, and then at Anlon, who could only look at her with astonishment and awe.

Cian pulled out his sling and reached into the leather pouch at his belt. The sling whipped over his head and a polished white stone flew through the night, striking the head of one of the terrified sheep.

The shaggy brown animal fell to its knees. It managed to get back to its feet but staggered blindly, clearly stunned by Cian's shot. From beside him, Anlon thought he heard Scahta whisper, though no sound came from her lips.

He watched in amazement as the sheep continued to stagger, now moving between two of the torches, past the unseen flames and coming unsteadily toward them.

There was a shout from the men of Dun Mor. "Look, there! Get it!" Two of them started past the line of torches where they had seen the sheep disappear into the night, and stood blinking in the darkness.

Cian's sling sang out again. So did Liath's. And each of the *dun*'s men leaped back as though bitten when the shining white stones struck them in the legs and shoulders.

The two men roared in rage, but ran back to the safety

of the flames. "The Sidhe! The Sidhe have taken that animal—they shot it and drew it to them!"

Three more men left off their work of slaughtering the beasts. One grabbed a torch from the ground, and the entire group, cold iron axes in hand, started toward the dark forest where the sheep continued to stagger.

The animal dropped and lay still, struck again by a flying white stone. The men stopped, then started forward again—just as their torch showed them the reflection of a pair of shining yellow eyes.

All five butchers froze. Another pair of eyes appeared, and another, and then a low and terrible growl reached out to the men from the forest.

"Leave it," said one, his voice furious and frustrated. The others obeyed, retreating back to the safety of the torchlit killing field.

Anlon lowered his sling. His stone had found its mark, bringing down the sheep, which had wandered toward them in its stunned condition. Yet he barely thought of how he had added greatly to the Sidhe-folk's chances of surviving the winter—he could think of nothing but the huge grey-white wolves that now crouched in the darkness, almost close enough to touch.

At last all the sheep and cattle lay still and silent on the earth. The human men quickly began the work of removing the fleeces and skins and cutting up the carcasses. A few were kept busy carrying meat and hides as quickly as possible into the *dun* and running back out to the field again.

None made any further move to go beyond the fires.

Anlon and Scahta and the three others remained in the forest while the men finished their work, waiting in darkness while the moon rose high. Finally they were done. They pulled up their torches and slammed shut the iron-hinged gates of Dun Mor, leaving only the low-burning bonfire and a faint mist creeping over the reddened fields.

Quietly, invisibly, Anlon and the folk of the Sidhe crept out over the cold and windy field to search for anything that might be of value to them. The wolves, too, moved in silence with them, snatching up a bit of bone here or lapping at a pool of blood there; but there was little left of the third harvest for the Sidhe. They found only a few handfuls of wool, the tail of a calf, a couple of hooves . . . and everywhere, blood-soaked earth.

Anlon stopped in the center of the field to catch a breath, his tension easing slightly as the wolves trotted away to vanish back into the forest. He could not help turning to look back at Dun Mor, silent now, its gates tightly shut.

Scahta, too, paused in the open field and followed his gaze to the distant *dun*. "It is not too late," she said. "You need only pound on the gates. They will take you. You can live with the king and all his warriors and women. They will welcome you. Even now they believe you are lost to the Sidhe." He could not read the tone of her voice.

Anlon closed his eyes, thinking of the security and pleasure of a winter spent at Dun Mor . . . the companionship, the games, the food, the wine . . . and then he opened his eyes again and saw the *dun* as it looked right now. He saw a wall hung with severed heads of the Sidhe, the light of the dying bonfire flickering across their dead faces as they stared out at the blood-soaked fields.

He shook his head. "Not on this night, Queen Scahta. There is no place for me tonight among those men." He looked into her eyes, shining in the moonlight, and thought of the warmth and beauty of Caher Idir. "I can only hope to find a place with you."

She smiled and turned toward the night-shrouded woods. Together they left the killing field and returned to the edge of the forest, where Anlon lifted the dead sheep to his shoulders, and all started on the path back to Caher Idir.

The next morning brought cold air and a grey sky and a world turned white with frost. Anlon wrapped his fine woolen cloak tightly around his shoulders as he stood in the center of Caher Idir, watching the play of mist around his feet.

The weight of the previous night and the endless work of the past several months lay heavily on him. In less than a year his life had changed in ways he had never imagined. First he had left his quiet home to ride with the lofty Fianna, and then he had left the Fianna to live among the mysterious Sidhe. He shook his head. Never would he have thought such things might happen to him!

It was wonderful, it was exciting, but it was also overwhelming. At this moment he could think only of how pleasant, how restful, the days ahead were going to be . . . all he need think about right now was a quiet winter wrapped in the warmth of this place.

He walked slowly among the houses, where the pleasurable smell of wood smoke hung in the crisp cold air. Most of the doors stood open, and he could see the folk inside as they began their winter tasks. The familiar rhythm of the loom came from one house; a group of women in another sat near the hearthfire with their spindles and baskets of dark- and cream-colored wool; and near the center of the fortress were several men already engaged in beautiful woodworking and delicate leather carving.

On the cold grey days he, too, would sit outside by the

fire with the men of the Sidhe, under the leaf-bare, frost-covered trees, making fine things out of leather or wood. He would pass the long, dark, fog-shrouded nights sheltered by the thick walls of the houses, snug within rushes and furs, playing games and listening to stories and to music. He smiled at the thought of what stories the Sidhe-folk would have to tell, of what beautiful music they would play.

There was also, he knew, one young couple among the Sidhe who had made a vow of marriage to each other on Samhain Eve. Their door was closed, their house quiet. Anlon smiled. They had certainly chosen a fine time of the year to begin their life together.

Such imaginings made his own thoughts turn to Scahta, and of how he had hoped, and believed, that he would be spending the long winter with her as her husband. Even now the mere thought of her was enough to send desire flooding through him. He was resigned to keeping that desire in check, though he hoped he could keep his disappointment in check also. He would never give up the hope that one day she would accept him . . . even come to love him. She would call him to her, just as she was doing now. . . .

He turned and saw her standing near one of the houses, watching him, as cool and delicate and beautiful as the frost that lined the branches of the trees overhead. She wore a beautiful cloak of the purest, whitest fur, and the two bronze disc pins that fastened it gleamed softly in the frosty white light of the morning. Anlon smiled as he walked to stand beside her, but Scahta's serious expression did not change.

"It seems that the world has turned to white," he said, gazing up at the frost-covered forest surrounding them. "Such a fine place to watch the winter. I never thought to live in such a beautiful . . ." He stopped as Cian walked up to them, glancing at Anlon from beneath lowered eyes.

"Come with me," Scahta said, and started toward the gates.

Only a little surprised, Anlon followed her and Cian to the gate. It opened as they approached. Scahta and Cian went striding into the frost-whitened forest, their boots silent on the cold earth, leaving Anlon puzzled and hesitating at the gate.

She turned, frowning. "Why do you wait?"

After a moment, Anlon spoke. "My lady . . ." He glanced at Cian, and then began again. "My lady, I am not sure why we would leave the safety of Caher Idir now, when the winter has just begun . . . when all have worked so hard to make it ready for the long season ahead of us. . . ."

Scahta stood framed by the ice-rimmed black branches of the trees and faced him with a gaze as cool as the wintry air. "I believe you said that you wished to be my husband. That you wished to be my king."

"I did." He could almost feel Cian glower. He turned and got the full force of Cian's angry, burning stare. Quickly Anlon looked back at Scahta. "To whom do you speak, my lady?"

"To both of you. Both of you have said these things, have you not?"

"Both—" Again he looked at Cian, and the truth hit him like a shot from a sling. "I see now," he continued, forcing his voice to keep steady. "Both of us are to be tested. You are considering us both."

"I am."

"As your husband, and your king."

"Do you object to my methods?"

65

"I . . . I thought that . . ."

"Thought what?"

"That perhaps affection would enter into your decision, somehow."

She laughed. "I am a queen, Anlon. I cannot rely on affection to find a king for me. Affection alone will not save the Sidhe." She studied him again. "You may leave anytime you wish. I will force no one to endure my tests. Cian will be only too glad to show you the way back to Dun Mor."

Cian actually smiled then, cold and hard, and held out his hand toward the forest as though politely allowing Anlon to go first. This time, Anlon met his gaze. "I thank you, Cian. But I will stay."

"Good." Scahta's voice was as light, and as cold, as a wind-touched spray of snow.

"Will I need my sword, Queen Scahta?" he asked.

"You will not. Come with me. I am here to lead you down the path of a king." She turned and started to vanish into the forest, with Cian close on her heels. Anlon moved quickly to keep them both in sight.

He was glad he was behind the two of them, for that meant they would not see his fair skin burning red with anger and shame. He had thought he was Scahta's chosen; he had believed he was special to her! But in reality, it seemed he was merely one more beast for her to choose from, the way she might select a stallion for a mare.

All right, then. If she wished to see a contest, a contest she would see.

The three moved deep into the white and silent forest.

Chapter Six

Anlon had always followed the winter routine of staying within the walls of his family's home during the cold barren months, when only the wolves moved about freely, and he was surprised to find that Scahta seemed quite unconcerned about walking openly through the wintry forest on the day of Samhain. She led him and Cian deep into the woods, saying nothing, apparently content to let them wonder what she might have planned.

As the day wore on, the sun generated enough pale light behind the clouds to turn the frost to dripping water and the ground to cold slick mud. Yet Scahta seemed to know exactly where she was going and did not care how difficult the path.

At last they heard a small sound in the silent forest—a hollow echoing almost like singing. In a moment, they reached a small stream that ran along the foot of a sheer and towering cliff. The bare, jagged rock face rose straight up over them, so far they had to crane their necks back to look at it.

It was the sound of this stream echoing against the cliff wall that they had heard. Now Scahta walked to the edge and added her own voice to the song of the water.

"Do you see the small shrub growing high up there in the face of the cliff, the lovely green yew with the bright red berries?"

Anlon and Cian looked up, and up, and nodded. Scahta smiled at them and sighed like a young girl. "Always in winter I miss the sight of green growing things. Might one of you bring me a sprig of that tree?"

Anlon looked up at the enormous cliff wall. It was so steep that it seemed to lean out over them, yet he saw its surface was broken and irregular, with what appeared to be fairly solid ledges and niches. "Of course, my lady, I—"

But Cian had already started up.

Quickly Anlon went after him. He had done little in the way of such climbing—cows and sheep were not known to scale cliff walls! Certainly there had never been any reason for him to attempt something this steep. Why would Scahta ask such a thing of them?

Then, as he began to work his way up, he had it: courage. Scahta wanted to see which of them could best demonstrate courage. Such a steep and dangerous cliff would cause even the strongest of warriors to hesitate. But he would show Scahta—and Cian—what courage was!

With strong and work-callused hands he grasped the rocks and hauled himself up. The soft leather boots he now wore were a help in finding and gripping the precarious footholds. Slowly, hand over hand, he crept up the face of the treacherous cliff.

Cian was still well ahead of him. The small and agile

Sidhe definitely had the advantage in a contest such as this. But when Cian was nearly halfway up, the wall grew smoother and the handholds fewer, and his progress began to slow.

It was not long before Anlon caught up. The two competitors hung side by side on the slippery slope, matching cold stare for cold stare.

Anlon could see now why Cian had paused. The rock wall would be much more difficult to climb from this point on. He looked up, squinting, at the bright green shrub growing from the top of the cliff, thinking only that Scahta wanted a branch of it—a green branch bright with red berries.

He was determined that he would be the one to get it for her, not Cian. If Scahta wanted to see a feat worthy of a husband, worthy of a king, he would make sure she saw one this day!

He moved up one more difficult step and glanced down at Cian. To his surprise, he saw that his rival had begun to creep back down the cliff, back down to the ground.

Cian had given up! He was quitting, backing away from the task Scahta had set for them. Anlon looked down and grinned. Now he could truly show Scahta what he could do. Now she would see who had courage and who did not!

He moved up one more handhold, one more foothold. The higher he went, the slower and more difficult it became, but he was determined. He would show them both what courage was; he would bring back a sprig of that green for Scahta. Just one more handhold . . .

With a shock he lost his grip and slid down the sheer face of the cliff, scrambling for a hold as the slippery rocks flew by. It was futile; he went crashing and sliding down with a rain of rock and dirt.

With a heavy crash he landed at Scahta's feet. Stones and earth and a cloud of dust slid down after him.

He gasped, fighting for the breath that had been knocked from him by the force of the fall. As soon as he could breathe again he sat up, rubbing the dirt from his eyes with the back of his arm, then got to his feet. Immediately he turned to the cliff and reached up once again for the first handhold.

A touch on his arm stopped him. "There will be no more climbing this cliff," said Scahta.

He stepped down and looked at her, puzzled. "I don't understand. You asked for a bit of green from the bush up there at the top. And I am determined that you will have it."

"Do you believe that greenery is what I desire most?"

"But I thought . . ." He paused. "You brought us far into the forest, to the foot of this cliff. You said you wished to have a piece of that shrub." He shook his head. "I know that bit of greenery is not what really matters. I believed this was a test of courage. The face of this cliff would make anyone hesitate. I wanted to show you that I would not give up, that I would have the courage to—"

A little pebble came rolling down the face of the cliff and landed at his feet. Looking up, Anlon saw Cian far above, all the way up at the top of the cliff, looking down over the edge.

In his hand was a branch of the dark green yew, dotted with red berries.

Anlon's face burned. "He did not climb the cliff as you asked," he said, both confused and frustrated. "He must have gone around. He took the easy way—"

"I never asked either of you to climb this cliff. I merely

asked if one of you might bring me a piece of that shrub. Climbing the cliff was not the only way to reach the top."

"But your test—"

"The test was not of courage, Anlon. It was of wisdom."

"Wisdom . . ."

"A king with a broken neck is of little use to me or my people."

Anlon closed his eyes. "I believed I could climb that cliff. I wanted to show you that I had the courage you require."

"No one can climb that cliff. Not Man, not Sidhe. Cian had the wisdom to recognize that. You did not."

Anlon felt as though every last bit of frost in the forest had settled over him. Cian reappeared from the far side of the cliff, walking along the stream looking quite pleased with himself. "For you, Queen Scahta," he said, and with a small bow he presented her with the sprig from the yew tree.

"I thank you," she said, accepting his gift and fingering the perfect red berries. "I am quite happy to see that you, Cian, know the difference between bravery and foolhardiness. Often, I find, the two are confused."

She smiled at him and turned to go. Cian followed closely, still wrapped in an aura of triumph. Anlon watched them go and then, head up, holding on to what little was left of his pride, walked after them. He was careful to keep them in sight all the long way back to Caher Idir, but also careful not to catch up.

The next morning, Scahta stood outside Anlon's dwelling. She watched as he shoved open the door with a bang and stumbled out of the house into the cool grey dawn, glancing left and right as he struggled to fasten his belt and pull on his boots at the same time. Dressed at last, he stood waiting in front of the house, clenching and unclenching his fists, his breath coming as fast as though he had just run all the way from Dun Mor.

She laughed.

Anlon froze. His gaze darted about as he searched for her, certain he had heard her voice. "Scahta," he called. "Scahta?"

She moved deeper into the shadows. He would never see her unless she wished to be seen. It was the way of her people, to hide, to watch. She quite preferred to remain hidden and study him at her leisure, coolly gauging his reactions to her tests and judging him as he—

"Scahta, please," he whispered, and closed his eyes.

She caught a little breath and found herself taking a step toward him, somehow moved by his unhappiness.

"I am ready for your next test," he called. "I will do anything you ask. Please, *Scahta* . . . please. Come to me."

With all her strength, Scahta halted and forced herself to stay out of sight.

What was this? Anlon had no powers, no knowledge of the wind-voice. He was a simple herdsman and had never been trained in the ways of the Sidhe. Yet when he had spoken her name just now, Scahta had felt it not just in her head but in her heart . . . and all thoughts of anything other than walking out of the shadows and into the sunlight surrounding this tall young man had vanished from her mind.

She could only watch as he slowly sat on the stone outside Cian's house and rested his head in his hand.

She had selected him as a possible king because he was a Man and did not seem to be so violent as the others— and he had needed little persuasion to come with her to Caher Idir. But now, gazing at Anlon where he sat in despair waiting for her, head down, shoulders bent, his soft dark hair falling over the smooth skin of his face and neck, a slow warmth began once again to spread itself around her heart. Strangely, Scahta began to wonder if perhaps she had chosen far better than she knew.

She had to beware, though. This was not a choice she could make for herself, but one for her people.

Anlon waited for a long time on the rock outside Cian's house. He was certain that Scahta was nearby, about to send him on another test, and this time he would be ready. He would think carefully of what she might really be trying to discover. Cian would not outsmart him this time!

But as the day wore on, he hardly caught a glimpse of Scahta and saw Cian not at all. The day passed quietly, with just the routine work that must be done to keep the fortress clean and its occupants fed and comfortable. The evening was spent sitting around the fire with a few of the other Sidhe men, carving a fine strip of leather for a belt.

The next several days passed in much the same way, with the hours of daylight becoming shorter and shorter as the winter solstice approached. Anlon's confusion only grew. He had thought Scahta meant to test him, but now he barely saw her. She would come and go in rare appearances, as hidden within the walls of Caher Idir as she had been in the whole of the forest.

Anlon would speak to her when he could, though she would permit only a few words here and there. She was never more than cool and polite, but he found that his attraction to her had changed not at all. Indeed, it only increased. She had to know how he felt, but she remained a distant, ethereal creature . . . and with a sinking heart he wondered if she was telling him she was no longer interested in him.

He forced himself to consider a bitter reality. Perhaps he had destroyed his chance of ever being Scahta's husband, much less her king. Perhaps he would never be anything more among the Sidhe than he had been among the men of Dun Mor. If he would never do more than be a servant during the day and sleep alone upon the reeds on the floor of Liath's house at night, then what reason could he possibly have to stay?

One day Anlon found himself standing at the gates of Caher Idir, left open for the morning while a few of the Sidhe took their bronze-finished wooden buckets to the stream for fresh water. He stood gazing out into the cold and silent forest, wondering which way he should step.

"It is a short way in either direction," Scahta said.

He turned, and there she was, coldly radiant at his side. "A short way?" Had she read his mind?

She began to walk, slowly, out into the open spaces between the great trees, and he followed her. "Why are you here?" she asked.

Anlon stopped. "I am sorry, my lady. If you wish to be alone, I will go back—"

She raised her hand a little, stopping his words. "I do not mean here, or now," she explained, almost smiling. "I mean, why are you at Caher Idir?"

"Why . . . you invited me." He looked at her and began to feel cold. "Are you saying I am no longer welcome?"

"You are welcome for as long as you wish to stay."

"Then what—"

"You came here thinking you would be my husband. That has not happened. So, I am asking you: Why do you remain, when still you sleep alone each night?"

He paused, staring at her, feeling somehow guilty. "Perhaps you *are* able to hear my thoughts."

This time she did smile. "Concerning women, no man's thoughts are a secret. You may as well shout it from the rooftops." She moved beside the largest of the trees and placed her hand on its rough bark. "So tell me, Anlon," she asked, gazing up at him. "Why do you stay, if you do not have the reward you thought you were promised? Why stay if you get nothing in return?"

"Perhaps . . . perhaps because I know that a prize too easily won is hardly a prize at all. Perhaps I dare to hope that the more difficult the contest, the greater the value of what is won."

She lifted her eyebrows. "Do you feel that I am naught but a prize for you to win? That a kingship is but a shiny toy a child might covet, hopeful of running faster or leaping higher than all the other children?"

"I do not. I—"

"Then why, Anlon, do you stay?"

"I stay because . . . I still hope one day to be your husband. I still hope one day to be your king. But if I cannot be those things, then I will stay and offer you whatever you are willing to take. You are a queen, both a queen of the Sidhe and of my heart . . . and never do I see that changing." He had begun intending to say what he thought she wanted to hear, but he had finished by saying what was in his heart.

Scahta watched him and nodded slightly. She made no answer, though her eyes shone. She started back toward the fortress and placed her fingers on his arm. Together they walked back through the gates of Caher Idir.

Three days later, Scahta again called Anlon and Cian to her side, and once more the three of them went into the forest.

This time, however, Anlon saw the suddenly moving tree branches, felt the little sprays, of water droplets from the tips of the branches, heard the tiny crackles of dead leaves. This time, it seemed, some of the other Sidhe had come along with them.

The forest lay wet and cold and silent in the heavy gloom of midwinter, almost in a state of perpetual twilight. The group walked on for a long time through a part of the woods Anlon had never seen, following a winding path that took them across streams and low valleys and then, gradually, higher and higher into the hills.

At last they stepped out of the woods and found themselves high on a wind-swept hill, on a field covered only with dry, green-brown grass. Anlon stood straight, gratefully stretching himself tall after the long time crouching and bending through the thick forest.

The view from the hill held him immobile. He looked down on the black and barren treetops, interlaced and heavy, stretching across the hills and valleys as far as he could see—except for one wide clear swath that ran from the field where they stood all the way down to the valley below. The swath was wide and bare and covered with the same half-green, half-brown grass.

The smooth grey sky curved over them, and the wind blew fresh and cold. Anlon stood tall, enjoying the sight of the endless countryside after the many days closed within the walls and trees of Caher Idir.

"I could stay up here forever," he heard himself say.

"I think not," Scahta answered. "Though it is a fine place to visit." She paused, brushing a dry leaf from her long hair. "Perhaps, if we knew a better path to this mountaintop, I could visit it more often."

She turned to him, looking as though a marvelous idea had just come to her. "Anlon—do you think that you and

Cian could circle 'round and find a smooth path for us to follow? You could start there," she said, pointing down the back of the mountain toward the thick woods, "and return this way." She turned to face the wide grassy valley. As she had before, when they had stood together at the foot of the treacherous cliff, Scahta sighed. "It would indeed be lovely to come up here from time to time, far from Men. We would have a safe place for the Sidhe to gather. Will you find the path for me?"

Cian had already dropped his green-and-white cloak to the ground. Anlon pulled the bronze leaf pin from his own, and before it could fall to the wet grass Cian had turned and bolted into the forest. Anlon dashed after him, knowing that he could not allow him to vanish.

There was no doubt that Cian knew this region well. This was the land of the Sidhe and they knew every step of it, no matter what Scahta had said about wanting to find a new path.

This was another test.

What could the test be of this time? Anlon thought, struggling to keep up through the heavy brush on the all-but-invisible trail. Perhaps it was just a simple race—a contest of speed and endurance.

Yet he knew it could not be so simple. Just like the first time, there must be something more she wished to see—some hidden test that would not be immediately clear.

Also unclear was how Cian knew where to go. He continued at a fast and steady pace, knowing exactly where to turn, where to leap, where to step, with never a moment of hesitation or indecision. Either he knew the land extraordinarily well and had spent much time here, or . . .

There! There, by the side of the faint wet path, was a neat stack of smooth white pebbles, carefully arranged—

so carefully it could only have been done by the hands of the Sidhe.

He had no doubt now that the trail was marked. Here was a small pair of slanted lines slashed on the edge of a tree trunk; there, another carefully arranged stack of white pebbles. It would all have been perfectly clear to Cian. Yet he, as a Man, an outsider, had no knowledge at all of how to read the markings.

Cian had every advantage here. If Anlon was going to keep up, he would have to keep his opponent in sight and stay close on his heels—though Cian was certainly using every trick he knew to disappear.

Anlon gave up trying to use the delicate tactics of the Sidhe to slip through the forest. He simply began crashing through the brush and cracking down the saplings and scattering the fragile mounds of pebbles. With his doubled efforts he was able to keep Cian in sight and continue on the path that Scahta had set for them.

So, that was it! This was a test of resourcefulness. Of perseverance. Had she thought he would give up when only Cian could read the signs? Let Cian read them! He could show Anlon the way, and Anlon would rely on the strength that only a Man possessed to get him through.

On and on they ran, with Cian flying through the wet forest like a bird and Anlon crashing after him like a wild bull. Slowly, very slowly, Anlon began to gain on him— but it was clear he could not possibly catch up. There was no way he could win.

Then suddenly they were out of the forest and running on the windy grass of a wide open valley. Now the field was even. Now they could compete as equals! He could see the top of the mountain where Scahta waited, could see her small figure standing up there alone with her white fur cloak blowing in the wind.

He redoubled his efforts. His legs drove at the ground, muscles hard as iron, and he began to pull close to Cian.

In a moment they were even. Now the contest was equal—more than equal. Now the Man, with great long legs and muscles made strong from hard work, could begin to pull ahead.

His heart leaped. How easy it was now! Cian had no chance, just as Anlon had had no chance in the dark and unfamiliar woods.

Anlon looked up again at Scahta, and another thought struck him. He knew this was a test. He'd thought it to be a test of resourcefulness. But perhaps there was something more.

Kindness is the measure of a worthwhile man.

As he ran he could hear the voice of Scahta as if she were right beside him. He stayed alongside Cian even though he could have pulled ahead.

Kindness is the measure—

Along the edge of the valley was a ditch, narrow and rough, spotted with rocks and puddles and patches of mud. Anlon swung off and continued running while down in the ditch.

Now the race was different. Now Anlon no longer had the clear advantage, as Cian had had in the forest.

Now the race was even.

The ditch led all the way up to the foot of the mountain. Anlon stayed there even as Cian, glancing down and clearly baffled as to why his rival should choose such a path, held his own and even began to draw slightly ahead.

But Anlon was relying upon his own abilities to win the race for him, not on the advantage his size and strength gave him in a foot race over open country. The two competitors, hearts racing, legs pounding, reached the foot of the mountain together.

They started up, and almost instantly Anlon felt his lungs aching for air and his muscles beginning to quiver and burn from the long and desperate race. He knew that now he and his Sidhe opponent were truly even, and he gave it his all, one last push, one last stride, and collapsed at the top of the mountain at Scahta's feet, one short step ahead of Cian.

Chapter Seven

Never had Anlon drawn himself up so tall as he did on the apex of the mountain that cold grey day. Cian still lay flat on the grass, his sides heaving, but Anlon knew it was not exhaustion that kept him down. Anlon had beaten him fairly—more than fairly. And Cian knew it.

"It seems that you have won the race, Anlon," Scahta said, turning to him with only the barest glance at his opponent. "But, tell me: Have you won the test as well?"

He raised his chin, breathing deep of the cold damp air. "I do believe I have, my lady."

"Then, tell me: What was this test meant to discover?"

"It was more than just a race. It was a test of honor."

"Of honor." She cocked her head. "How?"

Anlon took a step back as Cian got slowly to his feet, but he never looked away from Scahta. "A race not run over a fair course is no race at all. I wanted a fair race—

not necessarily a victory. And when the chance was mine, I made the race a fair one."

She smiled. "So you did. This contest *is* yours, Anlon." She glanced at Cian, who glowered and said nothing, and then she turned back to Anlon. "Walk with me to Caher Idir. Perhaps you and I will eat together, at twilight." She started back down the trail into the forest.

Anlon stood back and allowed Cian to go before him. "It was so kind of you to show me the way the first time," he said with a grin, still a little breathless. "Perhaps you will be generous enough to do so again."

Cian glared at him, seemed about to speak, but in the end said nothing. Anlon walked past him into the forest and stayed close beside Scahta all the way back to Caher Idir.

That evening, Anlon could think of nothing but Scahta's invitation. *Perhaps you and I will eat together*, she had said. It took him back to the first night they had shared together at Caher Idir. He remembered how warm and comfortable Scahta's home was, and how lovely and desirable she herself had been. Tonight, perhaps, he would not fall asleep in the rushes as he had before.

At twilight he presented himself at her door, which opened for him before he could touch it. He stepped inside, smiling at the sight of her beside the hearth as she waited for him. But much to his dismay, he discovered that he was not the only guest in Scahta's home that evening.

Cian was there, too, standing on the other side of the hearth, glaring silently in Anlon's direction.

Anlon and his rival spent a very strained evening on the fresh dry rushes of Scahta's home, while she herself sat cross-legged up on the soft furs of her sleeping ledge and looked down upon them. The entire time she seemed cool and unconcerned, nibbling at her barley-acorn bread and small joints of bird as though unaware of the glaring tension just below her. The evening ended shortly after the meal, and both Anlon and Cian left for their own cold corners of the dark fortress.

It proved to be one of the few times that Anlon would see Scahta, or even speak to her, for many days. Never did he touch her, except in his dreams—dreams where she came to him softly and gently, with a shining strength that was, in its own way, more than a match for his own. He would embrace her, and there would be nothing at all between them, nothing at all but their flesh touching, warming each other. . . .

And then he would awaken and find himself alone.

By day, Scahta continued to observe both Cian and Anlon—especially Anlon, who could not always sense her presence as easily as Cian could. Yet this Man had surprised her like nothing else ever had. Still, she recalled that morning when, it had seemed, his voice had held the power to call her to him.

It had not been strength or force making her take that step. It had been the sincerity and longing in his voice. That had brought such warmth to her heart she had been ready to walk straight to him, to look up into his hazel eyes, to raise her hand to touch his face. . . .

But she *had* stopped herself. Anlon was a stranger who might become her people's king. The last thing she could allow herself to do was form a bond with him, grow close to him, care about him, love him. . . .

If he fell in love with her, that was quite well; no harm would be done, for all men easily forgot one woman for another. But she herself could not afford to love him in return. She was a queen, a sovereign who might one day be forced to send Anlon back to his own people and set another in his place . . . and she knew it might not be possible to do such a thing to one who had stolen her heart.

Now, the nights were darker and quieter than any Scahta could remember. Though her three serving women always slept in the soft thick rushes below her sleeping ledge, never had she felt so abandoned, so alone.

Never like this.

Sometimes, deep in the darkness, she would find herself sitting up in the soft furs of the ledge and peering out of the small high window into the cold and cloudy night. She would place her hand over her chest and wonder at the intense longing that she felt. Had he called her again? Was he waiting for her, searching for her, longing for her just as she longed—

Scahta wanted nothing more than to throw off the furs and go out into the night, searching for the warmth that awaited her there. But always she would force herself to lie back down and close her eyes and think of things only with her head, not her heart.

How very easy it would be if she were just another woman of the Sidhe. She could take Anlon for a night or for a lifetime, and, if she were lucky, bring a handsome child or two into the world of the Sidhe. If she chose to love Anlon, she would be free to do so, for they would simply be one more bonded pair among her people.

But she was not like any other woman. Anlon required not her love but her most careful and dispassionate scrutiny. She had vowed the people of the Sidhe would always come first, and if Anlon were to be their King he would have to understand that, too.

* * *

The days grew shorter, the nights longer and colder, until at last it was the time of the Winter Solstice. And then the days grew hungrier, too.

The barley flour was gone. Even stretching it with ground acorn meal had not yielded enough to last the Sidhe through the winter. The clan's meager supply of dried apples, along with dark green wintercress from the streams and whatever roots they could pull from the dead dry rushes and the water lilies, were all they had to supplement the little meat and fish the men of the Sidhe could bring in.

Each day Anlon went out with several other men to find food. Anlon and Liath would tie thorns to thin strips of leather, bait them with worms and insects, and leave them up and down the stream as far as they could safely walk. The men would set snares and traps for any hares and foxes and birds and even mice that had not grown wary enough to avoid them. The trappers would slip and struggle across the muddy forest floor, the cold dampness soaking through their soft leather boots, ever conscious of the openness of the bare woodlands and the great possibility of being seen.

After that they might join together and look for a red deer to stalk, though the strong and wary creatures were difficult to kill. The Sidhe had only their leather slings and wooden, fire-hardened spears to use in bringing down game, and there were fewer places for the hunters to hide in the winter forest. Often some of the precious dried apples had to be used to lure the deer close enough for the Sidhe to strike. Even with their best efforts, they were lucky to get a kill perhaps once a fortnight.

From time to time they would catch a glimpse of the wild boar that populated the woods. One would have made an excellent meal, but the Sidhe did not even attempt to kill them. They simply did not have enough hunters to bring down one of the fierce, blood-thirsty animals.

"You have never spent a winter like this one," Scahta said to him one day, as he walked to the stream with his thorns and leather strips.

He looked up, startled as always whenever she appeared. She stood with her hand on one of the great trees, gazing over at him as if she had always been there. Her dark eyes gleamed, and her soft brown hair lay like a cloud over the pure white fur of her cloak.

Anlon took a few steps toward her. "I have not," he said. "We rarely hunted in the winter."

"Why did you not hunt?"

He looked away, almost embarrassed. "There was no need. We had sides of smoked meat hanging in the sheds, from the herds of sheep and cattle that we kept for Dun Mor."

"And for bread, did you eat acorn and barley flour?"

"Never. There was more wheat flour than we could carry. You have seen the endless fields of the *dun*." He tried to meet her eyes again, but could not. "We always had plenty of dried fruit and good cheese," he went on quietly. "Most of the time there was even fresh milk and pale butter, since there was usually at least one cow with a winter calf. We would keep them safe in a shed, bedded down with straw from the wheat."

"I see." She let her hand fall from the side of the tree. "The woods are so cold and wet in winter. Did you ever leave the warmth and safety of your farm during such days?"

He looked away again. "Only to go to the stream for water each morning. If the weather was mild, I might have done a bit of fishing or set a snare."

"But not truly out of necessity."

Anlon sighed. "You are right. It was never really necessary. It was more for sport than anything. Until now, never did the winter bring anything worse than a little boredom through the long hours of darkness."

She took a step toward him, and then another. "You find this winter to be different."

He paused, and looked into her eyes once more. "It is unlike anything I could have imagined."

"The gates of Dun Mor will still open for you, Anlon." She stood silent, waiting, her hands folded.

He only smiled at her, and picked up his thorn hooks and leather fishing lines. "Perhaps I will bring you a fine salmon today, Queen Scahta," he said, and with an effort turned away from her and continued on to the cold rushing stream.

It was no coincidence, he knew, that Scahta had reminded him of how much different his other winters had been. At his family home there had never been a worry about having enough food, but now each short day was a grim struggle for survival.

Anlon learned to work quickly so they did not have to stay in the open forest any longer than necessary. Almost immediately their work became a race between him and Cian—a race to see who could get the most fish, set the most snares, haul the most water, and get back first to the fortress.

Anlon even took a perverse pleasure whenever he was able to bring in an extra trout, whenever he discovered a struggling white-coated hare in a trap he had set. He was not just helping the people of Caher Idir. He was also defeating his rival and showing Scahta that he was as much a part of this place as any of those who had been born to it.

Yet his successes were small ones. A few trout, a few hares, even a winter-thin young deer did not last long among fifty-seven people. One day, Anlon watched as Liath cut long strips from the inner bark of a willow tree. It was all that the hunters brought back that day.

Late that night, Anlon was awakened by the wailing cry of a woman. Sitting up in the rushes, he threw off the furs and hurried outside.

Scahta and Ean stood in the misty darkness of the yard, on either side of the young woman named Cleite. She was doubled over with pain, gasping, and the two others quickly led her back to her house.

Anlon started to follow, but Liath stopped him. "There is nothing for us to do there," he said. "We can only hope that Scahta and Ean will be able to save yet another child of the winter." He returned to the house, leaving Anlon standing alone in the dark.

In the morning they took away Cleite's stillborn infant. A few days later, that child was joined by a small girl who had not seen the turn of one year. Each time a procession carried a tiny body away, the sorrowful wailing of the women of the Sidhe rose up on the wind and traveled with them.

Somehow the days went by . . . a fortnight, and another, and another. As before, Anlon saw little of Scahta. All he could do was follow the daily routines of Caher Idir and try to keep himself occupied until the next test, which he knew could come at any time. There would have to be at least one more. He and Cian had each been the winner in one competition. Scahta would require a third to break the tie.

The time passed, and the seasons turned. The air lost some of its chill, and pale green leaves began to appear on the black branches of the trees. Flowers blossomed and the air warmed even more, for spring was approaching.

The milder weather brought longer days and a little more food. There would be no more flour until the harvest the following fall, but now the Sidhe could gather dandelions, the young shoots and green flower spikes of rushes, and occasionally a few eggs from a goose or swan if they ranged far enough to search out a nest. And there was still the meat, fish, and birds that the Sidhe hunters struggled to bring in each day in an effort to keep Caher Idir one step ahead of hunger.

Spring also meant the start of planting. One morning, Anlon collected a digging stick and went with several other men to help break the ground and plant the barley. He expected to go to the high open spaces to find the fields, but instead Liath led them into the forest.

After a time, he stopped at a small clearing. There was just enough open space in the trees to permit a bit of daylight to get through. "Where are the fields?" Anlon asked him, in confusion. "I thought we were going to begin the planting today."

Liath glanced at him as he set down his sticks. "The men of Dun Mor can have their fields on vast tracts of cleared forest without a care for who or what might see them. What is there to harm Men?" He shook his head. "The secret gardens of the Sidhe must stay as hidden as Caher Idir. Otherwise they would lead Men straight to the gates of our home."

Anlon could only nod. "I do not think I will ever get

used to such fields," he murmured. "And this is why you grow nothing but barley? Never any wheat, never any flax?"

"The barley is all that will tolerate such fields as these," said Mactire. "Not a handspan of earth is wasted on trying to grow anything else. Bread is more important than linen." He, too, gave Anlon a cold look. "Now, perhaps, you understand why flour is in short supply and often made in part from acorns."

Anlon could only nod, slowly. "And I wonder why I never thought of such things before."

Yet even with the planting and the neverending hunting and food-gathering, Anlon found a use for the extra light at the end of each day. When all the tasks were done, he would go out alone to the forest with his bronze sword and practice swinging and handling the unfamiliar weapon. He did not know if, or when, he might be called upon to use it, but something told him he had best be ready.

Today, as on all the other days, Anlon got slowly up out of the rushes of Liath's house and walked outside into the early morning. The trees overhead had become a thick canopy of deep green leaves, leaving Caher Idir hidden in cool shade.

Yet there was something different about this particular morning. The moon would rise full tonight, the second such moon since the equinox of spring. Tonight was the eve of the festival known as Beltane.

"Good day to you, Anlon." He was startled to see Scahta walking past him across the village grounds. Then he saw that Cian walked close behind her. Instantly he knew that at last the day had come—the day of Queen Scahta's final test.

Halfway to the gate, she turned to face him. "Aren't you coming?"

Anlon tensed. "I am. There is just one thing I need—" Acting on instinct, he ran back to the house and grabbed the sword out of the rushes, strapping it on as he raced back to the gate.

Quickly he moved to join Scahta and Cian as they started into the fragrant depths of the awakening forest. The gates closed behind him, but he did not look back. He only wondered when—or if—he would ever see Caher Idir again.

They took their time on the path that day, which only added to Anlon's torment. While Scahta walked casually along, stopping frequently to admire a flower or point out a bird, he could think of nothing but what might happen when at last the sun went down.

At one point the trio sat down on the grassy bank of a stream to eat. Cian, it seemed, had thought to bring boiled water-lily roots and dried apples. Not to be outdone, Anlon caught a few fish from the stream with his leather line and a thorn, and soon he had the fish cleaned and baking on the hot stones in a firepit. Even Scahta and Cian seemed impressed by how quickly he had caught the fish and set up camp.

"Quite easy after serving the Fianna all those months," Anlon said. "There are only three of us."

"Three. So we are." Cian held Anlon's eyes for a short moment, then reached for another chunk of fish. Scahta, as always, seemed not to notice.

But Anlon could keep silent no longer. He finished his meal and turned to face the Sidhe queen. "My lady," he began.

She looked up, blinking, faintly surprised he had spoken. He hesitated, but plunged on. "It is clear to me that this last test will not be the same as the other two. This time, I recognize the path. I know where we are going."

"And where do you believe we are going, Anlon?"

"For Dun Mor. Straight for Dun Mor."

Cian sat up, his eyes flicking from one of them to the other, but he kept silent. Scahta merely shrugged. "This path is well known. It leads to many places. The fortress of your men is only one of them."

"Yet tonight is also Beltane." He struggled to keep the tension from showing in his voice.

Scahta glanced up into the sky—blue and vast and studded with bright white clouds—as if to examine it. "So it is," she said nodding in agreement.

"We are going to Dun Mor, on the eve of Beltane." Anlon's breath quickened. "I can no longer keep my silence, Queen Scahta. I know that this must be the third and last of your tests. What can you possibly mean to have us do at Dun Mor on the eve of Beltane?"

"You are so sure this is a test. Can we not simply go for a pleasant walk on a beautiful spring day?"

"Of course we can. But I am certain that today, we are not."

She smiled, but Anlon continued, his urgency growing. "I know well that the Sidhe are drawn to the Beltane rituals just as Men are. My own grandsire was a child of the fires, as are—"

"As am I," she interrupted calmly. Half-closing her eyes, she turned her face up to the sun and allowed the breeze to caress her skin and golden-brown hair.

Something like pain, like fear, rose in his chest. "Do you mean for all of us to participate in the ritual around the fires? Do you intend that Cian and I stand aside while you choose another partner on this night?"

The queen's eyes opened briefly, but quickly she closed them again, sighing a little as the clouds moved aside and the full light of the sun warmed her skin.

Anlon clutched the hilt of his bronze sword, not caring that Cian grew increasingly jittery across from him. "I know well the joy and abandon that is the very heart of Beltane," Anlon went on. "I know that possessiveness has no part in it. But I cannot deny that I want no one—not Man, not Sidhe—to approach you at the Beltane fires tonight." He paused and drew a deep breath. "Not unless I am the one."

He heard a low and furious sound from Cian. Anlon's grip tightened on the hilt of his sword. But Scahta merely rose to her feet, adjusted her deerskin gown and soft white wool cloak, and continued down the path to the human castle.

It was as if she had not heard a word.

Anlon closed his eyes. No test could be more difficult than this. He wondered if he could simply melt back into the forest as the Sidhe were so adept at doing. Cian could declare himself the winner of this particular test if he wished. Anlon would not, could not simply stand by and watch Scahta while she—

He and Cian exchanged cold hard glances, then quickly picked up the camp and caught up to Scahta. The three walked on, again taking their time and frequently stopping to rest. Scahta would sit calmly and watch the birds in the trees while Anlon and Cian could only stand and glare in silence at each other.

The day wore on . . . and after what seemed like a very long time, it began to fade into evening.

Chapter Eight

The night was fast approaching, but it was not so dark that Anlon could not recognize the place where they walked. They were very close to Dun Mor, just off the road where Scahta had left the bronze sword hanging from the blackthorn tree. As the little group reached the edge of the woods, Anlon caught his breath.

There ahead, in the deep twilight, were the massive walls of the fortress. And in the open field before it, in the same spot as it had been for Samhain, an enormous stack of wood waited for nightfall and Men's torches.

"Beltane," whispered Anlon.

"So it is. Beltane. A celebration of summer," said Scahta, "when all of us seek out partners in the hope of creating new life."

"New life," repeated Cian, and he took a step toward Scahta, smiling at her.

Instantly Anlon's feelings toward Scahta, so long held

in check, flared once again into an overwhelming jealousy. He knew what was about to happen out there in the field and in the forests—partners found, lust gratified, all of them, Men and Sidhe, caught in the power of the moonlit summer night called Beltane.

He moved to stand between the queen and Cian, ignoring his rival and keeping his full attention on Scahta. "I can respect your wish that I may not touch you unless and until I am your husband—but you must understand that neither will I watch you with another. Not on this night, not on *any* night!"

She gazed up at him, looking a little surprised. "Do you mean to tell me who may or may not be my partner, Anlon?"

He stared back, trying to calm himself, but the thought of the great mountain of wood that would shortly blaze into life kept his heart pounding and his breath ragged. "I tell you only that I will do everything in my power to see to it that I am that partner."

"Everything in your power . . ." She glanced out toward the field, where the luminous yellow glow of the rising moon showed just below the horizon. "Are you so certain that I am the one you want?"

"Oh, I am certain. . . ." Anlon gazed down at her small and perfect form, at the gentle curve of her waist where the soft leather belt wrapped around it . . . at the cloud of dark hair that fell down past her hip, at her smooth lips and shining dark eyes. "Never have I been so certain of anything."

He could not stop himself. He reached out to her, wanting only to draw her close, but she caught his gold-covered wrists and forced him to turn away so that he looked out toward the waiting bonfire.

The sight held him motionless. There, emerging from

the forest on the other side of the field, were the people of Dun Mor, laughing and dancing and draped with green leaves and colorful wildflowers. They formed a merry torchlit procession as they made their way to the mountain of wood.

The sky had turned to black, and the great yellow moon rose behind wispy clouds. The people began to circle the mountain, flinging their torches high in the air so that they landed on the wood and started it burning. In a few moments the dancers were skittering back from the billowing ball of flame and forming a wide circle around it, leaping and posing and vying for each other's attention.

"You have visited the fires before, Anlon?" Scahta asked.

He swallowed. "Always near my home, a bonfire would be built each Beltane Eve. All those who worked in the fields and cared for the herds would go there . . . and sometimes a few of the Sidhe. Never have I been to the fires of Dun Mor."

Scahta placed her hand beneath his arm and urged him to take a step toward the field. "Look at them," she said again. "Look at the beautiful young women of Dun Mor. I am small, and dark, and plain. They are tall and strong. They have skin white as milk, they have hair long and flowing as molten gold. And they are calling you, Anlon. They are calling you."

You are the one who is beautiful, he wanted to say to her, *fragile and beautiful as the white hawthorn flower, as luminous and magical as the moon.* . . . But he found he could not speak. Scahta's voice had him in its thrall.

"Look at them," she said.

He looked. The women of Dun Mor, all wearing twists of ivy and violets and primroses in their red and gold hair, danced and whirled and laughed as they circled the bonfire. Their simple linen gowns of vibrant red or deep blue or soft green clung to their bodies and clearly outlined their curving, long-legged beauty. Long necks, shining eyes, fair skin flushed by the heat—he could not look away, he could not . . .

"Scahta," he whispered.

Just then all the dancers dashed away from the flames, scattering in his direction. Blinking, he saw that some of the men had driven a herd of red-and-white cattle as near to the bonfire as they could force the animals to go. They used long sticks to make the cows run through the smoke and heat and light, burning away the cold stale air in which they had lived all winter and making them ready to return to the high summer pastures after their long confinement.

The animals lumbered off into the darkness. The dancers began returning to the bonfire to resume their merrymaking—all, that is, but one.

One of the women turned and saw Anlon at the edge of the forest. He stood staring out at the dancers, at the women, as if he had been enchanted by them . . . and so he had. He knew that he should get away, now, quickly, before it was too late, run back into the forest where Scahta and Cian—

Anlon turned and searched the night-black woods for his companions. They were gone.

In the moonlit darkness, Anlon felt slender fingers on his neck and gentle hands on his shoulders. Then a feminine voice called out, "Orla! Keavy! Come here! Look at what I've found!"

Beside him, so close that he could feel her warm breath on his face, was a tall and lovely woman with blond hair to her knees and chains of white and pink violets clinging to her soft blue linen gown.

"Morrin! What is it? Oh—*oh!*"

The other two women, one blond like Morrin, the other with flying red hair draped with yellow primroses, hurried over to them, breathless, to stop and stare at Anlon.

"Well, he looks like a fine one," said the red-haired woman, Keavy, looking him up and down. "But such strange clothes!" She reached out to run her fingers down the smooth leather of his tunic, allowing them to continue down over his hip until at the last moment her hand fell away.

Morrin studied him closely, catching both of his hands in hers and holding them wide apart so that she could see him better. "He looks almost like one of the Sidhe: the leather clothes, the high soft boots. . . ."

"And this," said the third woman, the other blonde, Orla. She reached out and lifted the end of his sword in its bronze-trimmed scabbard, raising it up until the tip pointed at her belly. Looking directly into his eyes, she stroked the smooth hard wood of the scabbard with her hand and smiled. "Very, very nice."

Morrin let go of his hands, but Anlon could not move. He did not know these women, they were strangers to him, yet they may as well have had him bound with chains. It was a shock to discover what power they held over him—the power of his knowing that they were his for the asking, completely and entirely his, on this particular night. And he knew that he could have one of them, two of them, or even all three together.

Orla released the scabbard and let it fall back against his leg. "Will you come and dance with us?" she asked, reaching out and catching hold of his hand.

"He may not wish to be seen in the full light of the fires, if he is one of the Sidhe," said Keavy. "Usually they are shy creatures, preferring darkness and shadow—"

"Keavy! He's not one of the Sidhe," said Orla. "Look at him. He's much too tall, much too strong!"

Morrin laughed. "Many of the Sidhe carry the blood of Men," she said. "And it happens in just this way—at the Beltane fires. No doubt, that is what he is."

"I would stay in the shadows with him," said Keavy, her voice low and enticing. She moved close and picked up his other hand. "I would not make him dance in the glare of the fires if I could keep him close to me in the moonlight."

"Oh, and I would do the same," said Orla, with a little laugh. "Why let him spend his strength in dancing?"

"Do you think there's enough of him to go around?" asked Morrin, running her fingers down his arms, his hands, his face.

"More than enough!" said Orla, and all of them laughed.

They pressed close to him, touching him, caressing him, and he could feel the curves of their bodies fitting against him. The scent of their hair and skin was warm and sweet, so very sweet. . . .

He closed his eyes tightly. He could have gotten lost in them so easily. This was what all men were meant to do, *expected* to do, on this one night of Beltane, when all should seek out a willing partner or maybe even several so that many strong children would be born the following spring. That was why he was here, that was why all of them were here—

Anlon stopped. He forced himself to think in spite of the presence of the three enticing women. Why *was* he here? If he had remained with the Fianna, he would have

99

stayed all winter at Dun Mor and been preparing to leave with them tomorrow for another summer riding across the countryside—after a carefree night spent with these beautiful young women of the *dun*, out here in the forest beneath the full moon.

Scahta . . .

Scahta had brought him here. She had led both him and Cian here, and he had known that she meant to test them yet again. He'd thought that she would test them by choosing another partner for herself and then seeing how each reacted. Would they respect her choice? Or would they insist that she wait until she chose either Anlon or Cian?

But, as with the other two tests, perhaps Scahta was looking for something quite different. She had brought him all the way to Dun Mor on Beltane Eve, of all nights—and then she had left him all alone.

Except, of course, for a crowd of beautiful and charming young women who would give him anything he wanted, all he had ever imagined, if only he would stay the night with them.

Now Anlon understood. Scahta had brought him here to choose. Did he want the women of Dun Mor and the pleasures they were so eagerly offering him? Or would he stay among the Sidhe, as he had said he would do, even though it might mean sleeping alone in the rushes until the day that Scahta made her choice?

The three women kissed and caressed him. Together they began to draw him deeper into the forest, where the soft earth and sheltering trees would make comfortable beds for—

With the last bit of willpower he possessed, Anlon pulled away from the women and fled.

*   *   *

Anlon raced through the forest, seeking the darkness and the shadows, wanting to leave the glare of the fire and the shine of the moonlight as far behind as possible. "Come back! Oh, come back!" called Orla and Keavy and Morrin, but he could hear their laughter too. Their disappointment would only be momentary, for he knew that they would quickly return to the bonfire and find new partners.

One day, perhaps, the three women would have an amusing story to tell about how they had met a man of the Sidhe in the forest on Beltane Eve, only to have him vanish back into the shadows when they tried to draw him close. It would only add to the tales of the elusive and secretive Sidhe, and might even help them to survive a little longer.

But right now, with every stride, with every dodge past a tree and every leap over a rock or fallen log, he strove to put the women out of his mind. He wanted only to find Scahta. She had to be here, somewhere nearby. She would certainly be watching to see what he did, she would want to see the outcome of her test—

Suddenly he slowed, then stopped. Off to one side was a glimmer of light deep within a thick grove of trees.

Slowly he walked toward that grove. "I've come back to you," he called, his breath still ragged. "I turned away from them. I have come back to you."

There was no response. He stood motionless in the cool dark woods, but his blood still ran hot and his heart pounded. "Scahta!" he cried out, desperate to see her. "Scahta, come to me! Come to me!" Where was she?

He looked wildly about, knowing she was close, very close—and caught his breath when he saw her standing calmly just a few steps away from him.

"Oh—you are here, I knew you would be here. . . ."

His mind had forgotten the three women in the forest but his body most certainly had not. The longer he stood looking at Scahta, at her glistening eyes and delicate curves, the longer the scent of her rose to his nostrils and went straight to his head, the more heat coursed through his veins and the more rigid his body became.

He reached for her—but another hand moved to clasp his wrist. Looking up, he found Cian glaring straight into his eyes.

Quickly he looked from the Sidhe warrior to his queen and back again. Neither had their cloaks on—the cloaks lay one atop the other, white upon green-and-white, spread out smooth and inviting on the soft earth beneath the trees. Cian was without his tunic. Scahta's hair was decked with blue violets and had fallen over her eyes.

"It is Beltane Eve after all, is it not?" she asked, pushing tendrils of her long dark hair back from her face. She gazed up at him, waiting.

In an instant the fire in his blood turned from lust to anger. Anlon tore his attention from Scahta and turned the full force of his rage on Cian.

"If you want her," Anlon hissed, through clenched teeth, "you will have to fight for her." He threw off Cian's restraining hand. Pulling off his own cloak and tunic, he whirled around to face Cian with open, reaching hands—but stopped short when he saw the gleam of bronze and realized that Cian's sword was pointed straight at his heart.

"Nothing would give me greater pleasure than to fight for Scahta," said Cian, his voice low and furious. "Unless it is killing you."

Anlon fought for control through his rage. "I will fight you. But I will not kill you. Put the sword away."

"Never," Cian answered, and lunged for him.

Anlon had gone through any number of wrestling matches with his brothers and childhood friends, and even with the Fianna, but the small Sidhe was faster than any man Anlon had ever fought. And never before had he had to fight for his life.

Anlon managed to dodge the gleaming sword, but it burned in the passing and left a line of blood along his bare arm. Cian was not just threatening him. He meant to fight to the death.

Anlon reached down and whipped out his own sword. Released from its scabbard, the bronze blade shone in the light of the moon. "You cannot hope to win, Cian," he said, in an effort to reason with him. "I am twice your size. I trained with the Fianna—"

"You are a Man, slow and bragging, and you will never be my king!" With that Cian swung at Anlon again, but this time the two swords clashed. Man and Sidhe faced each other down across three feet of deadly metal.

Anlon had the strength to force Cian's sword away, but it was his only advantage. His lack of experience was now fully evident. So quick was the Sidhe that Anlon found himself desperately blocking shot after shot with no chance to attack.

At last, with a shout of rage, substituting passion and desperation for skill, Anlon swung one last time with all his strength. Cian's sword went flying through the air, flashing in the moonlight as it turned end over end and disappeared into the shadows of the trees.

The Sidhe leaped back, his arms at his sides and rage and frustration in his eyes. Anlon stood over him, breathing hard, blood trickling down his arm, his own sword pointing directly at his enemy's throat.

"Now, Cian," Anlon said, "the fight is over. I will not

kill you. But if you attack me again, you will not use a sword again for a very long time."

Cian ground his teeth, too enraged even to speak, and finally looked over at Scahta. "Why did you not kill him, Anlon?" she asked, her voice as cool and neutral as always. Was she fighting her reactions? he wondered. He thought he could see pleasure in her eyes, but it did not come across in her tone.

Anlon stepped back a pace from Cian, and then another, slowly lowering his weapon. After replacing the sword in its scabbard he looked at her with a steady gaze. "I have no wish to kill anyone, my lady, much less one of your people."

She considered. "Yet he spared no effort in trying to kill you. You have every reason to take his life."

"For all these many months I have thought of nothing but someday being your king," he answered. "What kind of king would become one of the Sidhe only by killing them?"

She nodded, looking away, seemingly lost in thought. The she met his eyes again. "You understand that you are being tested this night."

"I do, my lady. Of course."

"And what do you believe the test is for?"

He smiled, beginning to relax slightly, though he was still mindful of Cian's nearness—and of the hatred that showed no signs of lessening. "I believe it is a test of loyalty."

"Loyalty. I see. And tell me, Anlon, do you believe that you have won this particular test?"

He glanced at the glowering Cian, then back to Scahta. "I do, my lady. It was a test the like of which I hope never to experience again. But I believe I have demonstrated my loyalty to you in ways that should remove any doubt you may have had."

She shook her hair back from her face, sending the chain of blue violets cascading over her shoulders. "Why do you believe that to be true?"

He frowned slightly, beginning to feel the first stab of worry. "You brought me to Dun Mor on Beltane Eve. No other place, no other night. You knew that the women of the *dun* would be seeking partners, that one of them would no doubt offer herself to me." He shot a glance at Cian and could not help feeling smug. "Indeed, it was not one, but three—three of the most beautiful."

He looked again at Scahta, directly into her eyes, for he knew that nothing he would ever say to her again would be as important as this. "I did not take the life of one of the Sidhe, although I had every reason to do so. He drew my blood. And worse—he led me to think that he was the one you had chosen on this night."

She cocked her head, and regarded him carefully. "Are you so certain that I have not chosen him?"

Anlon paused for a long moment, holding himself very still, and then answered her carefully. "Yes. Because— because I believe you are still testing me, Queen Scahta."

She looked at him for a time, and her mouth began to curve into a slight smile. "Then you believe that you have won."

He, too, began to smile. And so, to Anlon's surprise, did Cian. "I do not see how I could have failed."

"I believe that this particular test has had no winner, Anlon. I see only that it has been a tie."

"A tie . . ." He could not believe what he was hearing. "A tie? What more could I have done to prove my loyalty to you and to all the people of the Sidhe?"

"Nothing more. Nothing more was needed. You did

not take a partner at the Beltane fires, and neither did Cian. Therefore, neither of you has lost, and neither of you has won."

She gazed at Cian, who now gave her a sly smile. "It is always my greatest pleasure to serve you, my lady," he said, and walked a few steps into the forest to get his tunic and cloak.

Anlon stared at her in shock, but she apparently had eyes only for Cian. "I thank you," she said, as he returned to her. "Go now. Get your sword and go back to Caher Idir. We will meet you there at dawn."

Without saying a word, merely smiling at her once again, Cian turned away and vanished into the dark forest.

Chapter Nine

Now, at last, they were alone. Anlon had expected to feel joy when he was at last alone in Scahta's presence, but found instead that his anxiety and anger only grew. "You said that Cian took no partner at the Beltane fires," he said in a low voice. "But what about here, in the darkest part of the forest?"

Scahta frowned, her slender brows drawing close together. "Why do you care about such a thing?" she asked, then brushed past him to get her white wool cloak from the forest floor.

He caught her wrist. "Was he your partner this night, Scahta? I resisted, out of loyalty to you. But what about you? I have a right to know!"

She met his gaze, making no effort to pull away. "You have a right to nothing, Anlon. You are here because you may one day serve the Sidhe as king. But on this night, I am queen, and you are still nothing."

His frustration rising, Anlon released her, then pulled his sword from his scabbard. The naked blade shone in the moonlight as he threw it down at her feet. "If I am nothing, then I should not own this. It is yours, I believe."

She spared not a glance for the weapon. "Now I see what you are truly made of. Now I learn what I needed to know all along."

She started to walk away, but he caught her again and this time pulled her close, breathing in the scent of the violets in her hair, intoxicated by feeling her small strong body pressed up against him. "Scahta . . . Scahta, be with me tonight, on this night of all nights, on this Beltane Eve. . . ."

He expected her to pull away, but she remained close, so close that the warmth of her body began to spread through him. Her heart beat fast, and her breath came quick and short. As gently as he could, with desire taking hold and turning his body to iron, he released her wrist and embraced her shoulders, resting his face against the soft warm cloud of her hair.

"Scahta, I have wanted this for so long," he whispered, his breath coming as quickly as hers. "This night is ours and ours alone. I only wish that it could last forever."

She stretched up tall, sliding her slender body upward against his, as though reaching for him. He raised his head and then looked down into her molten copper eyes, for she had turned her face up to his and stood gazing at him in the moonlight.

With one hand he stroked the side of her face, his body tightening even more as he saw her close her eyes. He moved his fingers down to the delicate skin of her throat and began to caress it, moving upward so that she raised her chin. All he could see were her soft lips, wet and glistening with desire.

"*Scahta* . . ." His voice was barely audible as he lowered his mouth to hers. Yet he knew that she had heard him, for her body softened and eased into his arms as he kissed her.

Anlon kissed her again, and again, and each time she seemed to grow warmer and softer even as he grew stronger and more driven to possess her. At last he reached down and lifted her up into his arms, then turned to carry her to the soft earth beneath the trees.

But at his first step Scahta stiffened and pulled away. Throwing back her head, she twisted out of his grasp and came to earth a few steps away from him, stumbling a little as she landed.

She stood there staring up at him, panting like a wild creature of the night.

Anlon grabbed her wrist and pulled her to him again, quickly, roughly, before she could escape. "Scahta, you will not leave me tonight," he said, his voice low and his breathing fast. "Not tonight, not after all this time—"

But she only pulled back against his insistent grasp. "I cannot," she said. Her usually cool and steady voice was a mere whisper. "I cannot. I *will not.*"

He held on tight. "There is no reason why we should not." Anlon stepped close and bent down to her again, hoping to persuade her once more with arms made strong by desire and a touch made gentle by love. His lips brushed hers again, but she hid her face and with all her strength pushed him away with both hands.

"There is a reason," she said, throwing back her flowing brown hair. "I am a queen. And you are not my husband."

Anlon clenched his fists in frustration, knowing that

she would turn and disappear if he tried to catch hold of her again. "This night is Beltane. This night is for love and for desire. This night is for all who feel as you and I do. There is no reason why we should not—"

"It may be well for you think of me only as a faceless lover at the Beltane fires, but I can never think of you as such. I am trying to make a choice of a king for my people. I am not merely taking a lover for an evening."

"You would never be a 'faceless lover' to me, Scahta. I would—"

"You would become much more to me than a king, should I stay here with you this night. I could never hope to make a fair choice for Caher Idir if I—if we—"

He looked down into her large and luminous eyes, and there he saw what she could not put into words. He knew that he had sensed this in her, yet he had been torn by insecurity. "You fear you could love me, if you become my partner on this night," he whispered. "Is that what you are telling me?"

Scahta raised her chin, and he saw the pleading in her eyes. *Do not let me do this thing*, it seemed he heard her say. *There would be no going back. . . . Do not let me do this thing.*

"Ah, Scahta, but I want you to love me," he said softly. Slowly, gently, he moved to hold her again, bending down so his lips brushed her eyes and cheeks as he spoke. "You have had my love for so very long. Come to me and let us love each other . . . love each other here . . . now, on Beltane."

Once more she started to melt against him—but then braced hard and shoved him away and vanished into the deep black forest.

"*Scahta!*" All his lust and frustration and pent-up anger burst free in that shout. "Scahta, come back to me! Come back! You will not leave me tonight, not if I must search every leaf and path and clearing in this forest!"

He set his jaw and began to run through the woods, but then caught his breath as the Sidhe queen stepped directly in front of him and forced him to stop.

"I will save you the search, Anlon. This is something you must understand, if ever you are to return to Caher Idir."

He took hold of her wrist. She made no move to break away. Instead, she threw her head back to look up at him. "No man touches me unless he is my husband," she said, with some difficulty. "And I have never had a husband."

"Never . . ." He whispered the word and allowed her wrist to fall away. "Never . . ."

"You may well take me here, Anlon. I have not the strength to stop you. Cian has already gone. But it will be the last time you ever touch me, ever see me."

They stared at each other in the moonlight, both breathing deeply of the night air, the tension between them threatening to snap. Finally Anlon looked away, and Scahta too lowered her gaze.

"Let me walk with you back to Caher Idir, Queen Scahta," he said. "I will see you safely home. But be warned—I do not give up easily. I will find a way to make you want to be with me and only with me. I will find a way to make you want me for your king—and for your lover—and for your husband."

She looked carefully at him, into his eyes, then walked away to pick up her cloak. With only a brief glance at Anlon she walked into the forest.

He retrieved his sword from the ground and followed her in silence, certain he would never be able to still the racing of his blood and the longing in his heart.

* * *

The days grew longer, and softer, and warmer, one flowing smoothly into the next; and before Anlon realized it, fourteen nights had gone by. A fortnight had passed since that long evening beside the Beltane fire, where he had been close, so close, to claiming Scahta for his own . . . but had released her because she had asked it of him.

Yet he was not ready to give up the idea of being her husband, of being her king. He was determined to keep showing he was worthy of her, and he would take every chance he could find to prove it.

Today, he believed, he had found just such a chance. He rode Nealta bareback through the high forest, on a sun-dappled trail leading upward to the high summer pastures in the hills. On the day he had come to Caher Idir, he had promised Scahta that his old grey mare would be just the first of many more horses for the Sidhe. He was about to keep that promise.

As a herdsman's son, he had taken sheep and cattle over these tracks many times and knew the ranges of the horses. As he approached the edge of the forest, with the sun shining brightly just beyond, Anlon halted his mare and slid to the ground. Safely hidden within the trees, he and Nealta peered out at the wide, grassy hilltop field.

Anlon smiled. Nealta lifted her head and nickered softly.

Scattered across the lush green field were some twenty fine mares—black, bay, chestnut, and grey—some with the heavy sides of late pregnancy and some with foals already running or playing or napping in the sun beside them.

Nealta nickered again. Anlon looked toward her interest. The mare had spotted the herd stallion, a fine young horse with an iron-grey coat. Anlon was impressed with his size; he judged the stallion's back would reach up past his own waist. He also saw good bone, a fine arching neck, and an intelligent eye. He reached up and slipped the braided leather halter from Nealta's head, stepping back as she trotted out of the woods and into the sunlit field.

Instantly, the stallion's head came up. He whirled and trotted over to this new mare that had suddenly appeared in his field, his head high, tail flagged, neck arched, showing her what a fine young horse he was and clearly telling her that he found her quite beautiful.

Nealta stopped and let him approach, touching noses with him, swishing her tail as he nickered and squealed at her. He moved to her neck, her back, her flank, all the while talking to her in the language of the horse. Finally the mare stood very still and held her tail to one side as the powerful young stallion climbed up over her back and caught hold of her neck with his teeth.

Anlon watched them with some satisfaction, hoping that next spring Nealta would, indeed, give birth to a strong young colt and begin to rebuild the herds of the Sidhe, as he had promised Scahta. He thought of how pleased she would be to learn that the aged mare would still provide them with at least one foal—a beautiful grey foal, almost certainly.

But first he had to get her home. And he had to find a way to do it without arousing the suspicions of the horseboys, whom he knew would be at their encampment somewhere near the other end of the field.

After a time the stallion returned to his grazing, still keeping a watchful eye on his new prize. Nealta attempted to join the other mares but was greeted only with pinned ears, angry squeals and flying hooves. She was forced to stay far to the edge of the herd.

Anlon knew he would have to move quickly if he hoped

to get her back. It always took time for a new horse to be accepted into a group, but it would not be long before she found her place and would consider this to be her home. Already she was touching noses with another mare, a small dark bay with a sturdy black foal at her heel. No doubt that mare had been the lowest-ranking until Nealta came along, and she was glad to find a friend.

From a little bag at his waist, Anlon took out a folded scrap of thin leather. Inside were a few dried apples with a bit of honey. Cautiously he moved along the edge of the woods, the braided halter over his shoulder, until he was close enough to call softly to Nealta.

She raised her head from the grass and looked at his outstretched hand. Without hesitation the mare came over to get the apples and honey, and Anlon was able to slip the halter over her head.

He breathed a sigh of relief and was about to lead her into the woods when he saw the bay mare just a short distance away, staying close to Nealta and clearly interested in what was going on.

Anlon gently tossed a bit of sweetened apple at the bay mare's feet. She ate it quickly and looked up, taking a step toward him, licking her lips and clearly hoping for more.

A daring thought came to Anlon. The iron-grey stallion was out of sight on the other side of the herd. There was no sign of the horseboys, who were most likely gathered for their midday meal at the camp. He pulled Nealta into the shadows of the woods and tossed another bit of honey-coated apple to the little bay mare.

She followed them into the woods, with her foal close behind.

Anlon swung up on Nealta's back. And as he did, he heard the stallion scream.

Anlon froze. The stallion had caught sight of his way-ward mares and was trotting over with every intention of forcing them back into his herd. And right behind them were two of the horseboys galloping up on their ponies, knowing only that their stallion and at least one mare and foal seemed to be disappearing into the woods.

He kicked Nealta's sides and she lumbered off down the trail. The bay mare followed, startled by the shouting and galloping behind her and instinctively staying with the other horse.

Anlon concentrated only on the trail and pushed Nealta into the thickest woods, the deepest shadows, the darkest corners. These were the places only the Sidhe would travel—places that just might shield them from the eyes of Men.

He could only hope the difficult path would allow him to escape. The stallion would not pursue them for long; he would not leave the rest of his herd unguarded just to chase one or two. But the horseboys were different. They would have much to answer for back at Dun Mor if they allowed a good mare and her foal to be taken away.

Anlon pushed on and on. He could hear the bay mare and the colt still following them through the heavy forest growth, both horses breathing hard from trotting through the twisting, turning, slippery path. But his tactic seemed to have worked; there did not appear to be any-one or anything else following them.

He stopped. There was no sound, except for the puff-ing of the mares and the singing of the birds and the pleasant drone of insects making their way through the forest.

Anlon patted Nealta's damp shoulder and glanced back at the little bay mare. She stood close beside her bright-eyed foal, watching him from a few paces away, ears up and eyes anxious as if wondering just what she had got herself into.

Anlon grinned and started Nealta down the path that would take them to Caher Idir. "Come with me, ladies," he said, as they walked at a much calmer pace. "I know a number of folks who are going to be very happy to see you."

By the time he reached Caher Idir, darkness had fallen and the stars were out. Anlon could hardly wait to show Scahta his prizes. And more than that, he wanted to see the look on Cian's face when he rode up and announced that not only had he brought them Nealta but a fine young mare as well, and *her* foal, and *Nealta's* foal, and the *other mare's* foal in the coming spring. Because of him, the Sidhe had gone from no horses at all to a herd of three—and next spring, that herd would number five!

The gates opened for him as he approached. From the shadows of the forest several of the Sidhe moved behind the shy bay mare and foal, gently encouraging them to follow Nealta into the torchlit fortress.

Anlon rode triumphantly across the yard. He smiled and gazed down at the other Sidhe, who stood and stared in amazement at the little herd of horses that had suddenly arrived at their home. Anlon rode into the livestock enclosure with all three animals, dismounted and turned Nealta loose—and when he looked up at the gate he saw Scahta standing there, Cian at her side, surrounded by the people of the Sidhe.

"How have you done this, Anlon?" she asked, her eyes wide and flicking from horse to horse.

He could not help but grin. "I took Nealta to visit one of the herd stallions. If all goes well, she will present you with a lovely grey foal next spring."

Scahta seemed at a loss for words. "You—you took her to the herds of the Men?"

"I did."

"And you stole this other mare and foal?"

He frowned. "I did not steal them, Queen Scahta. The mare followed Nealta, and of course the foal followed its mother."

"Of course." Scahta studied them. Her face was serious, but he could see the twinkle in her eye as she looked at the beautiful bay and her greedily nursing foal. "Of course."

She folded her hands and walked toward Anlon. "Did any of the men protecting the herd see you?"

He paused. "A few of the horseboys tried to give chase, but we lost them in the woods. I kept to the deepest woods, the faintest trails—"

"Lost them in the woods!" Cian cut in angrily. He strode forward to stand beside Scahta, the fury plain on his face. "Then you *were* seen! Those men know that you stole two of their horses. And they know that you came here!"

"I lost them in the woods," Anlon repeated, looking Cian in the eye. "I stayed in the deepest part. I followed the hidden paths just as the Sidhe always do—"

"*You are not one of the Sidhe!*" Cian shouted. "You will *never* be one of the Sidhe. You are a loud and clumsy Man, and you could no more hide three horses in the forest than you could hide them in the open air! If you had carried a drum and beaten it as you rode, you would not have been any more obvious to our enemies! You—"

"Stop!" cried Scahta. Cian fell silent, but the rage was still evident in his red face and burning eyes. She ignored him and turned to Anlon. "You rode for half a day to

117

come home. Did you see or hear any trace of the men of Dun Mor during all that time?"

"I saw no one. I heard no one."

She twisted and glanced at the people gathered behind her. Her gaze stopped on Cian. "And do you, Cian, see or hear any trace of those men now?"

She waited but received only silence as a reply. The night wind blew through the trees, and the torches flared and guttered. One of the horses snorted.

Scahta turned to Anlon. "We thank you, Anlon, for bringing us these beautiful horses, and for seeing to it that the herds of the Sidhe will indeed be renewed. Considering all the animals they have stolen from us, it will cause the men of Dun Mor no great hardship if we keep just one mare and foal."

Anlon smiled at her, as happy and as pleased with himself as he had ever been in his life. As Scahta and her people and the furious Cian turned to go, he looked at the three horses standing peacefully together in their enclosure and thought that now, indeed, he was beginning to know what it must feel like to be a king.

A few days later, on a lovely summer's afternoon, Scahta sat beneath the trees with her women on the soft grass of the riverbank. Sunlight and shadow filtered down through the fluttering green leaves as high white clouds moved across the sky.

Each had brought a stack of soft tanned leather for clothing and a collection of things with which to decorate it—bronze beads, gold discs, and beautifully polished stones and shells. Geal and Ean patiently stitched the pieces together with long bone needles, while Maidin and Scahta worked at decorating other strips of the soon-to-be leather gown with the shining ornaments.

Their laughter floated out across the sweet summer breeze. "Scahta, you cannot mean to say that you are not enjoying the attention from these two who would be our king!" said Geal. "And I am even growing accustomed to the Man."

"The Man's eyes never leave you," said Ean with a merry twinkle in her eye.

"And he grows more like the Sidhe every day!" added Maidin.

Scahta laughed, too. "So, are you telling me that I should choose the Man to be my king?"

"Oh, that was not my thought, my lady," said Ean. "Surely you have not forgotten the Sidhe who also strives to win your favor."

"He, too, is agile and strong and wise."

"And his love for you is clear for all to see."

Scahta nodded, thoughtful. "It is difficult to choose when there are two such excellent choices."

"Every woman knows that!"

"Watching two men compete is most enjoyable!"

"Do not rush them—the longer you delay your choice, the greater the enjoyment!"

The three women laughed and laughed, and Scahta too joined in the merriment—until a small sound made her look up.

Quiet footsteps approached from within the forest. They looked up, and there on the grassy bank stood Liath and Mactire. The two men had stern expressions.

"You must know, my lady, that not all find this situation as enjoyable as you and your maids."

The laughter faded. Scahta set her leather work back in its basket and folded her hands. "I do not enjoy being without a king, Mactire. But even less would I enjoy having a king who is unsuitable."

Mactire walked a few slow paces across the grass. "That is understandable. But there is a third possibility that perhaps you have not considered."

Scahta gazed steadily at him, then at Liath. "Please. Explain yourselves."

Liath came forward. "Three times you have tested Sidhe and Man, hoping to see which is worthy. Is that not true?"

"That is true."

"And of those three tests, has a winner emerged each time?"

Scahta paused. "No. You know this to be true, Liath. Why do you—"

"Please. Tell us. Why have your tests not shown you which of them should be your king?"

Scahta glanced at the other women, and then stood up. "One test showed Cian to be the better choice. The other showed Anlon."

"And the third?"

"The third had no winner."

"And so we wait."

Scahta shook her head slightly. "Is a good king not worth the wait? But I will not make you wait forever. My choice will be made by Samhain."

Liath gazed steadily at her. "Samhain is many months away. If you wait that long, you may not have need of a king, for there will be no kingdom left."

A chill wind seemed to blow across the riverbank. Scahta frowned. "What do you mean, saying such a thing? Our difficulties are pressing, but not so much as that. Explain yourself!"

"Your kingdom has become divided, my lady. As with Sidhe and Man, as with your two candidates, the rivalry becomes increasingly bitter. One is now enraged because the other stole some horses—and because the one who did the stealing now believes that he has won."

"I am not unaware of this, Liath. It is as difficult for me as it is for the rest of Caher Idir."

Mactire came forward. "This waiting only allows our people more time to choose sides. None could be expected to remain neutral day after day, month after month."

Scahta raised her chin. "*I* am able to remain so."

"You are like no other, Queen Scahta. You are not in the same position as the rest of us. We who only observe cannot help but choose sides—especially with candidates who are so very different."

"I see." She looked down for a moment. "Then, tell me—what do you propose I do? Simply cast lots to decide which one I will have?"

"Not at all. We propose that you give them one additional test, and that you do it as quickly as possible." He tried to smile. "We know how difficult this has been for you. We know you are doing what you believe to be best for Caher Idir. We have come to tell you only that your people need your help, your wisdom, your strength.

"Please, Queen Scahta—help us now. Give us a king, and bring your people together."

Chapter Ten

The sun had moved only a little through the sky when Scahta, surrounded by all the folk of Caher Idir, walked out onto the damp bare floor of the horse enclosure. She could feel the eyes of all upon her, especially the gaze of Anlon, who stood near the two mares and the foal. She folded her hands and looked into the face of each of her people before beginning to speak.

"We stand in this place set aside to keep our animals safe," she began. "How is it that of all the creatures the Sidhe once cared for, and that provided us with food in return, only three horses remain? How is it that there are no longer any cattle? How is it that there is room for all of us to stand here?"

There was a silence, and then someone spoke. "All the animals were stolen or killed, Queen Scahta," said one male voice from within the crowd.

"They were driven from the hilltop pastures," added another.

"It was Men who did this," finished a woman with an angry cry.

"So it was." Scahta walked slowly across the damp earth until she stood beside Nealta. "Yet it was a Man who brought these horses to us." She stroked the grey neck of the mare, and looked up at Anlon. "Perhaps a Man can help to bring us something more."

Cian stepped forward. Scahta turned her attention to him. "What can a Man bring us that one of our own people cannot?" he demanded, and she could feel the subdued rage in his voice. He gave Anlon a freezing glance, and she noted it was returned with equal coldness.

"Listen to me," Scahta said. "The Sidhe have been without cattle long enough. Now that Beltane has passed, the Dun Mor's cattle will be out at the high pastures for the summer." She paused, satisfied that everyone's attention was again on her, and smiled. "Those men have taken so much from us. I do not believe it would be wrong to take one cow back for ourselves."

The Sidhe-folk all looked at each other. Anlon stared at her in silence, and Cian actually broke into a grim smile. "One cow for ourselves," he repeated. "My lady, I am certain that such a thing would not be wrong. And I will be the one to bring a cow for Caher Idir. Perhaps *several* cows." Scahta smiled at him, but then a strong voice broke in.

"I, too, will bring you a cow, Queen Scahta." Anlon left off stroking Nealta and walked toward the center of the enclosure. "I should have done it long before now. If you wish, I will go this night."

Cian glared at him. "I will not go this night. I will go

now." And the two of them turned and exchanged a look of such viciousness that Scahta felt her blood run cold.

Liath and Mactire had been right. Something had to be done so that she could make her choice and end this rivalry before it turned into a blood feud. Perhaps there was still a way to reconcile these two to each other, no matter her decision. "Listen to me," she said again, looking from one to the other and back again. "Both of you will go. And both of you will return—together."

They stared at her. "I charge you to get a cow for Caher Idir. It is a dangerous feat, and it cannot be done alone. You will work together to get a cow from the Men, and one of you will not return without the other. You cannot serve your queen if you are dead."

"I will do as you ask, Queen Scahta." Anlon bowed to her and walked out through the gate that led inside the fortress.

Cian watched him go, and his jaw tightened. "It will be done in the way that you ask, my lady. But I will be the one to bring you the cow." He, too, walked straight out of the enclosure and back into the grounds, the same way Anlon had gone.

Scahta looked into the crowd. She caught and held the gaze of first Liath and then Mactire. Both returned it steadily, and she knew, as the people began filing back inside the fortress, that they understood.

Night fell swiftly, just as the rain began, leaving Scahta to sit in her home with her women. All she could do was wait and wonder.

Ean brought a small stone dish with a tiny flame burning in it and sat down on the ledge beside her queen. Geal and Maidin sat in the rushes at Scahta's feet. For a time there was only the sound of the rain on the thatched roof and the small crackling of the fire in the hearth.

"They will be out in the hills by now," said Maidin.

"Out among Men to steal a cow for Caher Idir," said Geal.

"I wonder when they will return," said Ean.

Scahta took a deep breath, searching for the stillness of her soul, which had always come so easily but had recently begun to elude her. "It is the last test I will give them. But it is also the most dangerous."

"Indeed. This is not a foot race or a rock climb."

"Those men guard their cattle with their lives."

"They would be only too happy to kill a Sidhe who tried to take one."

"Or a Man." Scahta closed her eyes. "Even if they both come back with a cow for us, I will still have to choose just one of them to be my king. Our king."

"Liath and Mactire were right."

"The choice must be made soon."

"It must be made now."

Scahta nodded, almost rocking back and forth. "I meant always to make the choice of a king through dispassionate means . . . the head, not the heart, must choose a king, I believed. But I have found that method more difficult with each day that passes. I can only hope . . . I can only hope that the choice my heart tells me to make is the right one."

The following day passed slowly, very slowly, the skies as heavy and grey and threatening as the cold iron of Men. Scahta was conscious of every breath she took, of every beat of her heart, as she sat on a rock not far from the gates of Caher Idir and waited for Anlon and Cian to return.

She watched the birds in the green canopy above. Occasionally she saw the grey coat of the wolf that was never far from her. But as the shadows began to lengthen, and there was still no sign of the two warriors she had sent out, she told herself that this was only the beginning. She must be prepared to wait many days more if need be.

Then, as the light faded, she heard a sound just beyond the clearing. A footstep. Another. She could hear step after slow, careful step coming through the forest. Her wolf made no move to join her, but remained quiet in his hiding place. Scahta knew the creature would have been instantly at her side had a stranger been approaching.

Her heart beat faster. There was only one set of footsteps. Only one man was returning, and there was no cow. She slid down from the rock and made herself walk out to meet whoever was approaching.

The forest was thick and leafy in the place where she heard the footsteps approach. In the heavy twilight Scahta could see only the smooth leather of the breeches and tunic worn by all the men of the Sidhe. Then, atop the leather, she saw a fall of wool cloth. It was a cloak . . . a cloak of green and white.

Cian's cloak.

She thought her heart would stop. It was Cian returning. He was alone and he was not leading a cow. She had ordered the two to return together and no matter how great his hatred for Anlon might be, Cian would never disobey her.

They must have been seen. It was the only explanation. Cian was faster than Anlon, better at hiding in the forest, at escaping the iron javelins of the Men—

Scahta closed her eyes, moaning softly to herself as the pain started in her heart and spread outward through her body. He was gone. Anlon was gone, dead at the hands of his own people. He was gone, and *she* had sent him to his death.

The figure in the woods drew closer, pushing past the last of the low overhanging branches. And as the figure strode slowly into the clearing she found herself looking at the face of Anlon, pale and drawn—Anlon who was carrying a burden in his arms which was draped with Cian's green-and-white cloak.

"Anlon . . . ?"

He had returned. He was alive. She had not lost him; he was alive, he was alive. . . . Scahta began to breathe again as he drew closer and closer.

Yet he moved so slowly, so wearily. The burden in his arms did not look so heavy. What would cause him to move so deliberately, so slowly?

Now he stood before her, and she realized the green-and-white cloak was stained with blood. Then, as he set the burden down in front of her, she saw, as though from a great distance, that Anlon's bronze sword had been driven deep within it so that the hilt stood straight up.

And something was terribly wrong with the sword. It was dark and dull—almost black, as though it were dead.

Slowly, so very slowly, she knelt down and placed her fingers on the green-and-white cloak. Only one touch was needed to tell her that Cian's lifeless body lay beneath it.

Yet the sword, too, looked lifeless and dead. She reached for the hilt to draw it out but instantly pulled her hand away as if burned. The bronze weapon seethed with horror and fear. The emotions had been captured by the metal, and the metal had been perverted by them.

Scahta put the sword out of her mind and thought only of Cian. She wanted to see his face. She had to look upon his visage one last time, see the features of her subject and servant and friend. She had sent him out to die, she owed him that much. . . .

She reached for the edge of the cloak to turn it back, but Anlon stopped her with his hand on her wrist. "Do not, my lady, I beg you," he whispered. But she only stared at him and withdrew her wrist, and she saw him close his eyes.

Carefully she turned back the edge of the cloak, searching out Cian's face, wanting to see for one last time his silky dark hair, his deep brown eyes. But she could not find them . . . there was only the damp and mossy earth beneath the cloak, then his shoulders, stained with blood.

His head was gone.

Scahta's wail filled the forest, bringing the rest of the Sidhe racing out from Caher Idir. They gathered around as Anlon pulled out the blackened sword and Scahta fell weeping across the ruined body of Cian.

They carried him inside, into his house where he would be safe, where he could be prepared for what was to come. Scahta watched until the door to Cian's house closed and he was alone with those who would care for him. As if asleep, as if caught in a terrible dream, she walked through the darkness toward the center of Caher Idir where a fire burned and the rest of her people were gathered.

They waited in silence as she sat down on one of the logs that rested near the fire. Anlon sat on the ground a short distance away, head down, his face hidden by the shadows.

"Please, Anlon," Scahta began. Her voice was clear, and steady, but seemed to come from very far away. "Tell us what happened to Cian."

For a long time, he did not move. Scahta thought her heart would break if she did not go to him, if she did not see his face and look into his eyes and try to ease his pain; but she could not move. At last he raised his head and got slowly to his feet.

He was a tall shadow in the flickering firelight. "Queen Scahta," he began, but he did not look at her; he could do no more than gaze steadily at the ground. "Your good and loyal servant Cian is dead. And I am responsible."

There was a great murmuring and stirring among the Sidhe. Scahta could feel the sorrow and wrath of her people as they looked at Anlon. Here and there were flashes of light from gleaming bronze daggers; she knew they refrained from attacking only because she herself had not ordered it. Anlon must have seen the weapons, too, but seemed not to care.

"Tell us," she said to his shadow, holding up her hand to warn her people back. "Why do you say this?"

He stared into the flames, blinking. "You do not understand," he said with an effort. "I did not kill him. But I did not save him, either." He looked away again. "I could not save him."

Anlon pulled his blue-and-grey cloak close around him, as if he were cold. "We had no trouble finding the herds. And we did exactly as you asked, Queen Scahta. It was clear that Cian did not welcome my presence, but he tolerated me for your sake. Together we watched the same herd until well after nightfall, and together we chose a cow to take for Caher Idir."

He looked up at Scahta and tried to smile. "This was truly an exceptional cow. Almost pure white she was, with just a little red about her head. I am sure you would have been pleased with such a beautiful animal."

She gave him a little nod, barely able to speak. "Please. Go on."

"Under cover of darkness, we approached the beast, and without too much trouble we were able to get hold of her and slip a leather line around her horns. I felt hopeful this would indeed work out—that he and I together would get the animal home. But it was not to be."

He paused, and Scahta saw his shoulders move as he struggled for breath. "Cian turned to me and pulled his dagger. He told me that my help was no longer needed, and he wanted no part of me. He said he considered me an enemy no different from any other Man and he would see me dead before he would see me as his king."

Scahta closed her eyes.

"It was no use. I could not get through to him. I could only watch as he tried to lead the cow away, and hope to help him if I could. And though she was balky, Cian nearly succeeded. He had her just within the woods when she bellowed to her herdmates once, and then again. And that brought the men running."

There was a rustling and stirring and muttering among the Sidhe. "Surely you are not trying to tell us that Cian could not escape such men?"

"He would have had plenty of time to know that they were coming," a Sidhe in the back of the room called out.

"Never would any of those men have found him in the darkness of the forest."

Anlon nodded once, slowly, and then again. "On any other night, he would have escaped long before they reached him. But he was so enraged—so determined that he would triumph over me—that he held on to the cow until the very last moment. And then it was too late.

"He ran, but one of the herd's guardians threw a rock from a sling and struck him down. By the time he could rise they were close—but Cian was closer to me. I threw him my own sword."

Instantly, the other Sidhe responded: "You say you threw him your sword."

"Yet he was running for his life."

"Why did you not keep the sword and use it yourself to defend him?"

Anlon smiled, though there was no joy in it. "I knew that he had only his dagger. And he was far better with a sword than I, for never had I touched a sword until Scahta offered me that one. My strength is with a club.

"He tried to fight them. He struck down two of them before they brought him to heel with stones and finished him—with his own sword."

There was a silence. Then a woman spoke up. "What did you do while all this happened?"

"Did you watch?"

"Did you help them?"

Anlon raised his chin, and none could fail to see the anguish in his eyes. "I broke a branch to use as a club and used it to drive them away." When the Sidhe frowned and looked at each other in disbelief, he shook his head. "These were herdsmen. There was only one true warrior among them, their guardian, and he was the one who . . ."

He paused, and then there was a hint of a very sad smile. "I shouted out as if I were calling to companions, which made them think that more raiders waited in the forest. And I may be new to the sword, but I am good with the club."

The faint smile disappeared. "They retrieved their cow and ran away. It was left to me to carry Cian home." He turned his face away, then moved back into the shadows. "I am sorry . . . I am so sorry. I never thought that it might end like this."

131

Slowly, heavily, Anlon sat down again in the darkness at the edge of the yard. And then a soft sound began rising up from among the Sidhe, a hissing sound, ominous and frightening. The hissing began to form words:

"The rivalry between them had become fierce."

"It was becoming a blood feud."

"How could Sidhe and Man ever compete without it ending in death?"

"Never will I believe that the Man would give Cian his sword."

"How good it is for the Man that his rival for the kingship is now dead!"

Anlon stood up, and moved into the firelight so that they could see him. "You cannot believe that I would harm Cian," he said. "Surely if I meant to do so, I would have taken the chance long before now!"

But the angry hissing only intensified:

"What is one less of the Sidhe to any Man?"

"It has happened many, many times before."

"And each time it happens it becomes easier to make it happen again."

Then the voices stopped and the ominous, angry hissing rose up louder than ever. *"Death,"* they were saying. *"Death . . . death . . ."*

"Stop!" cried Scahta.

The hissing faded. There was only the silence of the night and the snapping of the fire.

The queen looked at her people, wanting to feel angry, wanting to feel frightened, wanting to feel anything at all . . . but there was only cold and emptiness and a terrible stillness within her heart.

"Why do you chant for death?" she whispered.

"He has killed one of our own!"

"He is our enemy!"

"He must never be allowed to do this again!"

Scahta flung out her hand to silence them, but the sound still floated on the air. *Death . . . death . . .*

"Listen to me," she said. "I will tell you how it will be." Slowly she stood up, though it was difficult, for the coldness and the stillness continued to hold her in their grip. "Anlon will not be killed," she said, in a clear and steady voice. "He will not be harmed. Do all of you understand this?"

There was only a short pause. "We do," came the murmured response.

"He will not be harmed. But he will be banished. He is to go from Caher Idir and not return—not unless . . . unless . . ."

It seemed that she could hear the silence holding its breath. "Unless he can restore the sword I gave him to its original state. Unless he can remove the fear and horror that now contaminate it. Unless he himself can purify it."

Her words echoed in the silent void and then faded away into the night. "Will you respect my ruling? Or shall I, too, leave Caher Idir and not return?"

This time the response came quickly. "We do respect your rule, my lady."

"Never will you leave us."

"You are our queen, now and always."

She drew a breath and listened to a few beats of her heart, just to make certain that it did indeed continue. From the edge of her eye she could see the shadow that was Anlon moving slowly away from the gathering. The gates opened for him, and he walked into the darkness, and then the gates closed once again.

Scahta rose slowly, looked at no one, and went into her house and shut the door.

Chapter Eleven

Her women found her sitting in darkness on her ledge, cross-legged, head down, eyes closed. Ean moved to stir the nearly cold embers and find a spark to light the lamp. Geal and Maidin sat beside Scahta, stroking her hair and holding her hand.

"It is not your fault, my lady," Geal said.

"Cian knew the danger of trying to raid the cattle of the Men."

"All of us mourn him."

Scahta raised her head a little, though her long hair still obscured her face. "It is my fault. I pitted Anlon and Cian, one against the other."

"But you hoped to find a king!"

"A king must be someone extraordinary."

"You did only what you felt was necessary."

Slowly Scahta shook her head. "I never meant for it to go so far as this. It was not to be a death match. I hoped

134

not so much for the testing to show me a choice—I knew which one I wanted—but to make certain that my choice was the right one. I needed to be sure that Anlon could not be driven away, that he would not turn his back on me and my people even when he should have every reason to do so."

She almost smiled, and brushed a few strands of hair away from her face. "And now that he has earned his place—now that he has passed every test I set for him, and more—now, I have ordered him away. And given him a task that he cannot hope to complete.

"He will never return. He will take his sword and go to Dun Mor and stay with those other men, as he once intended to do. Those men will never notice that anything is wrong with that weapon."

Scahta looked up and stared miserably into the feebly glowing fire. "He is no druid. He knows nothing of the mysteries. He is a simple man, the son of a herdsman. To purify that weapon would take the utmost strength, the greatest knowledge, the most intimate rapport with the elements. I am not sure I could do it myself. I cannot hope that he could ever find a way on his own to remove the evil, the horror, the fear that clings to that sword."

She lowered her head once more. "Now I have no king to offer you. Of those who were best suited, one is banished, the other dead. There will be no king . . . and no more children for Caher Idir." She felt an overwhelming dread fill her, then a nausea.

Scahta swayed, then slowly lay down in the soft furs. A great darkness descended upon her.

All night Anlon sat outside the fortress with his back to a great tree, very near the spot where he had placed Cian's body before Scahta. The terrible events of the day had left him sitting alone in the night, stunned and wounded, almost as if he were the one who had been struck down and not Cian. From time to time his eyes closed, but he never really slept. Yet he wanted to sleep, and do so forever, if it would keep him from remembering what had happened this day.

But he could not.

Cian was murdered and he himself was banished. It would be so easy to just get up and begin walking back to Dun Mor, or even to his family home, and leave this strange place and all that went with it far behind. He could go on with his simple life as if he had never met Scahta. But neither could he turn his back on a tragedy that he had brought about, in spite of his best intentions, even though the people of Caher Idir might never understand.

He must think of what was to be done next. He must find a way to make things right and once again take his place at Scahta's side—but right now all of it seemed impossible. One of her own was dead. Her beautiful sword was ruined. The future of her kingdom itself was in jeopardy, for both of those she had considered worthy of being her king were gone. And all had happened because of him.

He closed his eyes again as the relentless thoughts continued to fly through his mind. *Cian is dead, and I am banished . . . and I will never see Scahta again. Never again . . . never again . . .*

When the dawn came at last, Anlon got slowly to his feet. As he stood up, he found his gaze drawn to the bronze sword.

Now a discolored brown-black, it lay where it had fallen on the earth. Beneath it was a fern, bent down by the weight of the sword—but the crushed fronds were now blackened and dead wherever the dull metal touched them. They looked as if they had been burned.

Though he knew little about such things, it was clear to him that something was terribly wrong with the weapon. All its former beauty was gone. It seemed to writhe with evil, and Anlon recognized that the fairy blade had somehow absorbed all the terror and anger and pain of Cian's death.

He himself was loath to touch it, but he could not leave such a thing to lie out in the forest where an animal—or even one of the Sidhe—might encounter it. Anlon reached for the hilt to pick it up but dropped it almost instantly. The sword was cold, colder than any frost, so cold it burned.

He could not carry it as it was. And he did not want to place it back in its Sidhe-crafted scabbard, fearing it too would become tainted. Glancing around, he pulled up a few lengths of ivy from the earth and gingerly wound them around the hilt of the sword. Lifting those vines, he allowed the sword to hang and twist out in front of him, cautious not to touch the darkened, perverted bronze.

Anlon looked around. Everywhere was dense forest. Where should he go? He would not return to the world of Men, and the kingdom of the Sidhe was closed to him now. Yet he must find a place where he could live for a time while he did what he could to again make things right.

Then, from a little distance away, he heard the familiar singing of water where it flowed past the fortress. Here was life and swift motion in the midst of the impenetrable woods. He turned and began to travel upstream along the narrow sparkling brook, following it like a clear and shining path.

Anlon could only hope that the pristine waters would show him the way he should go, would help him discover what it was that he should do, if ever he hoped to see Scahta and Caher Idir again.

His chosen path led him gradually upward, higher and higher into the sheltering foothills. At last, after walking nearly all day and climbing over several smaller hills, Anlon reached the top of the highest one and found the source of the river.

A beautiful spring welled up among the rocks and tumbled down over several large boulders in a gently singing waterfall, and then continued down the hill to form wide pools and the icy stream. Tall willow and oak trees and flowering hawthorn bushes were scattered around the top of the hill. And there was no sign that anyone, Man or Sidhe, had ever frequented this place.

Here was water and shelter and solitude. Here he would stay for a time and think about what he might do next.

Just as he was looking for a spot where he could set down the sword, perhaps on a bare rock, the lengths of ivy snapped and the blade dropped to the grass.

Shocked, Anlon looked to see that the ivy had blackened and rotted. It had been strong and healthy when he had fastened it around the sword. Obviously the blade had the power to corrupt, the power to destroy. Even as he watched, the grass where the sword lay began to curl and brown.

Something had to be done. He could not leave this vile thing sitting out, but neither could he simply cast it away where anyone or anything might come across it.

He took a small flat stone from beside the stream and used it to dig out a narrow trench in the ground alongside the sword. Still holding the stone, he tipped the Sidhe weapon into the trench, then quickly used the clean loose earth to cover it up again.

Now it was safely hidden. Anlon moved from the site and went to make camp beside the spring, building a fire, catching a small trout, and searching out watercress and clover from the stream banks.

Later that evening, he rested beside the warmth of his glowing fire, staring into the blue twilight of the summer evening. He looked out across the hills in the direction of Caher Idir. Then he blinked and looked again. Small points of flame were moving slowly away from the fortress.

He sat up. The line of lights was winding its way through the forest and up over the hills, moving in his direction.

For a moment he was frozen to the spot. He could only believe that the Sidhe had decided to take their revenge on him. They were looking for him, following his trail. He could not hope to hide from them; they would come straight here and they would find him!

But the torchlit procession did not go far. The points of light gathered together below him, on top of a smaller hill, and Anlon could see them quite well. The small figures were indeed the people of Caher Idir, but the white-covered burden they carried could only be the body of Cian.

He watched quietly, knowing his small banked fire would not be visible to them. And even if it were, they had far greater concerns at this moment. They had gathered to say good-bye to another of their dwindling number.

The torch lights formed a circle on the bare grassy top of the hill. In the center of that ring they placed the body of Cian, and for a time the soft sound of their chanting reached Anlon on the night breeze. He could not tell what they were saying, but he knew it must be part of the ceremony that would give final release to Cian's spirit and send it safely on its way to the next world.

The circle began to move, rotating three times sunward around the center before it stopped. And then, to Anlon's surprise, the torches all moved downward and set alight the body of Cian.

The Sidhe mourners stepped back as the pyre caught and the flames billowed upward. Anlon stared, fascinated. His own people did not practice cremation; the dead were laid to rest in a cave or in the earth. He had heard that the Sidhe burned their dead and hid the ashes away, but of course he had never seen it. Now, though, he would help to keep the vigil for Cian here in this lonely place, along with the Sidhe who surrounded the blazing pyre, sending his own thoughts of peace and forgiveness along with the newly freed spirit to wherever it might be going.

For three days, Cian's fire burned. The Sidhe took turns keeping watch and feeding the fire with wood to keep it blazing. Anlon peered closely at the small distant figures in an effort to recognize them, and did sometimes see Liath or Mactire, but there was never any sign of Scahta.

At last, on the third afternoon, the fire was allowed to slowly die down. It burned itself out just as the sun vanished.

Darkness settled over the world once again. The only light came from the torches of three Sidhe gathered close to the pyre. Again the sound of chanting drifted up the hill. After a time they left in single file, visible only as three spots of light headed back to Caher Idir.

The next morning showed Anlon that the hilltop where the funeral pyre had blazed was now clean and smooth and covered with grass, just as it had been before. There was no sign that a great fire had burned there for three days.

It was as if Cian had never been.

Anlon felt as though he was awakening from a long dream. He had kept his unseen vigil along with the Sidhe, broken only by occasionally getting a little food for himself, but now the world was slowly returning to normal. And he began to remember something else.

He walked to the spot where he had left the sword. It was not difficult to find, for the grass was ashen and dead all around the place where he had buried it. Even the earth itself had darkened where it was heaped over the blade.

Anlon picked up the flat digging stone he had used to bury the sword and approached the dead strip of earth—but then he hesitated. Why not leave the poisoned object where it was? So long as it stayed buried in the earth, no one would come across it by accident.

Yet the odd-looking soil, the strangely dead grass, might rouse the curiosity of anyone who happened to pass by—which did not seem unlikely given that such a beautiful spring was only a few steps away.

He could not leave it here.

Using his flat digging stone, he pushed aside the stained and blackened earth until he reached the mud-caked sword. Oddly, and though it was difficult to tell beneath the clinging earth, the sword did not seem quite so dark and angry as it had been before; it was as if the now-discolored soil had absorbed some of the taint, some of the poison, from the weapon.

Yet he still could not touch it. The bone handle remained cold enough to burn. So he found another flat stone and used the two rocks together—one beneath the hilt, one beneath the blade—to lift it out.

He wanted to clean the mud from it, to see if the time it had spent in the earth had truly made any difference at all. But how could he clean it if he could not touch it?

The waterfall sang a little distance away. Still using his two flat stones, he carried the sword to the very beginning of the stream and let it slide beneath the water's glassy surface to a smooth boulder situated just beneath the falls.

The water hissed and roiled as the sword came to rest against the rock. Then, to his horror, Anlon saw a faint brown-black stain emanate from the sword and begin wafting down the crystal clear water of the stream.

He reached to pull it out, before it could poison the water that would eventually flow to Caher Idir—but the terrible cold of the weapon stung his hand again. Frantically he searched for the rocks he'd used to carry it here, hoping he could lift it out before it was too late—but then he noticed something else.

Just a short way down the stream, the hideous stain faded away and vanished. The water continued on its way down the mountain, clear. He tasted it, and it was as cool and pure as it had always been.

Anlon relaxed a little. It seemed that the water would do its part in cleansing the tainted weapon without any harm to itself, without any further help from him.

He returned to the trench where the sword had rested. Already the earth was losing some of its blackened stain as the wind blew over it. Anlon sat down to rest once more, knowing that his part was over, at least for now.

It was not until another three days had gone by that the terrible stain finally vanished from the sword. The water around it flowed clear and pure once more, just as it had always done.

Anlon reached into the cold water to lift out the sword, but quickly dropped it. The hilt remained colder even than the icy waters of the spring. Again he used the stones to lift it out—and then his gaze stopped at the firepit.

Something so terribly cold must crave fire. And so he placed the sword across the stones surrounding the pit, on the side where the flames and heat and smoke would be constantly driven over it by the winds.

As soon as Anlon placed the sword on the stones, the red flames and wispy black smoke that rolled over the weapon became fogged and stained a filthy brown—but not so much as the earth, not so much as the water. He began to hope he was indeed doing the things that needed to be done, that he might actually have a chance of purifying this bronze sword and returning to Caher Idir—and to Scahta.

That thought drove him onward.

Now Anlon's days were busier, for the fire had to be fed, and it would have to burn until the flames and smoke no longer took that hideous color as they rolled over the sword. It had taken three days in the earth and three days in the water for the elements to do their work. He felt sure the fire would be no different.

He spent nearly all his time searching out wood for the voracious blaze, which had begun to burn hotter and fiercer than any other he had ever built. On the first day, he merely scoured the forest floor for any deadwood or twigs he could pick up. The fire consumed them as quickly as he could toss them in, but the discoloration of the smoke remained as strong as ever. Something more was needed—but what?

On the second morning, Anlon began to search more carefully. He thought back to his days as a boy with his mother and grandmother, trying to recall the lore of the woods and plants that they sometimes spoke of. He remembered the stories of the Fianna, hoping for any bit of knowledge that might help him complete the task with which he was now charged.

Nearest to the stream were white willow trees, tall and graceful. His grandmother had used the leaves and bark in making a tea to ease pain. A man of the Fianna had once told him that poets loved to sit beneath the willows in hopes of finding inspiration for their work. And he himself, these past few nights, had admired the curving, delicate shapes of the trees as they moved in the breeze by the light of the moon.

He gathered up the fallen bits and branches of the willow, thinking of easing pain, poetic inspiration, and the magic of the moon.

High on the hill, where they could best reach the sun, was a small grove of apple trees. Here was sweetness and delicate beauty, in the flowers that appeared each spring; here was life, in the fruit all could eat in the autumn.

He picked up the fallen sticks of wood from the apple trees, thinking of sweetness and beauty and sustenance.

The final tree Anlon sought was the oak. Nothing that grew was as strong and enduring as an oak. He carried stacks of its wood back to the fire, thinking of power and endurance and strength.

That evening he sat down beside his enormous collection of branches and twigs and fed the fire through the night, throwing on piece after piece of wood. With each branch, each log, he commended to the fire, he thought of what he wished to add to the cleansing flames:

The easing of pain.
The inspiration of poets.
The magic of the moon.
Sweetness.
Beauty.
Sustenance.
Power.
Endurance.
Strength.

The fire leaped and flared with every stick he fed it, and at the last, it roared with a white-hot glare he had never before seen.

The next morning the fire burned with a little less fierceness, a little less anger, but the smoke and flames still held the ugly brown stain.

Anlon's task was not finished yet.

Again he walked into the forest, not sure just what he was searching for but certain he would know it when he saw it.

In the cool shade of the woods, the dark leaves of ivy grew all across the forest floor and up around the trunks of the great oaks and willows, shielding and protecting the trees where they grew. He pulled three long strands of ivy, thick with dark green leaves, thinking of protection as he did.

Leaving the cover of the woods, he saw a rare sight: low shrubs of heather with beautiful blossoms of the purest white. The flowers seemed as cool and fresh as snow.

He gathered a handful of the tender blossoms, thinking of the cooling and easing of terrible passions and emotions.

When he had almost reached the campsite, he took a second look around and smiled. As they did in virtually every place he had ever been, the three-leafed clover grew lushly and abundantly underfoot. They provided food for the animals and for Man and Sidhe alike, as well as a lovely green carpet over the land. He gathered generous handfuls of the clover, thinking of abundance and plenty and how the simplest things were what allowed life to continue.

On the third evening the sword had rested before the fire, Anlon sat before it and began casting in the plants and flowers he had gathered, thinking of the final things he wanted to give to the fire:

Protection.
The calming of violent passions.
Abundance.
Beauty.
Life.

At last, as the fire burned on and on, Anlon rested his head on the soft grass and slept.

Chapter Twelve

When dawn came again, Anlon saw, to his great relief, that the fire had burned down. The flames were gentle and quiet, and faint black smoke rolled out over the sword to vanish on the breeze. The weapon itself had lost most of its angry coloring and purified bronze now showed through in many places. Anlon found, as he cautiously closed his fingers around the bone hilt, that although it still felt cold after three days before the fire he could at last pick it up.

Yet the bronze still held some of the dull stain. The blade was heavy with smoke and heat, though it still felt cold when he tried to touch it. He carried the sword to the nearest of the willow trees, the one whose branches reached out over the stream into the air and light. He placed the sword there in the branch, wedging it tightly so that it would not fall no matter how the wind made the tree dance.

Anlon left it there and went back to the fire to rest and eat, believing he had done everything he could. All that remained was for him to wait and watch, and hope the elements had the power to remove the terrible stain from Scahta's once-beautiful sword.

For three days the sword rested in the tree. Anlon stood by as soft rains and gentle mists enveloped it, and from time to time the warm summer sun filtered down through the leafy branches of the willow to touch it with added warmth. Most of all the winds blew over it, the fresh zephyrs of the day and the cool breezes of the night. Anlon kept watch from the campfire, never approaching the sword, simply waiting—and hoping—to see a gleam of shining bronze within the willow leaves.

On the morning after the third night, he saw it.

He walked to the tree where the sword rested. The weapon looked almost as it had before—the bronze had a bright gleam, and the bone hilt merely felt cool as he took hold of it and lifted it out of the tree.

The bronze sword again showed its beauty in the soft light of the dawn. If he had never seen it before, he would think it was the finest sword he had ever encountered—but he knew this weapon well. The blade was still cold, too cold. Something was still missing.

But what else could be done? The elements of earth, fire, water and air had each done all they could. What could be left?

He was at a loss. It had seemed to go so well up to this point, and he had been so hopeful that he would indeed be able to complete the task and return the sword, once again beautiful and pure, to Scahta. But now he had reached an impasse. All he could do was hold the blade close to his chest, as close to his heart as he hoped to one day hold Scahta, allowing his body to take the final chill from the metal and hope that he would discover the answer soon.

Anlon started to set the sword down, and found he could not. It seemed to cry out for him, to draw strength from him, to take from him something that it had lost and desperately needed again. And so he continued to hold the sword, keeping it cradled in one arm as he went about his tasks or sitting with the hilt over his left shoulder so that the blade rested over his heart.

He was certain that with every moment, every heartbeat, the blade grew warmer and the bronze regained its gleam, until, on the morning after the third night, the sword was glowing and shining and more beautiful than it had ever been before . . . and Anlon knew that now, at last, it was time for him to go home.

He had been gone for fifteen nights. The bronze sword had been restored to its former beauty and now rested in its scabbard at Anlon's hip. But in that short time, Caher Idir had greatly changed.

Anlon stood outside the gates of the Sidhe fortress, beneath the green leafy canopy of the interlocking branches that spread over it. But the gates were shut tight and appeared not to have been opened for many days. The green plants and shrubs of the forest had grown up and over the gates and the high stone walls, as if the place had sat deserted for a great many years.

But that was not possible. They had all been here fifteen nights ago, on the night he had left, and while he was up on the mountain he had watched them carry out the ritual for Cian. Now there was no sign of life here at all. The air hung damp and still, with no smell of smoke. There were no footprints on the path that led away from the gates. Even the path itself had been almost covered over by ferns and moss and fallen leaves, as though no one had set foot on it for a very long time.

But where would they have gone? Why would they leave Caher Idir, unless . . .

His heart went cold. Had something happened to Scahta? Had the grief and shock of Cian's death brought her own life to an end? Had her people left this place because they no longer had a queen—and no more hope of a king?

He started to turn away, searching for any trace of a trail to follow, when a movement behind a stand of trees made him look up. He peered closely at it, and with a start he realized that yellow eyes watched him from the forest.

So. The wolf was still here. That wolf was Scahta's constant companion, and he knew the creature would never leave her so long as she was alive.

She had to be here!

Quickly, Anlon began tearing away the shrubs and growth from the fortress walls until he could reach the gates. He braced himself and shoved with all his strength against the heavy wooden doors, determined to push it open against the earth that had become heaped around the base—and nearly fell, staggering, into the courtyard of Caher Idir as the gate swung open easily.

The inside of the fortress was in the same condition as the outside. There was dampness and stillness everywhere, with green growth choking the pathways and doors—and no sign of anyone. Had the Sidhe vanished after all?

Slowly he walked through the fortress grounds, crushing the thick ferns and masses of sapling trees until he reached the ivy-covered door of Scahta's house. Pulling away the vines and throwing them aside, he placed his hand on the door and gently pushed it open.

"Scahta . . ."

The queen lay on the furs draping her sleeping ledge, her face turned up and her long golden-brown hair carefully arranged on either side. She wore her finest leather gown and white wool cloak, with her best jewelry of gold and bronze at her shoulders and neck and wrists. Her skin was fairer than ever he had seen it—so fair it almost looked white, almost as if she were—

"Scahta," he said, willing his voice to keep steady.

He stepped closer and saw that three of her women lay nearby, covered by their cloaks in the rushes. He could not tell if they lived or not.

At last he reached Scahta's side. She was near enough to touch. For so long he had thought of this moment . . . he had felt such pride, such joy, at the idea of being able to bring back her sword and show her that it had been restored to its former purity. It was all that had kept him going on those fifteen days and nights up in the hills with the corrupted weapon. She could not be dead, he *would not allow* her to be dead!

Surely nothing that remained so beautiful could possibly be lifeless.

He reached out and brushed her cheek with the lightest of touches. She remained cool and still, but he was convinced that what he felt was life—not death.

"Scahta."

His voice was steady now. He touched her hand, trying to clasp the fingers in his own, but still there was no response.

Slowly he drew the bronze sword from its scabbard. With the utmost care he rested the hilt against her shoulder so that the flat of the blade lay across her hands. Then Anlon stroked her hair and waited.

He was quite certain that he saw her lashes move. In a moment she blinked, once, and then her dark eyes opened. She lay very still, staring into the distance, as she ran her fingers over the glowing, shining bronze, taking the warmth and purity of it into her own heart, holding the sword close and cradling the hilt against her cheek.

Anlon knelt on the rushes beside the ledge and covered both of the Sidhe queen's hands in his own. To his joy, she turned and looked at him, and then she gave him a gentle smile.

He placed the sword beside her on the furs and helped her to sit up. Reaching out with both arms, he drew her into an embrace that took away all the grief and pain and loneliness of the many long months they had spent in each other's company, together and yet so far apart.

Anlon lifted her off the ledge and carried her through the house, past her now-stirring handmaidens. A small kick pushed open the door and he carried Scahta across the green-choked courtyard towards the fortress gates. She raised her arms to his neck and rested her face against his.

Anlon closed his eyes, nearly stopping as he felt the flower-soft touch of her cheek. But he continued, watching as all around the doors of the houses began to open and the people of the Sidhe stirred to life once again.

Holding Scahta close, he carried her out through the gates, well aware that all the folk of Caher Idir would see them go.

He took her to a quiet spot not far from the stream, deep within the sheltering trees. Setting her down on her feet, he unfastened his cloak and spread it out over the lush grass that grew all around.

For a moment he simply stood and looked down at her, deep into her bright and shining eyes, and he held her gently by her shoulders. "I love you, Scahta," he said softly. "I love you as my queen and as my wife. Will you come to me this day as a woman comes to her lover, to the man who keeps only her in his heart?"

She reached up and touched his face with fingers that were feather-light and warm. Her anguish was real, but it was fading. "I love you, Anlon," she whispered. "I am here as the woman who keeps only you in her heart."

Anlon drew her into his arms, and for a time they simply held each other close. For so long he had wanted nothing more than for the two of them to melt together like this and draw strength and comfort from each other. At last, they could forget all about the rest of the world and think only of their own feelings, their own needs.

Scahta turned her face up to him. He tasted her lips, and they were as soft and sweet and delicate as the first mists of the morning.

She pulled the bronze pins from her white wool cloak and let it drop to the grass. Carefully, her eyes never leaving Anlon's, she worked the gold half-rings from the neck of her deerskin gown and allowed it, too, to fall from her shoulders.

Now he could see her in all of her delicate beauty. He could allow his gaze to travel over the small gentle curves, could almost feel the skin warm and fair beneath the long fall of her shining golden-brown hair. Anlon, too, unfastened his clothes and let them fall away.

Again they embraced, and this time there was nothing at all between them. Anlon was conscious only of the warmth and softness of her skin, of her hair falling over his hands, of her quickened breathing . . . and of her rapidly beating heart so close against his chest.

153

How strong she was, for someone who had seemed so fragile and delicate! She pulled him close, her slender arms tight and insistent across his back, but even through his own passion he was aware that her legs trembled and her body was tense.

He placed his fingers gently beneath her chin, stroking the silken skin of her neck and throat, and Scahta let her head fall back so that he could kiss her lips yet again. At last she took a deep breath and he felt her body begin to soften and yield against his. He simply held her for a time, caressing her smooth curving sides and the soft full-ness of her breasts.

He drew her down with him onto the blue-grey cloak. Anlon held her close, becoming lost in her, until he could no longer tell where his body ended and hers began. She responded in kind, seeking him out not as a queen but as a woman, a lover, a wife. Deep within the quiet shade of the forest, seeing and feeling nothing but each other, they moved together in an embrace that was both as old as Time and as new as the violets which bloomed along the sparkling stream.

The long summer days went by in a kind of magical golden haze for Anlon. He was kept pleasantly occupied from dawn to dusk with hunting and fishing, and with working in the small hidden fields of barley with the other men of the Sidhe. Best of all, when he returned to Caher Idir after a day of work he no longer slept at Liath's house. He was now a part of Scahta's life, and they shared the house where once she had lived alone.

One warm night, when the moon again was full, Anlon could not help but notice how very beautiful Scahta looked on this particular evening. She seemed to have taken out all her best finery and put it on for him tonight, and she gleamed with bright gold at her neck and wrists and even in her hair.

They sat together in the soft twilight and watched as two of Scahta's women brought in plates of food and cups of fresh cold water. To Anlon's surprise there was even a beautiful gold cup with a little honey-wine inside. Scahta took a sip of it and then offered it to him, and he accepted, greatly enjoying its delicate spicy sweetness.

Scahta smiled and set the cup aside. When the two had finished their meal of salmon and dried apples and boiled dandelion roots, she took him by the hand and led him past the quiet houses to the forest.

It was a rare balmy evening at the height of summer. The moon shone brilliant and white high above the green trees, casting an enormous white ring across the surrounding blackness of the sky. At first Anlon thought Scahta meant for them to enjoy a fine evening alone together out in the woods, but this time she led him only a short distance to the edge of the stream. Releasing his hand, she hurried across the stepping stones, ran through a cover of trees and stopped at the edge of a wide and grassy clearing.

Anlon stood beside her, looking around in amazement. Within the forest surrounding the clearing were tiny flickering lights, as if the stars had come down from the evening sky and scattered themselves among the trees. As he and Scahta stepped out into the lush grass of the field, the lights approached it too—lights carried in small stone lamps by all the people of Caher Idir.

Scahta stood close beside him in the very center of the field, her small hand on his arm, waiting while her people gathered around. To his surprise, he felt that she was tense with anticipation, almost trembling; but her eyes shone, and when she smiled Anlon realized he had never seen her so happy.

"I thank you all for coming here with me on this night," she said, in a clear voice, to her subjects. "Now, I will tell you why we are here." She glanced up at Anlon and smiled. "There is to be a marriage."

He reached up to cover her hand with his own. "A marriage," he whispered, feeling shock and joy all at once. "I have waited a long time to hear you say you will marry me, Queen Scahta."

She stepped back a pace, sliding her fingers down his arm to clasp his hand, and then raised his hand up to present him to the Sidhe. Turning to face her people, she began to speak.

"Here is the one I have chosen as my husband. Here he is so that all may know him. Here he will stay so long as both of us wish it."

Scahta turned to Anlon again. "Because I am the one who has done the choosing, and because my husband has left his home to live in mine, this shall be a marriage of affection alone. Both of us are free to go our own way if and when we wish, and it shall be as if the marriage had never been." She paused, and then smiled gently as she looked up at Anlon. "Yet I believe that he is worthy of being my husband, and of one day being your king."

Anlon felt both proud and pleased, and strangely light, as if a great weight had been lifted from him. Now he and Scahta would be free to give their lives and their love to one another. Now he would find a place at Caher Idir and would no longer be the outsider. Now he could look forward to one day being a king—her king.

He turned to look at her, but a strange sight caught his eye. All around them, at the edge of the forest, the tiny lights were going out.

In a moment the only flames left were those held by the people immediately surrounding them. Many more flames had gone out than remained burning. Anlon turned to Scahta, wondering if this was another part of the Sidhe ceremony, but then realized that she was standing very still. Her glance flicked over the shadowy trees lit now only by moonlight and a few candles, and she scarcely seemed to breathe. She was as confused as he was.

"Why do your lights go dark?" she asked.

From the shadows along the line of trees, voices drifted to them. "Once you said to us that if you chose a Man, you would stay with him for only one year."

"This Man has already been here since Samhain last."

"He may be your husband now, but he may stay only until Samhain next."

"*Samhain . . .*"

"*Samhain . . .*"

"*Samhain . . .*"

She stopped their chants by throwing up both hands in a fierce gesture. "I have not said that he would stay past Samhain. I only wish to honor him by making him my husband. Am I not entitled to a mate, as any of you are? Do you not respect the choice that I have made?"

Not all of the Sidhe were against them—perhaps a third stood close to Scahta and Anlon, holding their flickering lights—but the rest were scattered around the field and in and out of the forest, and they were the ones who murmured and whispered and hissed.

"He may be your husband, for a time, but he is still a Man."

"Making him your husband does not make him one of the Sidhe."

"Or a king."

Scahta whirled, facing her people as she walked a circle before them. "This man has lived among you for many months. Has he not proven his trustworthiness to you?"

The voices grew louder and angrier. "Cian is dead!"

"Cian went out alone with the man!"

"Cian came back with the man's own sword in his heart!"

The sounds from the darkness were frightening, but Scahta faced them down. "Anlon did not harm him! You know as well as I that he did not. He was the one who purified that sword, all on his own. He alone removed the terrible stain that clung to it. Could he have done that if he were a murderer?"

There was a silence, cold as the moonlight.

"In the end, it does not matter."

"It was a Man who killed Cian."

"It is a Man who stands beside you now."

Scahta stopped and stood very still. "I have made him my husband. Is that not enough for you? Does that not say to you how much I honor him, how much I trust him?"

The words were whispered, scattered throughout the crowd.

"No Man should live among us."

"No Man can become one of the Sidhe."

"No Man will ever be our king."

She drew herself up and made a formal request of her people. "Will you accept Anlon as your king?"

The voices of the outer ring shouted down those closest to Scahta.

"We will not!"

"We will not!"

"We will not!" they called.

Anlon realized Scahta could do nothing more. She had

brought him to Caher Idir and married him in front of all her people, but that did not make him a member of the Sidhe. He was still a Man to them, still an outsider, still an enemy . . . and no matter how much Scahta might love him, she could never stay with him if her people refused to accept him.

Now it was up to him.

Chapter Thirteen

Anlon stepped forward and held out his hands to them. "I am here because of my love for your queen and because I too carry the blood of the Sidhe. What more can I—"

The hissing rose up around him again.

"*Man . . .*"

"*Man . . .*"

"*Man . . .*"

But he pushed on. "Listen to me, I beg you!" Silence fell again. "What more can I do to prove my worth to you? There must be a way. There must be something—"

"*Destroy the Men,*" came the hissing response.

"*Destroy the Men.*"

"*Destroy the Men.*"

Behind him he felt Scahta shiver. And he himself grew cold at the terrible whispered words which flew around him.

"Stop!" he shouted. "If we attack Men, they will do nothing but wipe out every last one of you and laugh while they do it! There is another way."

Anlon expected to hear more hissing and whispering, but there was no sound. Everyone stood motionless.

He took a deep breath. "I will go to the Men, and I will serve as mediator for the Sidhe. I will convince them that you are not their enemy and they should not be yours. I will persuade them to leave a part of the wild harvest untouched so that all might survive in peace. Will you allow me to do this?"

The silence continued. Then one by one, the hostile Sidhe—those who stood in darkness where the forest met the field—turned and started back to the fortress.

"We shall see," was all he heard.

"We shall see . . ."

"We shall see . . ."

In moments, the outer rings of the Sidhe had all gone away. Scahta and Anlon were left alone with the remainder of her people, those who still held their burning lamps or candles and were willing to stand with the two of them.

Scahta turned, surrounded by tiny flames, and looked up at him. "I can do no more to make my people accept you," she said. "If you cannot find a way to make them believe you are a king, the way I believe you are a king, then you will have no choice but to leave at Samhain— and I will have no choice but to watch you go."

Now closer, friendlier voices spoke to him out of the darkness.

"We respect the choice our queen has made."

"Even a Man can serve the Sidhe."

"Only a king could have cleansed that sword, whether king of Man or Sidhe."

Anlon closed his eyes. Beside him, Scahta rested her hand on his arm once again, and he felt the renewed strength and calmness in her. "Can you persuade the Men, as you said?" she asked. "Can you truly do such a thing?"

For a moment the chill threatened to return, but then he looked into her eyes and smiled. "I can, Queen Scahta, for I must," he answered. "There is no life for me without you. I will do whatever I must, so that I can stay with you forever."

The next morning, Anlon wasted no time in keeping his promise to the Sidhe. At the first sign of light in the eastern sky, he set out on Nealta for Dun Mor.

The journey was a long one, longer than he remembered. He had made this trek once before, on that Samhain Eve which now seemed ages ago. But on that night he had not been alone. Scahta had been with him, and many of the Sidhe, and he had been there as one of them.

Now, as Nealta stepped along the soft forest path, he felt suspended between the worlds as never before. He was neither Man nor Sidhe, belonging everywhere and nowhere, and wondering where he might end up . . . if he ended up anywhere at all.

The sun was high by the time he reached the *dun*. The last time he had approached the great fortress had been in the moonlit darkness, on a terrifying night filled with fire and blood and death. Now, on this quiet summer afternoon, where white clouds drifted in a clear blue sky and the only sounds were the sighing of the breeze in the trees and the sweet distant singing of the birds, it was as though he were seeing the place for the very first time.

As before, he saw the massive earthen walls, far bigger than the sheltered stones of Caher Idir, sitting boldly out in the wide open expanse at the high end of the field. But today the gates stood open and various ordinary folk walked in and out—men carrying buckets for water, women carrying baskets into the woods for gathering herbs, a group of workmen driving a team of oxen yoked to a wooden wagon.

Massive as it was, Anlon could see now that it was not just a fortress. It was also a home, just as his family's *rath* had been a home, just as Caher Idir was a home. As he started Nealta across the open field toward the gates, he felt as if he were floating between three worlds. Any of them could be his own. . . .

Or perhaps none of them at all.

A terrible thought occurred to him as he moved closer to Dun Mor. He had once believed that the worst situation would be if he were forced to choose among three places. But what if he had no choice at all?

He would be forced to leave Caher Idir if its people could not bring themselves to trust him. The men of Dun Mor could well reject him as one who had turned his back on them to live with a perceived enemy. And even his own family, far away at its quiet *rath*, would surely find it difficult to accept him back in the place he had once held among them, for he was no longer the person he had been.

For a long moment he felt as though he would simply continue forever on Nealta's back, drifting through the tall grass the way a cloud drifts through the sky.

But he did not have long to do so. They had seen him. Before Anlon was halfway across the field, six armed men had come out of the gates on foot to meet him. He did not doubt more were ready should these six prove inadequate.

He stopped Nealta and waited for them to reach him,

Janeen O'Kerry

allowing his old mare to drop her head and grab a few mouthfuls of the surrounding lush grass as he waited. He hoped that such a picture would assure these men he was not here to attack them, but he was careful to keep his hands from his bronze sword nonetheless.

"Hello, Fehin," he said, as they walked up. "Good day to you, Donn."

It was strange to see them again, having looked for so long only upon the smooth beautiful faces of the Sidhe. These six men were tall and bearded, and had long braided hair. They were garbed in rough gaudy wool and armed with cold iron. For all his life he had seen only such people—indeed, had lived among them—but now they seemed like something from another world entirely.

Yet he himself had once been as they were. He knew that he must look equally strange to them. His face was shaven clean each day with a small bronze razor, and his hair combed smooth. He wore the deerskin pants and sleeveless leather tunic the men of the Sidhe wore in the summer months, with the soft blue-and-grey cloak fastened over his shoulder with the bronze leaf-shaped pin. At his belt was the bronze-tipped scabbard holding his beautiful sword.

They all peered at him closely. A look of disbelief came over Donn's face. "Anlon! Can it be you?"

"It couldn't be him," growled Fehin. "Anlon was taken by the Sidhe and their glamyr—captured by their tricks and magic—" He stopped and shook his head, and started to grin. "But as I live, I do believe it is Anlon, come back to us from the Sidhe! How did you manage to escape them?"

Anlon only grinned back at him. "You do not ride with the Fianna this summer?" he asked.

"Ha! I am now a part of the king's own army, as is

Donn, and a few of the others you remember. Only the trouble-making youngsters are pushed out for the summer." He laughed again, then turned toward the *dun* and waved his arm.

"Come on, come with us now, and you can tell us the story of how you managed to do such a thing! We'll give you food while you tell us. You must be starving for real food, for great joints of roasted meat and whole cakes of bread made with wheat and dripping with fresh summer butter the color of gold! No more thistles and thorns and other such things as the Sidhe-folk eat, you must be so tired of—"

Anlon smiled and held up his hand to silence him, throwing his leg over Nealta's neck and jumping to the ground. "It is a fine offer you make, and I will be happy to accept it. I will tell you all you care to hear, and more, but I must tell you first that I have not come here to stay."

They all stood and stared. Nealta dropped her head to the grass once more.

"You have not come back to stay?" Fehin asked. "Even after you managed to escape the Sidhe? Where else could you go—back to the life of a farmer?" The huge warrior peered closely at him. "Just where do you think you belong, Anlon?"

Anlon stared back at the man, searching for the words. "I belong . . . among the Sidhe," he heard himself say, though his voice was only a whisper.

Fehin only shook his head. "Then, you have a great deal to tell us, Anlon," he said at last, and started on his way back to Dun Mor.

As Anlon walked with them toward the great walls of the fortress, he felt a growing excitement at the thought of actually seeing, at long last, what lay within those walls. And he found that he enjoyed being once again in the company of these men. They were his old fellows from the Fianna, and they were now offering him grand hospitality instead of expecting him to work like the lowest of the servants.

Yet still, as he led Nealta across the grass toward the great towering gates of the *dun*, he heard the call of the Sidhe, of Scahta, whispering to him on the gentle breeze, never letting him forget the magic and mystery that he had found deep within the forest so very far away.

Someone took Nealta's reins as he led her through the gates, but Anlon scarcely noticed. All around him rose Dun Mor.

It was as open as Caher Idir was hidden, as blatant and powerful as the Sidhe fortress was secretive and protected. The great earthen walls towered over his head—walls so thick they were grown over with grass—and as he passed the gates he was amazed to see a second earthen wall within the first, separated from it by a ditch half-full of water and piled high with broken thorny branches.

At long last he was inside. So numerous were the buildings, and so large, that he could not see across the grounds to the other side. Houses twice as big as those of Caher Idir were scattered throughout the great walled circle, houses with tall doors and smooth daub walls and thatched roofs of thick straw, bleached grey-brown from the rains and the abundant sunlight.

And plenty of sunlight there was, for everything was clear and open to the skies and the winds and the rains. It was as if these men had openly proclaimed that they had no need of a forest for protection and shelter, but would tear out the trees as it suited them and build their own houses and halls wherever they wished instead.

Anlon and the others continued through the *dun*, past house after house, past other buildings that appeared to be used for storage or metalwork or carpentry. All around the perimeter were sheds and fenced-off spaces for the horses and a few sheep and cows.

And everywhere, iron. Cold iron was used in the hinges, the wagon wheels, the cauldrons, the scythes, the swords.

He drew a breath. There were so many, many people here! Two hundred, perhaps even three hundred, easily four or five times as many as lived at Caher Idir. Anlon had spent the last few months living as a prince among the Sidhe, but in this place he felt like nothing more than the simple farm boy he had always been. It was hard for him to even think about the world being so big, or having so many people in it; but here they were, within the massive walls of the fortress called Dun Mor.

They all sat together on the floor of the enormous circular building that was the king's hall, quite comfortable on furs and fleeces thrown down on the thick rushes. Though he was surrounded by some fifty men, all that remained of the king's warriors for the summer, Anlon kept looking up, and up, amazed by the sheer size of the structure that towered over his head.

He had never thought a single building could enclose so much space, though he had heard tales of such things. It almost made him dizzy to see the vastness of the thatched roof covering so expansive a room, one which would have stretched halfway across Caher Idir all on its own.

The roof was so high over his head that three—four— at least five men would have to stand atop one another's shoulders to touch the straw of the thatching. So large was the room that there was no hole cut in the roof for smoke; it could merely seep out through the vast surface of the thatched straw.

As Fehin had promised, servants brought out great quantities of meat and bread and early strawberries topped with honey. The smell of the hot wheat bread thick with melting golden butter was fairly intoxicating. He grabbed a chunk in each hand and devoured them one after the other, marveling at how very good it was and how he had always taken bread and butter for granted until now.

The men around him ate, and talked, and laughed, waiting for him to finish eating before they asked him any questions. Then, just as he finished his third great slice of meat, dripping with juices and sprinkled with sea salt, Anlon froze—and slowly set down his plate.

Just inside the doorway, surrounded by the warriors and advisors who made up his retinue, stood a tall bearded man whose wide heavy shoulders barely cleared the door. He wore the longest, widest wool cloak Anlon had ever seen, dyed in deep shades of purple and red and blue in a beautifully woven plaid. An enormous gold torque rested around his neck and a huge circular golden brooch fastened the cloak at his shoulder. His wrists and fingers and belt were heavy and gleaming with gold and more gold.

He had seen this man before. This was the king of Dun Mor, the king he had seen walking across the field when the fires had burned at Samhain.

Slowly the king walked through the great hall, his hall, followed by his ever-present retinue of servants and druid and personal guards. Quickly Anlon wiped his hands clean in the rushes and got to his feet.

The king stopped a short distance away. He looked the visitor over carefully, his eyes flicking from the leaf-shaped bronze pin at Anlon's shoulder to the simple leather tunic to the soft leather pants and high soft boots. Anlon was well aware that his appearance was markedly different from that of everyone else, but he stood tall and looked directly into the eye of the powerful sovereign.

"You are Anlon," said the king.

"I am."

"Have you been made comfortable here?" he inquired. "Have you been served food and allowed to rest?"

"I have. And I thank you."

"You are most welcome. Now, Anlon, please sit down, that we might hear your story."

When the king had made himself comfortable on a deerskin and the rest of the men had formed a half-circle around him, Anlon too sat down again in the rushes as the king began to speak.

"Last summer, you rode with the Fianna, did you not?"

"I did."

"You were to come to Dun Mor with them at the end of that summer, at Samhain. Yet you left the Fianna."

"I left them," Anlon agreed, looking down at the rushes.

"Did you not care to be one of the Fianna?"

He looked up again. "I have wanted to be one of the Fianna ever since I was a young boy—ever since I first saw them ride through the forest past my home."

"And you were to come here and stay at Dun Mor at summer's end. You were to stay and serve me over the winter months."

"I was." He could say no more.

The king paused, looking him over again. "Your family serves mine. They are a part of Dun Mor, living under

169

its protection even as you did. Yet you turned away rather than stay with the Fianna, stay at Dun Mor, stay and serve your king. I would know why."

Anlon could not meet his eyes. He nodded, once, slowly, and then again more firmly. "I found a thing that I never thought to find," he answered. "I found . . . a place among the Sidhe."

There was a rustling and murmuring among the men. The king frowned at him. "I had heard that one of the Fianna was lured away by the Sidhe . . . but I did not want to think that it was true." Again he peered closely at Anlon. "Surely you will tell me that you simply returned to your family home because you had a beautiful wife there who missed your company."

There was some laughter among the other men, but he also saw them murmuring to each other and nodding at his clothes. "I wish that I could tell you such a thing— but it would not be true." He looked down at the rushes again and fingered the bronze pin that held his cloak at his shoulder. "It is as you said. I have been living among the Sidhe since just before the last Samhain."

All of them held very still. Finally, the king spoke again. "Tell me how such a thing could come about. Tell me how a loyal young man could ride with the Fianna on one day and abandon them the next to live with the Sidhe."

Anlon felt the words stab at him. *Loyal young man . . . abandon them . . .* He forced himself to smile. "It is a strange story, I admit . . . yet it is true." He looked down at the rushes for a moment, and then met the king's eyes once again.

"There was nothing I wanted more than to ride with the Fianna. Though there was hard work involved, I did it gladly that I might be one of them. And I thought of little else save the day when I would see Dun Mor—and see its king that I might have the honor of serving."

The king glanced at the men around him, watching as they all nodded in agreement with Anlon's words. "Then, tell me. What glamyr did the Sidhe throw over you that you would abandon your lifelong desire in the course of a single day?"

"Glamyr." Anlon stared at him. Then it was as if the scene before him faded and he saw only Scahta's face. He could feel her, taste her, smell the warmth of her skin. . . .

He closed his eyes.

When he opened them again he found the entire company staring at him, waiting for his next words. "It *was* a glamyr," he said at last. "It was a glamyr more powerful than any other. It was the glamyr of love."

He stopped, then, and looked at the king—who merely blinked. Anlon's glance flicked across the other men, waiting for their response. Suddenly, after looking at each other and then back to him, they all began to shout with laughter—every last one of them, even the king.

Anlon could not have been more shocked, or humiliated, if they'd picked him up and thrown him bodily into the mud outside Dun Mor's gates. "I tell you the truth," he said, with as much dignity as he could find, though he had little hope of getting through to them.

He got to his feet, standing as tall as he could, and placed his hand on the bronze-trimmed scabbard. "The people of the Sidhe made me a gift of this sword. They have promised me—" He hesitated, then stopped completely.

How could he tell them that he was the one chosen by the queen of the Sidhe to be her king? If they were laughing now, they would be fairly rolling in the rushes at that! "They have promised me a place among them," he went on, his head high and his gaze steady. "And a woman there has become my wife."

"Oh, *ho!*" roared the men of Dun Mor, and they looked knowingly at each other even through their laughter. "Now we know what that glamyr truly was! Gifts and promises—and beauty!" They roared together again, and Anlon, stunned, could only look at them and wonder if they were right.

Had it all been just the magic of the Sidhe? A spell, a glamyr, an illusion cast over him, to lure a simple farm boy away from home to serve their purposes? What power they must have, and how he must have underestimated it, for them to lure him away from all that had meant so much to him without even a backward glance!

His hand fell to the hilt of his mystical bronze sword. *The magic of gifts and promises . . . and beauty.*

Had they been all he required?

Chapter Fourteen

The laughter finally died down, and the king spoke again. "Tell me, Anlon, if you will . . . why are you here? Why have you come back to us now, at midsummer, a time of ease, if you have found a place among the Sidhe?"

Anlon paused and gathered his thoughts. He must put the last minutes' humiliation behind him, and he must not let the wonders of this vast fortress and its powerful king distract him from what he had come here to do.

He took his hand from the sword and looked up at the monarch. "I must apologize. I have indeed come here to ask you for . . . for an agreement."

"An agreement?"

"With the Sidhe."

The king frowned. The other men shot glances at each other, clearly suspicious. "What kind of agreement?"

"You despise and fear the Sidhe," Anlon said, taking a

deep breath, "and yet I have come here to tell you that they are dying."

The king's frown only deepened. "You say you believe we fear them. Why should we fear something that is dying?"

"They are not your enemy. And they need your help."

"Our help?" Now it was Fehin's turn to laugh, and the other men joined him. "I'll give them help!" And to Anlon's horror he reached for the hilt of his iron sword.

"They are your ancestors," Anlon pressed. "They are your past. They are in your poems and songs if not in your blood. I know that I cannot be the only one here who carries the blood of the Sidhe."

"I carry the blood of the Sidhe," another man said. Anlon looked up, encouraged at finding an ally—but then he saw the warrior's surly laughing face. "I carry it on my sword, and on the gates of Dun Mor at Samhain!"

Anlon felt cold, but he pressed on amid the laughter. "They are starving all through the long winters," he said. "They are dying. There are fewer of them born every year."

One of Dun Mor's warriors spoke up with a sneer, "Perhaps with the likes of you among them, there will be many more infants born!"

"Do their women need any more help from us?" another called. "Just show me the way, and I'll be happy to be of service to them!"

Anlon gritted his teeth. "They don't want *you*," he said in answer. "They only want a little of the harvest."

"The harvest?"

"Our harvest?"

"Are you telling us that they expect to share in the food we have worked for, while they hide in their caves and do nothing?"

"They are not asking for the things you have planted and grown yourselves. They ask only that you leave something of the wild harvest, the hazelnuts and the blackberries and even the wild red deer, that the Sidhe might not endure such hardship through the winter."

"Leave the wild harvest. . . ." It was the king's turn to speak again. "Are we so numerous, so widespread, that we can take all the food from the forest?"

"The Sidhe don't eat what Men eat, Anlon," said another. "Thistles and thorns and the dew from the grass— that's what they live on! Surely you've learned that by now!"

"They eat no such things," Anlon said, his anger rising. "And I have seen firsthand just what a troop of men can do to the wild harvest."

"You speak as if you no longer count yourself among us, Anlon."

He met the eyes of the king. "I am a Man. But I am also of the Sidhe."

The king slowly shook his head. "You cannot be both, Anlon. There will come a day when you will have to choose. Even now the question hangs above you—to whom do you owe your loyalty?"

Anlon looked at him, and tried to answer. "I am . . . I am of course a Man, as I said. Yet a part of me belongs to the Sidhe and always will." He looked at the king, almost pleading for understanding. "Why is it necessary to choose? Can I not be a friend to both?"

"You cannot be a friend to two who are enemies of each other. One will force you to make your choice—or else both will turn on you."

Again the cold feeling settled over Anlon, but as before he raised his head. "I cannot believe that . . . and I cannot, I *cannot* choose. It is as though my life belongs to one

175

world and my heart to another. How could anyone make such a choice?"

"I do not know. And yet I wonder if even you know which world has your life and which one has your heart."

Anlon shook his head, looking away, shutting out the sight of the men and their king and their magnificent hall. "Will you allow me to tell the Sidhe that you will leave them some of the wild harvest?" he pleaded. "They are not your enemy. They are people of peace. They are—"

"They are dying, as you say." The king got to his feet, as did the rest of his men. "And a starving, dying enemy is of no concern to us. Tell them whatever you like."

He glared down at Anlon. "Do you think it is so easy for us, that we need not gather all the food we can from the forest? Are the winters not as long for us as they are for the Sidhe? We do not expect them to help us. Why should they expect us to help them?"

"They are dying," Anlon whispered.

The king shrugged his massive shoulders. "Stay with us this night," he said. "You will have the best Dun Mor has to offer. Stay with us this night and remember what it is to live in the world of Men."

Anlon hesitated. For a moment he was back to last summer, riding with the Fianna, the king's own men, and looking forward to finding a home and a life in service to the king at Dun Mor.

And now he was here, and the monarch stood within arm's reach of him, inviting him to stay.

He wanted to stay. The pull of it was strong. Yet the new life he had found in a fragile and secretive world called out to him, as if it whispered his name on the wind and longed for his return. "I cannot stay," he said quietly. "But I thank you for your hospitality."

The king shook his head. "You truly intend to live

among them? To turn your back on your king and your own kind forever?"

"I . . . I am determined to find a way to serve both," he answered. Anlon turned to go, walking out of the great hall for what he well knew could be the last time—the only time. And as he left he heard the murmuring voices of the men behind him.

"We shall see. . . ."

"We shall see. . . ."

"We shall see. . . ."

It was well past nightfall when Nealta brought him back to the bronze-faced wooden gates of Caher Idir. The rain had begun to fall. Anlon slid down slowly, wearily, and allowed one of the Sidhe men to lead the mare away.

Scahta walked out of the dripping darkness. Her white cloak was drawn over her head, and she was accompanied by her three women, all carrying torches. She walked to him and smiled, placing her hand against his cheek for just a moment. "Come inside where you can rest. We will bring you some food, and—"

Anlon stilled her voice by taking her hands in his own. "I must tell you now what I have done," he said. "It cannot wait." Then, looking up, he said to the crowd of people: "I must tell you what I have done."

The Sidhe villagers appeared from out of the houses and shadows and quickly gathered around him.

"Did you speak to the men of Dun Mor?"

"Will they do as you ask?"

"Shall some of the wild harvest be left alone for us?"

Anlon only shook his head. "They will do nothing," he said, "for nothing has changed. I have failed you."

Scahta looked up at him. "Did you not speak to them?"

"I did."

The people broke in, their voices agitated. "But they did not care to listen!"

"Do they now mean to destroy us?"

"When will they attack?"

Anlon raised his hands to silence the voices in the rain-soaked blackness. "There will be no attack. They care so little for the Sidhe that the idea of attacking you is not enough to raise their interest. They plan to do nothing at all."

"Except continue to strip the land bare each fall. Except to watch us slowly starve and fade away." Scahta gazed up at him, her large eyes almost reproachful. "We thank you for your efforts, Anlon. But as we said before you left, those men have no concern at all for the Sidhe, and never will."

"*Samhain*," spoke a voice from beyond the lights, and in a moment the others joined in their hissing chant. "*Samhain . . . Samhain . . .*"

Scahta stopped them with a sharp gesture. "Why do you speak of Samhain?"

"At Samhain, we will take back what is ours."

"At Samhain, the men of Dun Mor will be forced to deal with us."

"At Samhain, there will be war."

Anlon's heart began to pound. Scahta placed her hand on his arm. "Why do you say there will be war?" she asked, and though her voice was strong, he could feel her fingers tighten on his arm.

"They will never allow us to live in peace."

"Man and Sidhe can never live together."

"It is for us to destroy them, once and for all."

Now the rest of the Sidhe began creeping toward Anlon. "*Destroy them*," they chanted, in that terrible hissing voice. "*Destroy them . . . destroy them . . .*"

"Would you destroy my husband?" cried Scahta. "Would you destroy my life?"

The people fell silent. "Would you have me destroy the one that I believe should be our king?" she called out.

"He is a Man," one of the voices shrieked.

"Yet he lives as one of the Sidhe," called another.

"He will have to choose between the two."

Now it was Anlon's turn to clench his hands as the words of the king came back to him. The Sidhe wanted him to choose, just as the Men did. Yet how could he choose between his life and his heart?

"What would you have me do?" Scahta asked, in a clear voice that left no doubt she was merely requesting their opinion—not awaiting their orders.

"Send the man away!"

"I will not send him away."

"Destroy the man!"

"I will not destroy him."

"Make him lead us in a war against the men of Dun Mor!"

Scahta was silent. Anlon could sense the pounding of her heart. The voices in the darkness continued to call out to her.

"He must help us drive the Men out once and for all."

"War is the only answer now."

"He can prove his loyalty to us in no other way."

The Sidhe queen's voice dropped to a whisper. "Why do you need him to lead you?"

"Bait," came the chilling answer. *"Bait . . . bait . . ."*

Scahta released Anlon's arm and stepped out into the crowd. "I cannot believe you would consider such a thing. If it were possible to fight those men, do you not think we would have done it long ago? How many more of you

179

should I watch die in a futile war? There are far too few of us—and the others are far away!"

"Then bring them here!"

"We will spend the summer gathering them together!"

"On Samhain Eve we will all make an end to the tyranny of the invaders! These were our forests once. We shall take them back!"

"They will kill you all," Anlon said, walking forward to stand with Scahta. "You will have gathered the tribes and brought them to the killing fields just as the cows are brought down from the mountains to the slaughter. Is that what you want for the Sidhe?"

"Tell us what chance we have if we remain as we are!"

"With the other tribes," someone added, "we have at least a chance of succeeding."

"If we do nothing, we will all die as Cian died—at the hands of Men."

The silence fell heavily over the clan. Their torches snapped and guttered as the rain dripped from the trees onto them, and to the wet ground below.

"Anlon," said Scahta, allowing her voice to carry to all the people surrounding her, "the Sidhe have asked you to lead them in a battle to destroy the men. They ask it of you as one who would be their king. How do you answer them?"

He looked down at her, but could only see her profile beneath her upturned cloak; she stood very still, staring out over the heads of her people, waiting for his response.

Anlon wanted only to reach out to her. He wanted to forget about the Sidhe and the other men and all their hatreds, so that he could touch her face and turn it toward him . . . wanted to leave the impossible problems of two worlds far behind so he might draw her into his arms and comfort her, and tell her that somehow he would make things right for her again.

But he could not do so now, not while all of Caher Idir stood waiting for him to answer; and so with an effort Anlon turned from Scahta and faced the tense and glaring crowd.

"Here is what I will do," he began. "I will go with you to find the other Sidhe. If we find them, then we will speak to them and learn whether they feel the same as the people of Caher Idir. Do you agree to this?"

Even from a few steps away, Anlon could feel Scahta relax ever so slightly. He had not agreed to go to war. He had said only that he would help them go and search for others of their kind. By the time they found those others, perhaps the feelings of her people might have changed.

He was gaining them some time—if they would accept his offer. Together he and Scahta turned to face the crowd.

"Find them," came the whispered response.

"Find them."

"Find them."

The people of Caher Idir dispersed, moving back into their homes and into the wet and dripping shadows of the fortress.

Scahta drew Anlon after her into the warmth and shelter of their home. He moved to the sleeping ledge and sat wearily, covering his face with his hands. Scahta closed the door and moved to stand in front of him.

"You must be so tired," she said gently. "You have had a long journey, a long day. Let me call for Maidin. I will have her bring you some food."

She touched his shoulder and stroked his long soft hair, but he did not move. Finally he shook his head and allowed his hands to fall. "There is no need to call her. I am not hungry."

Never had she seen him so silent, so still. Scahta tried to smile. "There was nothing more you could have done today," she said. "Indeed, you have saved many lives. You persuaded the Sidhe to go search for more of their kind instead of attacking Dun Mor." Again she stroked his hair. "You should be pleased. I will tell you that I am very pleased by what you have accomplished this day."

Slowly he looked up at her. She felt a chill when she saw the exhaustion in his eyes, the great weariness in his face. "I am your servant, Scahta. I told you once that I would be your servant until I could be your king. I thought I was a willing servant. But now I am not so sure."

Her hand stopped. She withdrew a step, then sat down beside him on the ledge. "Please, Anlon. Tell me what you mean."

Her shoulders moved as he sighed deeply. "This day at Dun Mor, even as I walked through its gates for the very first time, it seemed that I could feel your presence—that I could hear you calling me, holding me, drawing me back to Caher Idir and to you. I thought it was my love for you that I was feeling. But now I wonder if it was love alone, or something more."

Scahta gazed into the fire. "What did those men say to you?"

"They said to me . . . they said . . ." He shook his head. "I told them it was love that held me here, and when they finished laughing they told me that it was not love. They said it was a glamyr. A Sidhe glamyr."

"And you believe you are here because you are under a glamyr?"

He got to his feet and moved to the hearth, leaning on the stones with both hands. He kept his back to her.

"I do not know," he said. His voice trembled. Whether it was from anger or from pain, she could not tell.

"Tell me why you believe this." She willed her voice to keep steady, but was greatly disturbed by the sight of his lowered head and rounded shoulders. He looked as though he carried a unbearable burden of weariness and doubt.

At last he turned to face her. Again she saw the pain, the fear, the doubt that had never been there before. "From the first moment I saw you, I knew I was under your spell," he began. "I could not help but fall in love with your beauty and your kindness and your power. I thought it was no more than that . . . until today."

Scahta remained silent. He must be allowed to finish.

"I am one who has always been drawn to the beauty and the mystery of the Sidhe. I believed you held me here with love alone. But today, when the king asked me how I could have left the Fianna so easily, how I could have turned my back on Dun Mor and my king and even my own family without a second thought—I found I had no answer for him."

Anlon looked straight into her eyes. "Am I here because you love me? Or am I here because you hold me with magic, that I might serve you better?"

She gazed at him without a word, knowing he would think she was merely dispassionate. He would not realize how her heart raced and her knees trembled, would not know of the coldness that settled over her.

"It is difficult to prove what a thing is not," she said. "But if you wish for me to show you, then tomorrow we will go to a place that will have a stronger pull on you than Dun Mor, or Caher Idir, or even my love for you."

"And where is that?"

"Home."

Chapter Fifteen

The summer's day in the forest was much like any other: green leaves fluttering on the soft warm breeze, birds singing and calling high in the trees, hares and red deer and wild boar moving among the trees and shrubs. But on this day there was another motion . . . a constant waving of the ferns and leaves along a faint path that ran beneath the largest, oldest trees.

Something made its way through the forest on a determined and secretive path, something that lived among the shadows and now moved through them on a single-minded hunt.

Anlon led the group of five. He followed the path in the general direction of Dun Mor, knowing that eventually it would curve away and take him to the place where he had grown up—the place where, as a boy, he had once made a gift of milk and bread to the shy members of the Sidhe and received a bronze cloak pin in return.

They passed one night in the shelter of the forest, then traveled nearly all of the rest of the following day until at last they climbed to the top of a low tree-covered hill. There, beneath a grey and rainy sky, they looked down on a small peaceful settlement.

Like Dun Mor, it was a ringed fortress in the middle of a field, but this place was only a *rath*—it was much smaller and had only a single ring of piled earth and stone. There was a single house within the ring, fairly large in size, along with a couple of lean-to sheds for storage and for livestock.

"Home," whispered Anlon.

Scahta looked up at him. "So it is," she said softly. "This has always been your home. The place where you were born, ran and played as a boy, and grew to manhood."

Anlon continued to gaze at the settlement. A wisp of blue smoke drifted up into the damp grey sky from the open space in the thatched roof. Someone was clearly working inside the dwelling.

"My mother is surely in the house. And my two sisters," he said. "My father and uncles will be out taking care of the fields, my brothers away in the mountain pastures watching the cattle at their summer grazing. But my mother is here. . . . My mother, my sisters . . ."

"You should go there, Anlon," said Scahta. Her voice was so soft that he felt the words rather than heard them. "They are your family. You should go to them. I will not try to hold you with me. You are free do to as you wish, as you have always been."

Anlon closed his eyes. He felt as if the weight of three

worlds lay upon him. "How simple it would be to just go home, to lay down all the burdens I have gathered in such a short time. It seems impossible to me that only one year ago I was riding with the Fianna, with nothing more to concern me than how quickly I could prepare a meal.

"Now death and destruction lie heavy on my shoulders. There is blood on my hands and a terrible fear like a knife in my heart that the woman I love might never be fully mine . . . that I may never find a place among her people . . . that if I cannot save them, her people might vanish from the world altogether."

Your home waits for you, Anlon, he heard Scahta say. *Your family waits. I will not force you to stay with me.*

Go back . . . go back to the simple, comfortable ways of tending the earth and the animals, with good food and a warm place in front of the fire each night. There will be a simple farm girl to become your wife and give you children and work alongside you the rest of your life . . . so simple, so comfortable, so easy . . . never a worry, never a care, never a doubt that each day will be just like the one before. . . .

"So easy," Anlon whispered, feeling as though he were in a dream. "So easy . . ."

He got up, steadying himself against a tree and reached down to help Scahta to her feet. "Come with me," he said. Together they started down the wet grass of the hillside while their three companions stayed behind, hidden in the woods.

The two walked close to the edge of the trees, with Anlon drawn to the clearing and Scahta holding back. At last he let go of her hand and left the forest, taking a single step out into the open.

Through the open gate of the *rath* he could see the

door to the house. As he watched, the door opened and two young women walked out into the misty rain.

They were younger than Anlon and just coming into the first fresh beauty of youth. They wore simple gowns of natural undyed linen and allowed their dark hair to fall unbound past their shoulders. Laughing and talking, carrying baskets piled high with cheese and hot loaves of bread, they went striding through the gate and started toward the distant fields.

"Morna," Anlon called. "Riona!"

They paused, looking at each other. One of them turned around to face the trees. "Morna," Anlon said again.

The two young women started toward him, walking quickly, and then setting down their baskets and running to the edge of the clearing. "Anlon! Is that you?" asked Morna, stopping just a few paces away.

She started to go to him, but then both she and her sister hesitated. They looked him over in bewilderment, their glances flicking from his high soft boots to his deerskin pants to his beautiful blue-and-grey cloak . . . and especially to the bronze sword in the scabbard at his belt.

Morna quickly clasped her hands together. "You have my brother's face, but do I know you? Who are you? *What* are you?"

Anlon stepped toward them. "I am indeed your brother. I do look different now, I know, but it is only an outward change." He smiled, wanting so much to reassure them, for he was genuinely happy to see them both.

Hoping to ease the tension, he raised his forearm beneath the cloak and held out the beautifully dyed wool for them to see. "A lovely thing, isn't it? Never have I worn anything with such color, such softness."

"Never have I seen my brother wear anything of the kind," agreed Riona. "And never a sword . . . much less a sword of bronze." She shook her head. "Our brother's family are all herdsmen. Farmers. They wear only the natural shades of the land. They do not wear bright colors as if they were kings and nobles."

"All I recognize is the pin," whispered Morna. "The bronze leaf pin he always said was given to him by the Sidhe."

"We heard that our brother had been lured away by them. We thought we would never see him again. . . ." Riona shivered. The sisters looked at each other, then back at the *rath*, as if they were about to flee.

"Wait. Wait!" Anlon said, stepping toward them again. He unfastened his cloak, letting it fall to the forest floor, and moved a little more into the daylight where they could see him better.

"I am your brother. Look at me! It is true that I have found a place among the Sidhe. But I have not forgotten who I am or where I came from." He smiled, then held out his hands to them. "I hope that you have not forgotten, either."

"We will never forget our brother," said Riona. "But you are so very different from the way that we knew him . . . it hardly seems possible that such a change could happen."

Morna looked straight into his eyes. "Why are you here?" she asked.

Anlon's hands fell back to his sides. *Why are you here . . . ?*

Scahta had asked the same question of him. So had the king of Dun Mor. And now his own family wanted to know.

"I am here . . . I am here to see you." They did not

look convinced. "And because I am searching for the world in which I belong."

His sisters looked at him, their heads cocked, clearly baffled by his reply. "You left your family to join the Fianna," said Morna. "Then you left the Fianna to live among the Sidhe. Now you have come back to us. Why are you here?"

"You wear the deerskin clothes of the Sidhe, the bright colors of the nobles of Dun Mor, and even the bone dagger of the herdsman you once were." Riona shook her head. "You are all those things, and yet you are none of them. Why are you here?"

"I will show you why," he said, and took a few steps into the forest. "Scahta," he called softly. "Scahta . . . please allow my sisters to meet you."

For many moments there was no response. Then, as Anlon waited and his sisters held their breath, there was a small movement deep within the shadows—a glimpse of white, a faint gleam of bronze and gold. And the small figure of a woman appeared in the misty forest.

"This is Scahta," said Anlon, with a glance at his sisters. "I am her husband."

"A woman of the Sidhe!" whispered Morna.

"Never have they shown themselves to us in this way," said Riona, her voice beginning to shake.

Anlon looked at them, confused by their reaction. "You have never feared the Sidhe before," he said. "You have heard the stories about them all your life, just as I have. You know that our own grandfather was one of them! Why would you fear this shy and gentle lady now?"

Scahta had moved out into the grey and dappled light beneath the trees and stood gazing at Anlon and his sisters with dark and shining eyes. Her hair and white cloak were sprinkled with wet green leaves from the forest, and her deerskin gown gleamed with touches of gold from the curving half-rings that held it closed at her neck and wrists. The bronze pins on her white cloak, with their ancient design of concentric circles on their discs, seemed like strange, staring eyes.

"They are so strange, so strange," murmured Riona.

"Their place is in the deep forests beneath the moonlight," whispered Morna, "not on our doorstep on an ordinary day."

Anlon turned to his sisters. This time he did catch hold of their hands—and was dismayed to find that they were trembling. "They are peaceful. Beautiful," he tried to tell them. "They live in the world as we do. They—"

"They do not live in our world, Anlon. And we do not live in theirs. It cannot be any other way." Morna clasped her free hand on top of his, and Riona did the same. "Stay here, Anlon," Morna said urgently. "Come back home, where you belong. Leave the wildness of the Sidhe and the troubles of the king far away, where they have always been for us."

"We would all be so happy to have you home again," said Riona. "Mother—Father—Colm, Fionn, all of them. We need you. And I believe that you need us."

Anlon looked at his sisters, feeling stronger than ever the pull of family and home. *So easy*, Scahta had said. *So easy . . .*

He glanced over his shoulder at the place where she had stood. There was nothing there but dense green forest, dripping with rainwater and moving gently in the wind.

"I . . . I cannot stay," he whispered, his voice beginning to crack. "I cannot. I belong . . . in another place."

Morna looked at him for a long moment, and then she

reached up and touched his hair with one hand. "I know that you cannot," she said. "I can see it in your eyes."

She tried to smile. "We wish you well. You are our brother, and we will always remember you. But—" Her hand fell away.

Riona looked him up and down again, and her mouth trembled. "I can see, now, that you are not of our world, either. Not any longer. After all that you have seen and done—after living with the Sidhe, after making one of them your wife—you could never forget all that and simply go back to tending sheep, with never a thought for the life you left behind."

Anlon looked at her and started to answer, but he could not find the words. At last he let his gaze drop. "You are right," he whispered. "You are right. I am not the man I was one year ago. And yet—"

His sisters gently squeezed his hands.

"We will not tell Mother," said Morna.

"Keep safe," said Riona.

With that they released him and hurried away, leaving Anlon standing alone in the wet and windy forest.

He was not sure how long he stood gazing at the *rath* in the field. "It is difficult to go home again, once you have left it," Scahta said.

With an effort Anlon turned from the sight of the old earthen walls. Scahta stood quietly a few steps away, beneath the dripping trees. "It is my home no longer," he said, in a clear and steady voice.

"You are so certain."

"I am."

"Your mother awaits in the house. Do you not wish to speak to her one last time?"

He closed his eyes, still standing at the very edge of

the field. "When I left last year to go away with the Fianna, I knew that I might not see my family again for many months . . . if ever. I made my farewells at that time. I would not make my mother go through that again, nor would I wish it for myself.

" '*Why are you here?*' she would ask, just as my sisters did. '*Why are you here* . . . *?*' and how could I answer her? By saying that I had come here because I could find no other place in the world where I belonged?"

He managed a small smile. "Look at me now. My sisters hardly recognize me and neither would any of the others of my family. They would all consider me one of the Sidhe now, and though they do not think of the Sidhe as their enemy, I will forever be strange to them . . . lost to them. I am not the man they remember."

Scahta nodded, slowly, though her eyes studied him carefully and she held herself away from him. "When you returned to Dun Mor, did they not invite you to stay?"

"They did."

"Yet you came back to Caher Idir. Would your life not have been much simpler if you had remained with your king and his men?"

"It would . . . oh, it would."

"Then we will go there now. They will take you in, no matter what they might have said to you before. Come, we will tell the others." She turned to go.

Anlon caught her by the arm. "There is no need."

Scahta stared up at him, her face as serious as he had ever seen it. "You must be certain that you are with me by choice. There can be no doubt in your mind, or in your heart, about why you stay with the Sidhe—or of why you stay with me."

Gently he took hold of her shoulders. "When I walked to this place today, I could feel you pushing me away just as surely as I have felt you calling me in. And yet not even my home, my family, could make me want to leave you."

"It was only a gentle push that I gave you. And I would remind you, it was not so long ago that your king and his great fortress did indeed take you from your home."

He paused, and then he smiled. "I never thought I would say such a thing, but I know, now, that he is not my king. Never would I do anything to harm him or his men—but I know that I do not belong among them. Mine is a different path to walk."

Scahta stayed very still, as if scarcely breathing. "And that path has taken you away from the simple world of your family, away from the glorious world of Men. What world is left for you, Anlon?"

He stared into her large and luminous eyes, brown and shining. "A world of beauty and magic like none I ever imagined . . . a world that has need of me, a world where I can make a difference."

"And if that world will not accept you?"

He closed his eyes. "I simply cannot allow that to happen. We will find a way, you and I together, for me to live among the Sidhe and serve them as best I can . . . for that will allow me to stay with you and love you with all my heart, with all that I am."

Her voice was quiet and steady, but Anlon could hear the faint tremor in it. "You are certain that you trust me now? You are certain that I am not forcing you to stay among the Sidhe?"

He sighed, then drew her close in an embrace. "With or without a glamyr, I am yours. I do not believe it is possible to know where love ends and magic begins."

She rested her head on his chest. "I do not know either,

Anlon. And I do not know how I can ever prove it to you."

"I do not require proof," he answered, stroking her hair. "I only want you to know that I am yours, Queen Scahta, for as long as you will have me."

For a long time they held each other silently, in an embrace that was both as gentle as songbirds with wings entwined and as strong as eagles facing the wind.

Chapter Sixteen

Now it was Liath's turn to lead them on the faint and nearly nonexistent trails, moving back and forth through the woods in an effort to find another tribe of Sidhe. At one point, Anlon and the others stopped and waited while he examined the forest thoroughly, closely. Finally he turned to Scahta. "I can find no sign at all, my lady."

"They must have lived somewhere near my home," Anlon said. "I used to see them from time to time, catch glimpses when they would come to take the milk or the bread I left for them. They could not have lived far from here."

Liath glanced back at him. "How long has it been since you saw them?"

Anlon looked down. "Years. Many years. I was only a boy."

None of them said a word. Liath turned and resumed

his slow walk through the dark woodlands, looking for the smallest sign of others of their kind.

For a day and a night they found no trace at all. "Perhaps they have all gone," he said to Scahta. "Or perhaps I just imagined them."

Scahta reached out and touched the bronze leaf pin at his shoulder. "I do not think you imagined them," she answered.

"My lady!" It was Liath who had called out. They all hurried over to him. "Here," he said, pointing to the ground.

Beneath a thick growth of ferns were three small white stones. Anlon would never have noticed them on his own. Even now they seemed to be just an ordinary scattering of pebbles, but—just as Cian had done during the race through the woods—Liath had read a message in the little stones. "This way," he said, and turned down yet another barely discernible path.

Anlon leaned down to Scahta as they walked. "I would give something to learn to do that, as the other Sidhe can," he said.

She glanced up at him, smiling. "You will learn, Anlon. I promise you." And she turned and followed the others through the woods, toward the meeting with the long-lost tribe that all hoped against hope they would find.

At last, that evening the five stood at the edge of a rushing stream, looking across its clear waters to a small cave. The cave was little more than a small crack in the face of a rock cliff, well-shielded from view by ferns and fallen trees and by a little waterfall that cascaded over it from the cliffs above. The narrow opening would scarcely be large enough for a full-sized man to come and go, but for one of the Sidhe . . .

Anlon began to hold his breath. It would be a good

place for the secretive folk to hide . . . if any were still here.

"Wait for us," Scahta said to him. "Do not show yourself." He paused, not wanting to leave her side for a moment, wanting to be a part of all that happened here; but she continued to gaze steadily at him, and at last he stepped behind the trees and crouched behind a mossy fallen log.

She nodded to Liath and Mactire and Amhran, and together they stepped carefully across the stream to stand before the opening in the rock wall. The three men of the Sidhe formed a half-circle behind their queen. Then, as they stood motionless, she began to sing.

As he had on several other occasions, Anlon seemed to feel her words rather than hear them. Scahta allowed the faint wind to carry her song to the cave, and then she stood quietly and waited.

After a long time there was a small movement at the slender opening in the rock face. From behind the falling water a tiny figure, wizened and bent, moved slowly out to meet them.

She was small and old, with long grey hair past her shoulders and a thin fur cloak that was worn and stained. Yet Anlon saw with a start that she also wore the soft deerskin gown of the Sidhe, just as Scahta did. There was a curving torque of bronze around her neck and a black raven's feather tied in her hair.

The woman stood very still with her head bent down and her hands folded in front of her. She peered up at Scahta with brown eyes that were still clear and bright. "I thought never to see any of you again," she said, in a creaking whisper.

Scahta walked to her and took the old woman's hands

in her own. "We have been searching for you," she said, in an equally soft voice. "We need you."

"You need me?" The old woman looked behind Scahta at Liath and Mactire and Amhran, and then made short sounds that alarmed Anlon until he realized she was laughing.

"Let us speak to your king," Scahta said, gently releasing the woman's hands, "or to your queen. Are they here? Please, tell them we wish to speak to them."

The woman only looked at her, still laughing. Anlon started to rise from behind the fallen log but then thought better of it. Scahta glanced at her three companions, saying nothing, and the little group continued to wait.

Before long the grey-haired woman regained her composure. She stood blinking in the soft light of the day, staring at her visitors as if she had never seen another person before.

"Your king, your queen. Will they come?" inquired Scahta, with great patience.

The old women shook her head. "Here before you is all that remains of our tribe. I am the only one still alive."

Anlon felt a shock, and a great sadness. The tribe of Sidhe he remembered so well from his boyhood—was this lone woman all that was left of them? He had to know, he had to find out for himself—

But before he could move Scahta spoke to the woman again. "You are all that remains?" she asked. "The tribe that once lived in this place—where have they gone?"

The woman regarded her. "Gone," she repeated. "And so they are, all gone, lost in battles with those men who wished to destroy us. And destroy us they did."

"Lost . . . in battle?"

The old woman paused. "It was so long . . . so long

ago." She took a few steps toward Scahta, and she reached out to touch the younger woman's arm with a thin and trembling hand. "Call your hidden companion to your side, and come with me for just a little while. I will tell you my story. I will show you what happened."

Scahta hesitated, then smiled. The old woman had known of Anlon's presence all along. Quietly he rose from his hiding place and walked across the stream to stand with the others.

"We will wait here for you," said Mactire. "Go. We will be here, if it takes all night."

Scahta nodded briefly at them and then turned back to the strange woman. "Will you tell us your name?" she asked.

"I am . . . Greine," the old woman answered. "Greine, for the sunset." She looked into the twilight sky, then at the little company that had come to her strange home. "I suppose it was a proper name after all."

Greine moved to stand between Anlon and Scahta, and reached up to touch each of them on the face. "Come with me, children," she said. Together the three of them walked inside the cave, behind the singing falls.

The opening to the cave was very slender, and Anlon had to turn sideways in order to slip inside; but then he found himself in a surprisingly large and high-ceilinged space. There was plenty of room, but it was cold and damp, lit only by a little flame burning in a flat stone dish.

There was a pile of rushes and furs in one corner and only a few possessions nearby on the dirt floor. He saw a bronze cup and bowl, a bronze knife in an old leather sheath, a handful of apples and acorns, a few small sticks and twigs broken up to burn in the lamp. There was also a flat round piece of wood, like a section of a fallen tree.

It was a curious object, perhaps to be used for placing food while eating or simply to sit on. But he noticed that it was covered with dust as though it had not been touched for a very long time.

Greine followed Anlon's gaze. She walked slowly across the dirt floor until she stood beside the strange flat piece of wood. "I have been keeping this for you," she said, gazing at Scahta. "Please. Open it," she instructed Anlon.

Anlon glanced at Scahta, and then knelt down beside the flat wood to inspect it. *Open it*, the old woman had said. He brushed away the heavy dust and found it was made of good oak that had once been rubbed and polished. It even shone a little in the tiny light of the lamp. There was a line carved around the sides, as if it were actually two flat pieces fitted together. With just a little effort he worked the top loose and lifted it away.

He heard Scahta catch her breath. The cave was filled with a soft reflected light as Anlon set aside the piece of wood. Scahta came forward to stand beside him, and together they stared down at Greine's treasure.

It was a flat and curving piece of gold, shaped like a wide crescent moon, gleaming and shining in the flickering lamplight.

"A lunula," Greine whispered. "It has been in my keeping for a very long time." She looked up at Scahta. "Put it on," she said. "Put it on, while I lie down to rest for a little." She moved toward her bed of rushes as Scahta lifted out the gold piece.

"So beautiful," Scahta said softly, holding it out. "And so very old. Such things have been used by the kings and queens of the Sidhe tribes for a very long time, but I have never worn one."

"Could you not have one made for you?" asked Anlon.

"I have seen how beautifully the Sidhe work in bronze and gold. I am sure that—"

Scahta glanced at him. "The lunulae are older even than the Sidhe, Anlon. We believe that they were made by the same ones who built the great stone monuments out on the plains. The monuments and the lunulae are all that remain of those long-ago tribes. We would not dare to attempt to copy either one. We do not have the knowledge they possessed."

With the greatest care she placed the lovely gold crescent across her chest, just below the hollow of her throat. Anlon lifted her long hair and fastened the gold wire around the back of her neck.

Scahta turned around to face him, her hair swinging behind her. The light from the gold collar lit her face and set her eyes to shining. "I always looked at you and saw a queen, but now I see a queen who is dressed in a way that suits her. The lunula is beautiful, Scahta, as are you."

She smiled up at him, and then moved to the shadowy corner where Greine had lain down on the rushes. Anlon followed her and took off his blue-and-grey cloak, leaving the bronze pin still run through the fabric, and covered Greine with the warm wool.

The old woman smiled up at him as Scahta pulled the stone lamp closer. The walls of the cave disappeared into shadow as the three of them gathered close together in the soft light.

After a little while Greine began to speak.

"I thank you both for coming here to me. It is a great comfort . . . something for which I have been waiting, all these many days, all these many years. Now I will tell you my story . . . the story of my king and my people."

The lamplight gleamed on Scahta's lunula collar. An-

201

lon blinked as it flashed into his eyes, but he could not look away. . . .

He blinked again when he found himself outside, walking along a path on a beautiful autumn day. There were a great many men walking before and after him, talking and laughing as if they had not a care in the world—but these were not Men, these were Sidhe, all wearing leather breeches and good wool tunics and cloaks. Each had a shining gold disc-shaped pin holding his cloak at his shoulder. Scattered throughout the procession were wagons, three in all, big wooden wagons with strong fat oxen pulling them. Each of those wagons was piled high with newly cut wheat and barley.

Red and gold leaves whirled around him on the fresh breeze. "Anlon!" shouted one of the men with a laugh. Anlon did not recognize any of them, but clearly they knew him and took him to be one of them. "Anlon, how can you walk so quickly after all these days in the fields? Did you not work as hard as the rest of us?"

"Why, don't you know?" called another of them. "He's saving himself for the beautiful lady who waits only for him!"

Beautiful lady . . . Scahta . . . Anlon grinned back at the two who were teasing him. "You would not want me to disappoint Scahta, would you?"

"If I had one such as her waiting for me, I would not be seen out at the fields at all!"

All of them laughed out loud, and Anlon joined them. What a wonderful place this was, so open and safe, so bountiful and rich! He wondered who this tribe could be—a tribe that had cattle and wagons and fields full of barley and wheat. How strange it was to walk with the Sidhe so boldly, so openly, in the bright light of the day, fearless and entirely at ease. Strange—and wonderful.

He did not allow himself to wonder why or how he was here. Somehow he knew that he was being shown this tale like a waking dream, and it was not a thing to be questioned. Scahta was here, too, somewhere, and together they would learn what Greine wanted them to know.

The happy group walked on as the sun approached the horizon. All were suffused with the satisfaction of seeing their very long days of work take substance in the shape of the well-filled wagons, the ripe grain piled so high that some of it spilled out onto the roadway. No one even bothered to pick it up.

Then, from the distant woods along the road, came another sound. A shaking, thundering sound, coming at them fast.

The Sidhe barely had time to look at each other before a band of riders came bursting out of the forest. They were tall white-skinned riders with red and gold hair and swords made of cold heavy iron.

"Here's a harvest!" they shouted, as the men of the Sidhe fell back. "Just the way we like to find it!"

A few of the Sidhe, stunned by the sudden appearance of wild-riding strangers, tried to pull their oxen off the road. But to Anlon's horror the riders simply kicked their horses close and struck down the Sidhe with their swords, once, twice, three, four times. Their bodies lay in the road. The men grabbed hold of the oxen and began dragging them back the other way, then. Anlon and the remaining Sidhe raced behind the trees at the edge of the woods, pulling out their slings and sending stones flying into the midst of the men and horses.

The men roared their rage as the stones struck them, and a few turned back to ride straight into the forest. More of the determined Sidhe were struck down by their

203

cold iron before the rest of the group fled for their lives. Anlon could only watch from his hiding place until at last the men rode casually away, having collected six oxen and three wooden wagons full of grain for their trouble— along with heads of eight of the Sidhe.

All that was left for the Sidhe were the bodies of their companions, lying headless in the road and in the cool shade of the forest.

The wind suddenly blew colder. The sun grew dim. Anlon looked up to find himself deep in a half-bare forest, with some golden leaves still clinging to the trees and others falling here and there to cover the damp forest floor.

Others of the new Sidhe tribe, men and women both, moved through the forest in search of the wild harvest. He saw Scahta walking with a group of women, carefully inspecting every tangle of shrubs for blackberries, while he and the other men brushed their hands through the leaves covering the ground to find the acorns and hazelnuts hidden there.

Anlon was acutely aware of how very different this harvest was from the last one. Gone was the laughter and the shouting and the openness of the Sidhe as he had seen them before, when they had walked along the sunny road with their wagonloads of grain.

Now there were only hand signals and whispered conversations among them, with total silence all the rest of the time. They even moved more cautiously, taking care not to crack the twigs or crush the crackling dry leaves. They stayed in the shadows instead of the daylight. And every single man carried a bronze sword at his belt.

For a time, there was little food to find. It was as if another tribe had been through here before. The Sidhe continued to move through the forest, across a little stream, up a small hill—and then came the soft calls of "Here! Here!"

The women had found an untouched part of the forest. There were plenty of berries and even a few stands of apples. Several of the men climbed up into the oak and hazel trees and shook the branches hard, sending the nuts showering upon the others below.

Anlon began to relax just a bit. With so much of their grain harvest stolen, the Sidhe would have to rely even more on the wild harvest to get them through the winter. He worked as quickly as he could to fill the leather bags with acorns, occasionally catching a glimpse of Scahta as she worked with the women to gather the blackberries and apples.

There was a great shaking in the oak tree above him. He looked up, shielding his face from the falling acorns, and realized that the man above was not trying to free more of the nuts. He was climbing down just as fast as he could, as were the others who had gone up in the trees.

"Hide! Run! Hide yourselves!" came the hissing call. "They're coming! They're coming this way!"

Anlon's first thought was for Scahta and the other women. They were all some distance away from him in the grove of apple trees. He pulled out his sword and began running straight for them, leaping over the shrubs and crashing through the brush.

"Hide! Run! They're coming again!" he shouted to the women, but they were already vanishing into the deep woods, running down a hill that dropped away from the grove to another stream far below. Once he saw to it that the women were well out of sight, he raced back up the slippery hill with sword in hand—and found himself in the thick of a battle.

The men on horseback had returned. As before, it was clear they intended to take what the Sidhe had worked so hard to collect. Riding through the woods, the horde of raiders picked up the leather and woolen sacks the Sidhe had dropped in their haste and began taunting the terrorized folk.

"We should thank you for showing us where the best was to be found!" the men shouted. "You've saved us the trouble!" Their laughter rang out through the trees. Anlon flinched, thinking of all that these men had stolen—and all they still intended to steal.

But this time the men of the Sidhe were better prepared. Stones flew from the shadows, striking their assailants and their horses. The scrape of metal echoed through the forest as the Sidhe drew their swords and raced out toward the men who struggled to control their frightened, stone-struck mounts.

Anlon, too, jumped into the battle with them. In a rage he swung his shining bronze blade at the first man who rode past him, and was rewarded by the sight of the warrior's iron sword flying out of his hand and into the underbrush.

But in the next instant, Anlon was horrified by the sight of his own weapon. The force of its strike against iron had left it bent and disfigured. All around him he could hear the clashing of weapons and the laughing of the raiders, as their cold iron swords bent and hammered the fragile weapons of the Sidhe, rendering them all but useless.

The man he had challenged swung around and attempted to ride his horse over Anlon, but Anlon struck at him again and again, slashing with the sharp pointed tip of his bent sword and driving the invader back by sheer fury and desperation.

Finally the warrior rode away, dismissing Anlon as he might brush off an angry insect. All the men were far more interested in grabbing up the sacks of hazelnuts and blackberries and apples than they were in engaging the Sidhe in combat.

At last, they rode off into the forest, their laughter giving way to the grieving wails of the Sidhe women when they discovered two more of their own were dead, their heads taken back to the fortress of Men.

Chapter Seventeen

The wind blew colder and sharper now. For a moment, Anlon could not see. He rubbed his eyes and then found himself in heavy grey twilight, on a great open field surrounded by thick forest. In the field was a milling, bawling herd of red-and-white cattle and dark brown sheep.

He could catch only glimpses of the moon behind the thick and fast-moving clouds, but he could see that it was not quite full. Anlon judged that they were perhaps three days from Samhain.

In his hands was a stone axe. He stood in a close group with the other men of the Sidhe, waiting in silence and watching as a pair of women, white-cloaked and sparkling with gold and polished stones, walked forward and began to speak.

"This is the third and last of the harvests," said the first.

"This is the blood harvest," added the second.

"This is the harvest which gives us the strength and the shelter to live through the winter."

"Respect the creatures which provide us this strength."

"Release their spirits swiftly and cleanly."

The women stepped back, and Anlon walked with the other men toward the cattle and sheep.

He did not dread what he was about to do. For every year of his life that he could remember he had helped with the third harvest, the harvest of meat and hides. This was the harvest that would keep all his people strong through the winter. He would see to it that no creature suffered, that the slaughter was all finished as quickly and painlessly as possible.

But before any of them could get to the animals, the forest around them began to tremble and shake.

For a third time, men on horseback galloped out of the woods. "Look at how kind these folk are!" they shouted, laughing all the while. "They have brought in all of their beasts just for us!"

Anlon's grip tightened on his axe. This could not be happening again! These men could not take their cattle and sheep. They had already taken the best part of the grain and more than they could ever use of the wild harvest. They must not take the animals!

As before, the Sidhe on guard in the trees sent bullets flying from their slings. But the raiders were better prepared this time, too; they had small wooden shields strapped to their arms and used them to ward off the worst of the stones.

As one, the Sidhe cried out in rage and frustration. They leaped to the ground and ran forward with their knives and axes raised.

For a moment it looked as though they might succeed in driving off the invaders. Their sudden charge, and another volley of stones, startled the raiders' horses into running wildly around the field and created chaos for a few moments. The Sidhe were able to get close to their cattle and sheep and begin to drive away the scattered riders—but then the men forced their horses back under control, swung them around, and drove them into a single sweeping charge over the tribe.

Anlon leaped out of the way at the last moment, swinging in vain at the men as they rode by. But, as he watched, many of his companions were struck down by pounding hooves or iron swords and left to lie on the cold wet ground of the field as their killers drove off every last one of their bawling cattle and bleating sheep.

And there was nothing Anlon could do.

Cold rain blew in Anlon's face. He shut his eyes against the wetness, and when he opened them, he saw that darkness had fallen. An enormous full moon, orange behind the dark clouds, hung just above the horizon.

Samhain.

He sat on a fine bay horse, high on the side of a hilltop, in the midst of a great crowd of Sidhe warriors on horseback. All wore leather and bronze armor and carried round bronze shields inscribed with concentric circles. Below him stretched vast hills and forests he did not recognize; but in front of him were high round walls of stone, set with heavy wooden gates faced with bronze.

For a moment he thought he was looking at Caher Idir, but no—this was another Sidhe fortress, one set on the top of a hill instead of hidden away in the forest. This one was also much larger, home to many more of the Sidhe.

Tonight the great fortress blazed with firelight, from the torches set around the tops of its walls and from the bonfire burning at its center. The sound of insistent drumming came from within it, along with the deep and ancient humming of the bull-roarer as it whirled around and around and turned the night wind into a low and ominous singing.

All of the Sidhe riders surrounding Anlon were tense and silent. Their horses shifted about uneasily, snorting in dismay. Then, just as the rising moon cleared the stone walls of the fortress, the gates swung slowly open.

Silhouetted by the glaring light of the bonfire behind him was the king.

Tall and graceful on his noble grey stallion, his long black hair falling past his shoulders, the leader of the Sidhe rode out among his warriors. Bronze gleamed from his horse's bridle and at the corners of the leather pad on its back, and at the king's wristbands and breastplate and shining leaf-shaped pin that held his dark cloak at his shoulder.

His was a noble face, young in appearance, though Anlon knew he must be older than he looked. His dark eyes flicked across the gathered warriors as he reined in the stallion. A crowd of torch-bearing women moved through the gates to stand behind him, their cloaks pulled over their heads against the rain. Their torches crackled and flared in the wetness.

"Men of the Sidhe," the king began in his clear and ringing voice. "Though we are a people of peace, we have suffered at the hands of these tall invaders who have lately come to our land. Though we have done naught to harm them, they have stolen our crops and our animals and even the harvest of the forest in the hopes that we would starve . . . and they have killed outright any of us who dared resist them."

Anger and bitterness were evident in his voice. "Even now, the heads of the Sidhe—of our brothers and cousins

Janeen O'Kerry

and sons—hang from the walls of the fortress of Men."

The gathered Sidhe warriors could contain themselves no longer. "Death!" they shouted, slashing at the night with their bronze blades as their horses pranced. "Death to Men. Death to them all!"

The king grabbed one of the flaring torches and galloped through the ranks of his fighters. Twisting, he rode down the hill toward the moonlit forest. His warriors turned and followed him, all racing faster and faster until it was impossible to tell where the thunder of the hoofbeats ended and the lashing of the rain began.

On and on they rode, through trees and rain and darkness. It seemed to Anlon that time began to slow, that they had been riding forever, that this night would never end. Then the king's torch burned itself out, and there was nothing to see but the occasional gleam of bronze and moonlight, nothing to feel but the rhythmic rising and falling of the horse beneath him.

Far ahead, he could see the fairy king ride out of the shadowy forest and into an open field. At the end of that field he saw the walls of Dun Mor, ringed with torches and hung with the bloodstained heads of his murdered people.

"Stay here," ordered the king. His warriors halted their horses just within the edge of the treeline and watched as their leader galloped alone across the windy land, his dark cloak flying out behind him above the grey stallion.

Straight to the iron-hinged gates he rode, drawing his bronze sword and using the hilt to pound on their rough wooden surface. "Come out!" he cried. "We are here to end this now! Never again will you attack us in secret as though we were animals! Come out! Come out and face us!"

He wheeled the horse and rode back to the center of the field. With a quick motion he pointed his sword at his warriors, then raised it overhead once more.

Instantly the Sidhe galloped out of the forest and across the field to join him, crowding close behind their king on his stallion. As they halted, one of the gates of the fortress creaked partly open.

The Sidhe drew their swords.

The men of the keep had clearly been caught by surprise. There were only ten, perhaps twelve of them at the gate, and some were still hastily strapping on swords and even pulling on boots.

Anlon found his confidence rising. The Sidhe glanced at one another. Their enemy was not so powerful now, caught asleep in their beds and barely even dressed! This time they would be no match for this ancient Sidhe tribe and their noble, powerful king!

"Come out here and meet us face to face!" the monarch demanded. "You are murderers and thieves. We will not leave until we have destroyed you, until we have taken back what is ours! Come out! Come out!"

The twelve men at the gate got themselves ready at last and walked out into the cold storm to meet their fate. But as the Sidhe lined up close together, preparing to charge, the king swung his stallion around to face them.

"Wait. Wait!" he warned his army. "This is not all that will come. They mean to draw us in with these stragglers and trap us within the walls. The rest of their fighters will come. When they do, we will meet them out here—and it will be on our terms and not theirs."

A rumble of hooves made them all look up. From out of the fortress rode a host of men, fifty, a hundred, two hundred, their deadly iron weapons all but invisible in the heavy darkness. They shouted in anger and bloodlust, and then they charged straight toward the shining bronze army waiting to meet them.

Instantly, the king of the Sidhe whirled his horse and galloped out to meet them, his warriors racing with him. With a terrible thundering crash, the two armies collided in the center of the field.

Anlon was conscious only of shouting and clanging and jostling and shoving. He struggled to push his horse into the midst of the fighting and search out a target to strike. Raising his shield to ward off the heavy blade of the nearest attacker, he felt the bronze crumple and bend as the man struck it.

He slashed and swung with his sword, again and again and again, and was rewarded with the sight of first one man and then a second falling from their horses in an explosive spray of blood. But when he struck at a third enemy, his violent swing was stopped by armor of iron—and he felt his own sword weaken and give.

He tried to pull it back for another strike, but a terrible blow struck him in the back. It knocked the breath and strength from him, and he began to feel lightheaded. The world moved slowly, distantly, and began to tilt as his legs weakened and he slid from the horse to the muddy ground below.

Again he struggled to breathe, but it seemed as if his lungs were no longer his own. He felt only a terrible sensation of coldness. Looking up toward the battle, it seemed the ranks of the Sidhe had greatly thinned; he could see only a few bronze-trimmed horses running wildly about, leaping over the still forms and dented bronze shields littering the dark battleground.

Anlon sighed, and as he did he heard the scream of the king's grey stallion. The horse rose up on his hind legs with the Sidhe sovereign still on his back, striking with its forelegs at the mob of men on foot who surrounded him; but both stallion and King were soon overwhelmed. In a moment, they crashed to the ground and disappeared beneath the shouting men of Dun Mor, ground under by a horde of angry iron blades.

Scahta waited in darkness, a torch in her hand. She stood before the bronze-faced gates of a round stone fortress, but this was not her own Caher Idir. This was another place, another time, and she was now experiencing Greine's story just as Greine herself had done so many years before.

Was this the power of the lunula?

They should have been back by now. The king and his army had left at moonrise, and now it was nearly dawn. She raised her torch and peered into the darkness, but there was no sign of them . . . no glitter of metal, no sound of hoofbeats . . . only the black rainswept forest and the creaking of trees in the wind.

Scahta walked back inside the fortress. Beside the fire circle, staring at her, were a gathering of women and children and bent, aged men. She could only look at them and slowly shake her head.

Another woman stepped forward, a fragile dark-haired beauty whose luminous eyes held a poignant combination of courage and pain. The gold lunula collar at her neck gleamed brightly in the firelight. "Tomorrow," said this tribe's queen. "If they have not returned by tomorrow, we will go search for them."

Scahta and the others nodded to her. "Tomorrow," they answered. One by one they put out their torches as the sky began to lighten.

* * *

The journey was a long one, for they had no horses; all the riding animals had been taken by the king and his army, and there would be no more, for the men of Dun Mor had stolen even the mares and foals out of their pastures.

Scahta walked in the twilight through the heavy forest. She stayed close to the other women, following the path that the Sidhe warriors had taken to the fortress of Men.

No one spoke, for there was nothing to say. Their husbands and sons and fathers and brothers had gone into battle against a fearful enemy, and not one had returned . . . not even one of their horses. The women dared not think of what they might find, for if they did they would never be able to make themselves go on.

Finally, as the moon hid her face behind the clouds, the women reached the edge of the forest. There, at the far end of the field, was the great iron-faced fortress of Men. A single torch burned over the gates, but it was enough to show them the heads hanging from the walls— the heads of Sidhe. Otherwise, all was dark and silent.

Softly, quietly, giving their voices only to the gentle wind that blew across the field, the women began chanting. Scahta joined them after a moment, realizing what they meant to do; and then the clouds parted, allowing the bright moon to shine down onto the field.

There was little to see, but enough remained to show that this had been the scene of a terrible battle not long before. On the chill, muddy ground were small bits of bronze shining in the moonlight, along with scraps of leather and strands of long dark hair . . . all that remained of weapons and bridles and the proud, graceful Sidhe army.

One at a time, the women crept out over the field, tiny shadows in the faint light of the moon. Each came back with a broken piece of metal, or carved bit of leather, or a carefully folded length of hair.

At last it was Scahta's turn. Moving over the damp and trampled field, she realized there was little left to find; the other women had done well in picking up any trace of their army. Yet she continued to search carefully with hands and with heart.

There!

All but hidden under a clod of mud was a last gleam of bronze. She pried the delicate shard from the grip of the earth and hurried back to the others waiting in the forest.

Just as she reached the trees the moon began to vanish once more behind the clouds; but in the last of its light she opened her hand and looked at the dirt-covered object she had found.

It was a long slender pin, wrought in the shape of a curving willow leaf.

The winter passed slowly for the women who remained at the fortress on the hill. It was an empty, quiet place compared to what it had been. All the animals were gone. The children remained, but even these young boys and girls were silent and subdued and no longer ran and played as they had once done.

Also remaining were five aged men. They were long past the days of being able to mount a horse, or even walk without the help of a stick or a supporting arm, and so they had been forced to remain behind when the king had ridden out on that last Samhain Eve.

And when the spring began to come again, there were only women and children left within the walls of the fortress.

The five elderly men had known that their king and

all his warriors were gone, never to return. They also had known that there was no part that they themselves could play in restoring the tribe to life once again . . . indeed, they would only be a burden. And so one night they lay on their beds in the rushes, and slept, and they did not awaken again.

With the fresh breezes of spring blowing through their hair, the women, too, began to look at their children and at each other and at the walls of the lonely fortress crowning the hill. *We cannot live our lives with no men at all*, they would say. *There would be no more children . . . no more life*.

Scahta would nod at them in understanding, as did two other women whom she knew were Greine's sisters. Then, one day, the tribe's queen stood at the gates with the assembled women and children. Each carried what belongings they could.

"We must go and find the other clans, if we can," said the queen. "There is sure to be at least one other which has not been destroyed by Men. We will find them, and we will start our lives anew."

Scahta and Greine's two sisters smiled sadly at her. "We will stay," Scahta said in Greine's voice, "so that if those other tribes also search for us, we will be here to greet them. Then we will all find each other and live together as we once did."

Scahta and the queen gazed at each other and smiled through their tears, neither of them believing a word that she had said.

Then the queen reached up and unfastened the beautiful gold lunula collar that rested around her neck. She handed it to Scahta, the gold flashing and shining in the sun.

"Why would you give this to me?" Scahta asked in

dismay. She could hardly bring herself to touch the brilliant gold. "It is yours, for you are the queen!"

"I am a queen no longer, Greine," the other woman said. "My king is dead. I will never have another. Keep it for me and for the new queen of the Sidhe, wherever we may find her."

Carefully, Scahta took the lunula and held it against her chest. Then she stepped back as the women and children of the tribe began to file past her, walking slowly through the gates. She followed them out, then watched for a long time as they moved down the hill and finally disappeared into the woods.

When she turned back to the fortress, she saw that the grass-covered earth seemed to rise higher around it than she remembered. And she noted that ivy and shrubs and all manner of green growths were rising up from the forest's edge and creeping higher and higher up the stone walls. The fortress, knowing it was being abandoned, was giving itself back to nature.

The three women stayed for several fortnights. They made journeys into the woods to set out small signs of their existence and to search for any indication of another tribe of Sidhe. But there was nothing. And each time they returned to the fortress on the hill, there was more green growth on the walls, and it began to creep within to cover the ground and take hold of the buildings inside.

At last came the day when the stone walls were completely covered with thick green ivy and sapling trees, as were the houses and sheds within. Even the earth itself had gradually risen until it was heaped halfway up the walls.

Scahta and the two other women took a few belongings and walked through the gates for the last time. They turned to face the place that had been their home. Standing side by side, they began to speak, softly, so that the wind would take their voices to the fortress. They said goodbye.

After a time, the three turned away and started down the hill. As they walked, the earth and grass finished their work, and by the time the women reached the forest, there was nothing on the hill except a smooth field of grass crowned with sapling trees, their fresh new leaves rippling gently in the wind.

Chapter Eighteen

They wandered in the forest for many days, concerned only with hiding from Men and keeping safe—and with finding a little food from time to time. They wanted nothing more than peace, after the terror of that Samhain night and the irreplaceable loss of their husbands and brothers and sons . . . and of their king.

Scahta knew, as had the queen and the rest of the women, that all the other tribes of the Sidhe had almost certainly met similar fates to their own. Their women and children, heartbroken and left without hope, would have been left alone to wander deep in the forest until they became one with it, even as the fortress had become one with it, finding what peace they could in the sheltering arms of the natural world.

Yet Scahta and her sisters had been given a task. They were the ones who held the lunula of the old queen. If there were another clan of Sidhe anywhere in the world, they were the ones who would have to find them and pass on the beautiful lunula—and tell them the story of a tribe that had dared to fight Men on equal terms, and lost everything. Otherwise, the story would die with these last three women, the only three who had found the strength to go on, if only for a little while.

After many days of walking through the deep wood, they reached a part that was completely new to them. There, the trio found a small hidden cave beneath a waterfall and knew right away they had found their place. There was clear water and fresh fish and the wild harvest of an untouched forest—more than enough to sustain three women.

It was the haven they had searched for, and they soon became a part of it, moving among the rocks and trees and shadows just as the deer and birds might, attracting no attention and leaving no mark of any kind to show they were there—at least, none that any mortal man might read.

They stayed for many months . . . months that turned into years. One cold day while she was far out in the forest, Scahta came upon a little earth-walled *rath* where a herdsman lived with his family. She saw a young boy setting snares in the woods and stopped to study him, caught by his graceful build and beautiful features. The nobility of his character was apparant to her, though he was simply the son of a Man.

The late winter had brought with it a shortage of food and so Scahta waited in the forest, thinking to take one of the boy's small trapped animals for herself and her sisters. She knew the boy's family would not suffer for it; they had a great surplus of grain and fruit and slaughtered beef within the walls of their *rath*. But a little extra meat could make a great deal of difference to three aging women living alone in the forest.

She took one animal with her that day, and a few days later returned to get another. Though she moved cautiously, silently, and stayed always in the shadows, she could not help pausing from time to time to study the handsome young boy. His face, young as it was, reminded her so much of the king who had lost his life in trying to save his people.

A fortnight later, when Scahta returned to the *rath* a third time, she went to the tree where she had raided the trap—and was surprised to find that there was no trap there any longer.

There was, instead, a bowl of fresh milk and a newly baked piece of wheat flatbread spread thick with pale winter butter.

She paused. This was clearly an offering, a gift, left deliberately in the spot where she had been taking the animals. The boy must have seen her. There was a reason why he had some of the grace and beauty of the Sidhe— he must indeed carry some of their blood if he had been able to spy on her without her ever knowing.

Here was the blood of the king, the strong and beautiful sovereign who had fought so hard to save and protect his tribe . . . and who, it seemed, still lived on in the dark eyes and fair form and kind heart of a young boy.

Scahta reached up to her shoulder and carefully withdrew the leaf-shaped bronze pin from her ragged cloak— the same pin the king had worn, the same pin she had found on that terrible battleground. She placed it on the earthy ground beside the boy's gifts, gathered up the milk and bread, and hurried back to the cave and her two sisters.

* * *

More years went by. The handsome young boy grew to manhood and she did not see him again. First one of her sisters, then the other, lay down and closed her eyes—and did not rise again. Scahta cared for them and returned their bodies to the elements, then settled once more into a quiet and secretive life beneath the waterfall and within the surrounding woods.

Yet she began to know, after a time, that it would not be long before her own life would come to its close. She still had a story to tell but had found no one to listen. If she were going to find any other Sidhe, it would have to be soon.

Over the next several days, she ranged a little farther than was her custom and left more of the careful arrangements of small white pebbles along the last of her people's hidden trails. If any other Sidhe encountered them, they would know how to find her.

Yet the time went by, and more years passed, and never did she see any sign of either Man or Sidhe. She was beginning to fear that she would have to die with her story untold, when one evening she heard the sound of wind-chanting beneath the singing of the falls.

She invited the strangers into her cave. For the first time since the loss of the king her heart was full again, for this young Sidhe visitor was the queen of her own small tribe—and her companion, who seemed to be both Man and Sidhe, had a familiar and handsome face.

Scahta gave the lunula to this new queen, feeling as if a new sun were rising when she saw the shining gold filling the cave with light. Then she lay down on her soft bed of rushes and began to tell them her story, allowing them both to live through it as she herself had done, that they might better understand what had happened. When it was finished, she looked up at the woman, at this young queen of the Sidhe. "You are a queen," she whispered. "Where is your king?"

The young woman hesitated. "I have no king."

With an effort, Scahta shook her head. "You are wrong, lady. Your king is here beside you, with the touch of his grandsire shining upon him. He is the way to your future . . . the only hope of a future you have."

Slowly, with a great effort, she reached out and clasped the young queen's hand. "You are not just any woman," she whispered. "You are a noblewoman, meant to be the mother of your tribe. You are a daughter of the sky and a sister of the moon . . . and you must have a king who is your equal."

Her story told, her task complete, she released the queen's hand and lay back on the rushes with a sigh. Then she closed her eyes as peace descended over her.

Scahta seemed to be awakening from a long and comfortable sleep . . . and oh, the dream she'd had. She opened her eyes and found that she was leaning against Anlon's shoulder—and he himself lay up against the wall of the cave. He was so still, so still, and as pale as . . .

"Anlon," she whispered, as it all came rushing back to her. The king and his warriors had gone to destroy the Men, and they had all been killed, all of them. . . .

"Anlon," she said again, and to her profound relief he began to stir, and to sit up, and then his eyes met hers. And she knew in that moment that he too had moved through Greine's story, just as she had. What had he seen?

They looked at the bed of rushes. In the flickering lamplight Greine lay still and pale. Anlon cautiously reached out as if to touch her, but Scahta stopped him with a gentle hand. "She is gone."

Scahta smiled down at the old woman, and touched the lunula at her own neck. "Thank you for telling us your story. You have helped us more than you will ever know. And I will try to be a queen worthy of this beautiful thing you have entrusted to me."

She got to her feet, as did Anlon, and together they walked outside. The stars were just appearing, and the sky was turning from deep blue to the black of night. Amhran and Mactire and Liath sat around their newly made campfire. All three looked up at Scahta and Anlon in surprise, blinking in the reflection of the gold lunula collar she now wore.

Scahta tried to find the words to tell them what had happened, but she found her throat tightening. She could only smile gently and stand close beside Anlon as the singing of the falls filled the night.

"There are no others."

Scahta stood in the center yard before the assembled people of Caher Idir. "We found only one woman, a very old woman who died on the evening that we came to her. Before her death she gave me this beautiful gold lunula that her own queen had worn, and she told me her story.

"She showed me that all the others of her tribe are long gone . . . the king and his warriors all killed in trying to fight Men, and their women and children lost in the deep forests and in their hiding places beneath the earth. None are left. We are all that remain of the Sidhe."

"This woman told our queen another thing," said Amhran. "She said that this man—Anlon—wears the pin that belonged to their king. She gave it to him years ago, because that long-dead king was his grandsire. Even Anlon himself did not know."

Scahta looked at Amhran with gratitude in her eyes,

and then turned to face the rest of her people again. "And she told us she believed our best—our only—hope for the future was for us to take Anlon as our king."

She paused. "I ask you again. Will you accept Anlon as your king?"

"*We will not.*"

"*We will not.*"

"*We will not.*"

With a sinking heart Scahta listened to the silence, broken only by the rustling and murmuring of her people.

"Let him prove himself to us—not just to our queen."

"Let him show us where his loyalties truly lie."

"Let him lead us against the men of Dun Mor on Samhain Eve."

Anlon took a step forward. "We saw what happened to the last tribe of Sidhe, the clan who tried to make war on Men. They were all destroyed, every last one of them! How can you think of trying to attack Dun Mor? What can you hope to gain?"

The gathered Sidhe stared hard at Anlon. Scahta could feel him brace himself for what else they had to say. So few of them remained firmly on the side of their queen and her chosen man—fewer and fewer each day, it seemed.

But they said nothing else. She saw only disdain and single-minded purpose in their eyes. Slowly they filed away, leaving Anlon and Scahta alone to look at each other.

"We have three full moons to find a way to stop them," she whispered. "The fourth one will be Samhain Eve."

The nights passed quickly. Anlon could only watch as the Sidhe became ever more single-minded, ever more determined in their preparations for the coming winter—and for the coming war.

"We will not go through another winter hungry," they said to him, when they would speak to him at all. "We have done so for the last time. And we will begin with the first harvest."

As soon as the hazelnuts and acorns began to fall from the trees, groups of men and women left Caher Idir for the forest. Anlon went with them, growing more and more tense as the foraging parties ranged farther each day. They spread themselves thin and scoured the forest for every last apple and blackberry and hazelnut and acorn they could find—and came closer than they ever had before to the fields and settlements of Men.

Anlon ran himself to exhaustion in trying to keep them all in sight. He was driven by the feeling that it was up to him to protect them, that somehow it would be his fault if they were attacked. Each day his heart pounded, never slowing it seemed, from both the pace he kept while trying to watch all the Sidhe at once and from the certainty he felt that Men were bound to appear at any moment.

"We must stop them," he said to Scahta. "They will be picked off by one—until the men of Dun Mor grow angry enough to hunt us all down. We must find a way to stop them."

"How can you tell them to stop gathering food?" she answered. Her words were short, but he could hear the pain in her voice. "Did you not suffer with us last winter? Have you forgotten how that was? Do you not remember the deaths of the children, and of how—"

He stopped her with a gentle hand to her shoulder, but she turned away. "I am not ashamed to tell you that the fear never leaves me," Anlon said. "I am not afraid

for myself, but for a desperate people engaged in an all-
or-nothing battle for survival. I fear they will throw cau-
tion to the winds to such an extent that not one of them
will be left."

Scahta looked at him again. "I have no more answers
for them, or for you," she said. "All the Sidhe can do now
is fight to the last to survive. A few more acorns, a few
more berries, might make all the difference. It just might
keep them from thinking that they have no choice but to
go to war. And if they do not make a difference—then
we will vanish from the world knowing we tried the best
we could, and did not simply lie down and die."

He pulled her close, pressing her face against his chest
and stroking her long golden-brown hair. "I cannot let
them die," she whispered. "I cannot let them die."

"I will find a way, I promise you."

"Help them," she said.

"I have tried—"

"You cannot stop them, Anlon. Help them with what
they are trying to do. Help us all to live through the
winter."

He sighed, and rested his head atop her own, closing
his eyes. "Through the winter . . . and after that?"

"If you help them, perhaps it will go more quickly.
Perhaps they will not spend so much time in harm's way."

He looked down at her. "Do you truly believe that is
true, Queen Scahta? Or do you simply tell this to yourself—and to me—because neither of us has an answer?"

"At this moment," she said, drawing a shaking breath,
"I would give all that I am, or ever will be, to find an
answer."

Anlon could only hold her close. Together they walked
back to her house, went inside, and closed the door.

Safe within those sheltering walls, they could forget for

a while the terrible fate that hung over them. They could think only of finding comfort and solace in each other's arms . . . yet Anlon was chilled by the thought that now, each time he and Scahta embraced each other in the warmth of the furs beside the fire, he had to wonder whether this time would be the last.

The first few weeks of the wild harvest went by, and Anlon almost dared to breathe easier. None of the Sidhe had been injured or killed. Indeed, Men seemed not to have noticed them at all.

"Perhaps the king is holding to what he told me last midsummer," said Anlon. He stood with Scahta in the evening light, near the door of their home. "He said that the Sidhe were of no concern to his men . . . that they cared nothing for a starving, dying enemy."

He smiled down at Scahta. "I was angry when he told me that—angry that he would simply dismiss us as something not even worth his notice. But now I have reason to hope that he will do exactly that. The best thing that could happen would be for his people to give no further thought to the Sidhe. I believe we can survive if they will simply leave us alone."

Scahta looked up at him, her expression grave. Then a movement behind her caught his eye, and his heart sank when he saw a gathering of Sidhe men carrying leather sacks and small bronze sickles.

"We must continue to hope that Men will turn their attention elsewhere," Scahta said. "Beginning this night, the Sidhe are determined to take what they require of the second harvest—and they will take it from both the hidden fields they themselves have tended, and from the great open fields of the men of Dun Mor."

She continued to gaze up at Anlon as her people began

filing through the gates into the night with their shining sickles. His heart began to pound once more, and with a last touch to Scahta's face he left Caher Idir and hurried after the determined group.

At first, the Sidhe only went to their own hidden fields in the forest to harvest the small amounts of ripened barley. Anlon worked with them, as quickly as he could, to bring in the grain and get them all back to the safety of Caher Idir. There was a fair amount of barley, a little more than what he remembered seeing last year, and with the extra acorns they had gathered he felt sure that there would be no need for them to raid the fields of Dun Mor.

But he was wrong.

The Sidhe made good on their bold and reckless gathering of the harvest. They behaved as if there were no danger at all. To his horror they began a systematic raiding of the crops of Dun Mor, even going out sometimes in the light of the day. "They won't be expecting us in daylight," said Mactire, with pride and boasting in his voice. "We'll be in and out of the fields before they have any idea of what's happened."

Anlon took to climbing in the leafy branches of the trees with his sling and a bag of polished white rocks. He could only wait for Men to come across them, as they surely must . . . and so they did before the first day was over.

Silently, he flung his tiny white stones at the two men who had ventured within range. They were just farmers, not warriors, and were quite unnerved by the sting of the tiny invisible missiles that struck them out of nowhere. The dropped their tools and fled, and Anlon knew it would not be long before everyone at Dun Mor had heard the story of the magical weapon that had attacked them at the fields.

The Sidhe went to a different field each day, and soon more farmers came by. Anlon did not hesitate to send the tiny pebbles flying at them, too. It did not matter to him whether the men came near by accident or because they were searching for the Sidhe. He had no wish to harm any of them, but he was willing to do almost anything to avoid having another of the Sidhe meet the same terrible fate as Cian—and of those other long-ago tribesmen he had seen in Greine's story.

Soon there were not just farmers coming to the fields. Warriors came, too, guarding the farmers so that they could do their work. Most of the time Anlon was able to send the stones flying into the arm of a man or the rump of a horse, causing confusion and fear among their ranks—but not death.

It was clear to Anlon that all the men—warriors and farmers alike—hated and feared the Sidhe missiles, for they could never be sure of where or when they might strike. His tactic was effective enough to prevent any more terrible ambushes on either side. Anlon dared to breathe just a little easier when he realized that his plan seemed to be working, but he knew that the danger was far from over.

Chapter Nineteen

The clan grew bolder with each day. They had been robbing the fields of Dun Mor almost at will and nothing had happened at all. They had begun to think they could do anything they wished. Anlon know that boded ill.

Until now, the Sidhe would never have touched anything made by Men. They hated the iron that caused them so much agony. But now, determined to cause as much trouble for Men as they could and take away the tools their enemy needed for farming and fighting, anything left near the fields was stolen. If it were made of iron, the Sidhe would throw it in the bog; if it were of bronze or wood, they would keep it for themselves.

They would creep around the *dun's* herd of horses, getting close enough to the animals to touch them. They did not attempt to take any of the mares or foals, for it was going to be difficult enough for them to get Nealta and her two herdmates through the winter. But they braided and twisted the animal's manes into awful tangles, just to show they could have taken the beasts had they wished.

Some journeyed to the high pastures where Men guarded their cattle, and they could sometimes manage to catch hold of a young calf and steal the milk from its mother. Once they even managed to drag the calf far enough away to slaughter it and take the meat back to Caher Idir.

Its head was left behind for the herdsmen to find.

Anlon could only shiver as he watched the wild tribe, feeling more and more powerless with each night that passed and dreading more than ever the eve of Samhain.

In the darkness of one cloudy night, the Sidhe worked fast to cut the heads from the stalks of the just-ripened wheat. Anlon was right in the middle, wanting to get them out of this place as quickly as possible and hoping that if he helped them get what they wanted they could leave that much sooner.

He constantly glanced around as he hacked at the golden stalks with a small bronze sickle, though he could see almost nothing in the gloom. Several more of the Sidhe moved along the edges of the field not far away. He could hear the faint swish of their sickles as they worked. They kept low and stayed as close as they could to the forest, for, bold as they were, all knew they might have to flee for their lives at any moment.

He had a very uneasy feeling about this field. It was closer to Dun Mor than any they had raided so far. It had to be guarded. And the Sidhe had found it much too easy to creep inside and begin harvesting.

Resolutely they cut and bagged the wheat. The tribesmen had a way of cutting off only the ears of grain, leaving the tall stalks standing in the field, which infuriated their enemies. Anlon was certain that this tactic, along with his invisible missiles which stung and confused them, had combined to once again turn the Men into the active enemies of the Sidhe.

The moments went by in darkness and in silence. Perhaps Scahta had been right. Perhaps if he helped them to get in and get out quickly, there would be less chance of their being caught by the Men. Perhaps this could work after all. There was still a hope that he could save her people, find a way to lessen their anger and—

The sound of something rushing through the air high above him made him look up. He knew that sound!

A rain of iron-tipped javelins thudded into the earth, right in the midst of the Sidhe.

The tribesmen instantly turned and fled, vanishing like smoke in the woods. Anlon too dashed away, but then tripped and nearly fell over something heavy. Looking down, he realized to his horror that it was Amhran he had stumbled over, Amhran who lay pinned to the wheat field by the still-quivering javelin through his chest.

Already the light was fading from his eyes. Anlon tore himself away from the scene and raced after the others, cold with shock and with the fear that he would find others who had met the same fate.

But he found no other Sidhe at all. Either they had fled so quickly for Caher Idir that they had left him far behind, or else all of them . . .

It was a long and terrible journey back to the hidden stone fortress. When at last Anlon returned home, he was greatly relieved to see the remaining twelve Sidhe who had gone with him gathered together in the yard. "You are alive," he said. "Cogar, Mactire—all of you—you are alive. I was so afraid that—"

But they only glared at him. "Samhain," was all that they would say. *"Samhain."*

In the deepest, blackest part of the night, where only a few stars glimmered in the void behind the heavy clouds, Queen Scahta led a group of her people from Caher Idir out into a clearing in the forest. It was the same field where her marriage had taken place, but Anlon knew that this ritual would be far different.

Thirteen women and thirteen men followed in a long single line, alternating male and female so that Anlon walked directly behind Scahta. When they reached the grassy field they formed a double circle, with the women creating the inner circle and the men the outer one.

Scahta stood alone in the center.

She wore only her deerskin gown and boots, but paid no attention to the damp and cold of the night. The gold lunula collar rested around her neck and shone brightly even in the faint light of the stars. It seemed to Anlon that the collar gathered and reflected the starlight directly into her eyes . . . and she would need it this night, for this was the dark of the moon, the new moon, and the only light would be that from the stars and from the shining stones and glittering gold and bronze adorning Scahta and all the rest of the Sidhe.

The circles formed, the men and women stood silent and still for a time. Scahta stood at the center with her face raised to the sky, eyes closed, arms outstretched, and breathed deep of the quiet and the shadow of this darkest of all nights. Slowly she began to move, her eyes still closed, walking in a small circle to her right—and all of the men and women, too, began to move as she did. One carried a drum, and he began to keep time as they all stepped around the circle.

Three times the dancers circled, and then Scahta brought her arms down. The drumming ceased. She opened her eyes and began to speak.

"Here we stand in darkness, in silence, in hiding, even as our people hide themselves always in the still of the night. Yet we come to this place now, in hiding, even as the moon is hidden from us, to seek an end to our long night of seclusion. We seek a new beginning, a beginning of power, of brightness, of light, even as the moon must renew herself and wax to brightness once again.

"Ours will remain a soft light, a gentle power. Forever shall we be as elusive and unreachable as the moon—yet we must use that strength so that we might continue on through the years, through the ages, even as the moon continues, though she waxes and wanes, and yet continues."

Scahta raised her arms and the rhythmic drumming began again. She was about to close her eyes and begin the circle once more—when something in the distance caught her eye.

She stood very still, staring into the darkness. The ritual was forgotten. The drumming faded away to silence as all the men and women in the circles stopped and stared at her in bewilderment, then tried to follow her gaze.

They all saw it. Out among the trees on the far side of the clearing, for just the briefest of moments, was the unmistakable gleam of bronze.

Anlon was the first to move to her side with sword in hand, offering her strength from his presence. "What could it be?" he whispered to her. "Are the others coming from Caher Idir to join us?"

She shook her head slightly. "They would not come out here. And they would have no reason to circle around and come to us from the far side of the forest."

Again they saw the gleam of bronze. The dancers crowded around Anlon and Scahta, their circle forgotten.

Anlon drew Scahta close. He could feel the tension and trembling of her body. It seemed that she struggled even to breathe. "Another tribe," she said, her voice so soft it could barely be heard. *"It is another tribe."*

She started to move toward the shining bronze, but Anlon caught her arm. "You are so certain, Scahta?" he said, and knew that she must hear the fear and doubt in his voice. "How could it be another tribe? We know what happened to Greine's tribe. And there has never been sign of any other. . . ."

She looked out into the forest once again. He felt her shiver when there appeared first one and then a second gleam of yellow metal. "It could be nothing else. No animal could cast such a light. And Men would never bother to creep up so silently, nor be abroad on the dark of the moon." Scahta drew a deep breath. "Somehow, another tribe has survived, even as we have. And now they have found us."

"Then speak to them," Anlon said urgently, letting go of her arm. "Before you go to them, speak to them as only you can do, in that voice of yours which travels only on the wind. If it is another tribe, they will surely answer you, and we can be certain."

Scahta stared straight ahead into the darkness, then took a few slow steps toward the woods. Anlon tensed, but then she paused and began singing to the soft night wind and letting it carry her words toward the spots of light out among the trees.

The moments went by. The wind sighed in the branches. The men and women of the Sidhe waited quietly behind her. At last Scahta turned around and looked up into Anlon's eyes.

"They do not answer," she said to him.

Anlon stared back at her. "Then we must return to Caher Idir. We cannot know what this is. We cannot—"

"Perhaps they do not understand our words," said one of the people.

"Perhaps they are from a strange tribe very far away."

"Perhaps they are simply afraid."

Scahta looked into the forest again. "I too would be afraid, if I had come upon a new tribe—even though I had tried with all my strength to find them." The bronze gleam showed itself again. It appeared to be closer now. "I will go to them. I cannot let them leave—"

But before she could take a step, a dark grey shadow moved across the field between the Sidhe and the forest. It was her wolf, and as she swung toward the people, all could hear his low, ominous growl. The animal continued on, growling all the while, and disappeared again into the blackness of the woods.

"That is enough for me," Anlon said. "Please—let us go back to the fortress where it is safe. There could be anything out there. There are so few of us. How can we dare to take such a risk?"

She looked up at him. "And if I go and hide in my fortress—walk away from a frightened tribe of Sidhe, one that Wolf does not recognize, one that has come from very far away to find us—what am I risking then?"

Anlon straightened, and held his bronze sword close. "*I* will go and see what is there."

Her lips parted, and before she could speak Cogar stepped forward. "They would only flee from one they would recognize as a Man. I will go, my lady." And then he was gone, walking into the darkness toward the intermittent gleam in the woods.

Anlon could only watch as Cogar disappeared into the night. The clouds obscured the stars, and it was so dark that it was impossible to see where the field ended and the forest began. He could do nothing more than wait, his heart pounding and his hand tightly gripping the hilt of his sword.

Come back, come back! he wanted to cry out; but the black night had swallowed Cogar utterly, and there was nothing they could do but wait for his return.

The silence and the darkness stretched on around them . . . and then Anlon heard a sound.

All of them heard it. Near the place where Cogar had vanished, and rapidly spreading outward, was a rumbling, crashing sound, like a great herd of horses galloping through the brush and over the sapling trees of the deep black forest and coming straight for the group of Sidhe in the clearing.

There was no time to run, no place to hide. Anlon pulled Scahta behind him and prepared to meet whatever was coming. The rest of the Sidhe men drew their swords and moved quickly to stand with him. The women gathered in behind them, each with her bronze dagger in her hand.

Yet just as it reached the edge of the clearing, the noise began to subside. Then it stopped. In the forest there appeared a single spot of flame, hovering within the trees.

Anlon turned to Scahta and the rest of the women. "Run, now, run while you can! This is no tribe of Sidhe. We will hold them here while you escape. Go. *Go!*"

Scahta hesitated for only a heartbeat, then began moving with her women toward the other side of the field.

Anlon turned back to the forest ahead of them. The single spot of flame had now become two.

As he watched, the two spots became four, and then six, and then eight—and then the entire half of the clearing in front of them was ringed with spots of light, and the lights surged forward all at once as a band of shouting men on horseback galloped straight for the Sidhe.

Anlon thought his heart would stop. A thousand questions burst into his mind: *How did they find us? How did they get so close? Where is Cogar?* But there was no time to think, for the clearing flared with a sudden blinding light as the men's torches reflected in their cold iron swords and javelins.

The men dragged their horses to a halt just a few steps from the closely gathered Sidhe. Right in front of Anlon was the mortal warrior Fehin, and across the shoulders of his horse was the slim body of Cogar—captive!

Anlon knew that if he paused for even an instant he would have no chance. There was only one thing these men would not expect him to do—

Sword high, he threw himself straight at Fehin with all his strength. Fehin's horse half-reared and whirled away from Anlon's charge. Cogar fell heavily to earth. Anlon slashed down hard with his bronze sword, and it struck the face of Fehin's wooden shield and bounced upward with a shock. By the next swing Fehin had got his horse turned around and was meeting Anlon's bronze sword with his own iron blade.

Anlon knew that his sword could not last long against his opponent's iron. Still, he swung and slashed with all the speed and strength he possessed, sometimes using one hand on the hilt and sometimes swinging with both, hoping to overpower his attacker as quickly as possible.

He knew that it might well be the last action of his life, but Scahta and the other women just might get a chance to escape if he and the other men of the Sidhe engaged the invaders in combat.

He was dimly aware that Cogar had managed to get away from the battle scene, for the captured Sidhe was no longer underfoot. And as Anlon pressed Fehin with all his strength, he began to hear another sound—a sound that was the last thing he expected to hear.

Laughter.

The men around him were laughing. He wanted to look up at them and see what was happening, see what had happened to the rest of the men and women of the Sidhe—but he could not. Fehin leaped off his horse and threw down his shield and began circling around Anlon, grinning, laughing, holding the hilt of his cold iron sword with both hands. He brandished the weapon but made no move to attack. He just circled, watching Anlon and laughing.

Anlon spared a glance at the other Sidhe. They stood huddled together near the center of the clearing, men and women both, with the points of the men's cold iron javelins aimed straight at them.

Anlon crept backward a pace, and then another. The shadows jumped and danced in the light of the mortals' torches. Slowly he lowered his scarred bronze sword, his cold stare never wavering. "Why are you here?" he said to Fehin. "Why have you come here?"

Two of the *dun*'s men rode their horses up behind Anlon and aimed their javelins straight at him. He stayed very still. "We are here to speak to you, Anlon!" Fehin answered, as though they had both just come to the house of a friend to share a meal and a story and a few cups of blackberry wine.

Anlon glanced at the Sidhe again, and to his despair he saw Scahta standing fearless and proud near the front of them. She was there with all the rest of the women; none had escaped.

"I want to know how you found us," Anlon said through clenched teeth. "How could you find us, a tribe of Sidhe, deep in the forest in the dark of the moon?"

"Oh, it was not easy," Fehin answered with a laugh, "but it can be done, if one rides out on enough nights, and looks in enough places, and listens carefully enough for the sound of a drum." He grinned at Anlon, looking very pleased with himself.

Anlon closed his eyes and struggled for breath. "Why have you not killed us?"

Fehin's eyes narrowed. "I am not here as a warrior, Anlon. I am here only with a message from the king." He lowered his long sharp sword and stood up straight.

Anlon, too, stood up taller, and stepped back, touching the iron points of the men's javelins. Yet he held his ground. "Give me your message, then."

Fehin glanced over at the surrounded Sidhe, making sure they all still watched him. They returned his gaze and stood silent and unmoving, refusing even to acknowledge the rough men who held them captive with glaring torches and hard-edged weapons.

Fehin began pacing back and forth between Anlon and the rest of the Sidhe, his iron sword still in his hand. "It is the dark of the moon, and only a fortnight until Samhain," he began. "And every year the Sidhe come around to harass us and steal what is ours."

The smirking grin disappeared. Again his eyes narrowed. "The king has sent us here to warn you to stay away from Dun Mor. Your presence will be tolerated there no longer.

"Nothing would please me more than to destroy you all. We could do it as easily as we might wipe out a nest of mice. But the king has ordered us to leave you untouched this night, for he believes you are a poor enemy." He turned and glared straight at Anlon. "It is also true that one of our own lives among you. That is why all of you still breathe."

Anlon raised his chin and glared back at him. "Your king is right. We are not a threat to you. We have asked you only for a share of the harvest, just enough that we might not suffer through the winter. That will in no way harm anyone at Dun Mor."

Fehin caught hold of his horse and swung up onto the animal's back. "Thieves are not tolerated at Dun Mor, whether they be mice or Sidhe." He pointed his iron sword at Anlon and at the gathered Sidhe in the center of the field. "If ever you come creeping 'round Dun Mor, whether it be on Samhain Eve or any other night, we will cut you down like the thieves you are. You have been warned."

The party of warriors turned and started to gallop away—and, as if to emphasize Fehin's words, an iron javelin flew out of the darkness and thudded into the earth at Anlon's feet. It quivered there as the men and their horses and their torches vanished into the night.

Chapter Twenty

The next few days passed with no more signs of the men of Dun Mor, though the Sidhe kept guards posted near the fortress and throughout the woods at every moment of the day and night. The visit by the *dun*'s warriors had achieved the opposite of their intended purpose. The Sidhe tribesmen's fear and anger grew with every sunrise, every sunset. They redoubled their efforts to prepare for the attack at Samhain.

Each day the Sidhe men made new javelins and sharpened their swords. Each night they gathered small mountains of polished white sling stones just as diligently as they gathered their stores of food.

That food was the one thing that gave Anlon some small measure of hope. Beneath the smoke shed, where the meat of the trapped animals was hung to dry and cure, was a small souterrain. It was like a small cave, dark and cool, and he reassured himself each day by looking at the rows of green apples and dark brown waterlily roots stored on long flat slabs of wood to dry, along with basket after basket filled with hazelnuts and acorns.

Most importantly of all was the deep narrow pit, sealed over with clay, which Anlon knew was more than half full of barley. That grain would keep perfectly and would be waiting for them in the spring, when they would use it for seeding and, perhaps, for a little bread.

With each bit of food came a better chance of the Sidhe surviving the coming winter. They had gathered a much better store than they'd had at this time last year, even though it had cost them the life of Amhran. One life for many, though, did not seem to trouble the Sidhe at all.

If only they could survive long enough to make Amhran's sacrifice worthwhile. . . . He had to stop them from attacking.

Seven nights before Samhain Eve, Anlon followed the Sidhe men as they made one final journey into the darkness of the forest in search of sling stones and any bit of food they might have missed. He stayed close enough to the others to keep them in sight, but did not attempt to work with or speak to them. The tension was high and he knew that his words would only be met with glaring silence.

Yet when he found a spot that yielded several handfuls of acorns, he filled his leather bag with those instead of sling stones, and on the way back to Caher Idir he could not resist showing his find to Liath. "There may be even more out there that we have not yet found," Anlon whispered, with hope in his voice.

Liath nodded, but in front of them one stopped and

turned to face them. Anlon's heart sank when he saw it was Mactire.

"Acorns alone will not get us through the winter," Mactire said in a cold voice. "The third harvest is yet to come, and we will have our share of that, too."

"I will help you hunt," Anlon said quickly, still hoping that somehow he could persuade them to listen to him. "If we go out every day and set snares, we are bound to get enough meat, to last throughout the winter—"

"Or we may not!" cried Mactire. "It is a great risk to rely on the hunt all winter long. How can you so easily forget how it was for us last year? We must have food stored away before then, and the men who stole our herds are going to give it to us. They will have no further need of it. They will all be dead."

Anlon closed his eyes. "No. All of you will be dead," he said quietly. "I have seen it. I have seen what happened to another tribe who tried to do what you intend . . . they were killed, every last one of them."

Mactire glared at him. "What are you talking about? What do you mean, you have seen it? I will tell you what you have never seen—the Sidhe at the height of their power!"

"Oh, but I have. . . . I have seen them, shining and strong, and even then—"

Mactire cut him off. "You are so intent on preventing us from attacking the men of the *dun*. Why is that, Anlon? Is it because you wish to weaken us and keep us off guard, so they can come for us when they wish and destroy us at their leisure?"

"Of course not. You have seen their weapons! You have seen their strength! You have seen their horses and their iron swords and spears! How can you believe that you could ever defeat them?"

247

"And if we do not fight? What will happen to us then, if we simply stay here huddled like a little nest of frightened mice? That is what the man called us, was it not? Mice?"

Mactire gave him a cold stare, then continued, "I will tell you what will happen. If we stay here and do nothing, we will starve, and they will come and kill us all. They already know where we are! They found us even in the darkness of the new moon! They will be at the gates of Caher Idir itself if we do not stop them!"

"But if you attack them—"

"If we attack them, we have a chance! We have a chance to turn them back and force them to leave us alone, if we show them that the price of molesting us is too high!"

Anlon looked at him, at the pent-up desperation and anger and despair in the eyes of Mactire and all the rest of the Sidhe who stood behind him, and his own resolve hardened. "I will not let you do this," he said. "I will not let you throw your lives away. You may well be the last tribe of Sidhe in all of Eire. I will not let you do it."

The coldness in Mactire's eyes flared into fury. "And I will not let you stop us! You have interfered here for the last time!" With that he pulled out his bronze sword and crouched down to face Anlon, glaring, angry, determined to make an end to this.

"Mactire, listen to me," Anlon pleaded. His own anger and despair were growing, but the last thing he wanted to do was injure one of Scahta's own people—or be the cause of his death.

"You already have the blood of one of us on your hands!" Mactire cried, as if he had heard Anlon's thoughts. "What is one more of us to one of you Men?"

Anlon backed away a step, then another. Then he

could go no farther, for he and his assailant were surrounded by the other men of the Sidhe. "I will not fight you," he said, one last time.

Mactire lunged at him and slashed with his sword. It flashed and the sharp tip caught Anlon's leather tunic, slicing it open. A line of blood ran down his chest.

The sting of his wound ended any words Anlon might have used to reason with Mactire. He tore off his cloak, pulled out his own sword and charged the smaller Sidhe with all his strength.

It was a difficult and terrible fight, for Anlon's rage and long frustration at being forever the outsider, forever looked down upon—not Man, not Sidhe, not anything at all—threatened to rise up and overwhelm him.

Mactire's face, only inches from his, held all the contempt for him that had been repressed by so many of the Sidhe for nearly one year. It was all Anlon could do to keep from driving his sword straight at that face, all he could do to simply defend himself instead of killing his opponent.

At last, with a two-handed shot that risked taking off Mactire's arm, Anlon knocked the sword from the Sidhe's hand and sent it flying. Instantly he tossed his own sword to his left hand and swung his right fist at Mactire's jaw, sending his enemy dropping hard to the earth. Before Mactire could move, Anlon straddled him with his feet and stood there, breathing hard, the sharp point of his sword held at his opponent's throat.

"Stop this!"

He glanced toward the sudden cry. Scahta pushed her way to the front of the crowd and looked around at them all, trying to comprehend what was happening. She could only stand and look at them, at Anlon with blood running down his chest, at Mactire at the point of death, and at her people, divided and angry and desperate.

"I told you Anlon was never to be harmed," she whispered. "Has it come so far as this?" she whispered.

"It has," said a voice from the crowd.

"Many of us believed that Man and Sidhe could never live together."

"Here is our proof, and yours."

The stricken, horrified look in Scahta's eyes made Anlon forget Mactire. "And you still intend to attack the fortress of Men on Samhain Eve?" she asked.

Voice after voice responded to her. *"We do, lady . . . we do . . . we do . . ."*

Scahta looked carefully at each and every one of her subjects. She drew a deep breath and seemed to compose herself. "Very well," she said. "I understand. And I will put an end to this now."

She looked up at Anlon. "All of you go back to Caher Idir. Wait for me there. Anlon—stay here with me."

No one moved. Scahta turned and looked hard at all her people, and slowly they began to move off toward the fortress, leaving her alone in the clearing with Anlon.

For a long time, as the people filed away and returned to Caher Idir, Scahta stood in silence looking up at her husband. She stared closely into his eyes as though searching for something there.

"What can I say to you?" he asked at last, gazing back at her with rising anxiety. "I am sorry that Mactire and I fought. I tried every way I knew to avoid it—and when I could not avoid it, I did all I could to keep him from harm. He walks away now unscathed, back to his house as though nothing happened."

She stopped him with a gentle hand on his face. It was clear to him that she had heard nothing of what he had said. "Come with me," was all that she said. "Come with me."

They walked within the shelter of the forest, familiar even in the darkness, to a place deep within the trees where the stream sang clear as crystal. She led him to the edge of it and lifted his tunic off over his head. With her hands, and with the edge of her large white cloak, she washed the sword slash across his chest with the cold clean water. When she was done, she drew him down to sit beside her on the soft grassy earth of the stream bank.

"I do not know what I could have done to stop the fight, Scahta," he said again. "I am sorry . . . I am so sorry."

Her hand tightened on his fingers. "That is over now," she answered, staring at something far away in the night sky. "There is a far more serious battle which concerns me."

He looked up at her face. It was only a profile shadowed in the darkness. "They intend to attack Dun Mor on Samhain Eve. We must find a way to stop them." But even as he spoke, he knew what she would say.

"Nothing will stop them. Nothing that you or I can say or do will turn them from it now. They are determined to fight for their survival. I cannot argue with that."

"If they attack Dun Mor, they will die. All." Anlon's voice was quiet. "Their king should be able to stop them. It should be clear to you now that I am no king. And for that, too, I am sorry."

She seemed to smile, though her eyes still looked at something far away. "You have done all you could, and more. I never thought to find anyone, Man or Sidhe, to make a better king than you. I never could."

"Yet your people do not feel the same. Even though I

know my home is here, and my love for you could never be matched . . . even though I carry the blood of a Sidhe king . . . your people look at me and see only a Man. They see an enemy."

He sighed in frustration and in pain. "I am the enemy of both and of neither . . . and I do not know how to convince either one to trust me. Perhaps it is no longer possible."

Scahta tilted her head, but still she would not look at him. "It has not ended yet. There is a long night yet to come. Perhaps—"

He stopped her with his hand on her wrist. "There is no reason to give me false hope. No matter how it goes tomorrow night, I will never be your king. The best the Sidhe can hope for is a truce of some kind with Men, and how long could it last? I tried to persuade the men of Dun Mor to do just such a thing. They simply laughed.

"The Sidhe have no chance, *no* chance, to defeat those men in combat. There are simply far too many. All of them have iron swords and iron javelins. You know as well as I that the bronze of the Sidhe is no match for the iron of Men. If every last warrior of the Sidhe is not destroyed, you will be fortunate indeed, Queen Scahta."

She nodded, slowly. "I know this, Anlon. I too have tried to dissuade them from going. They feel that they must go, though. They feel they have no choice but to defend their own as best they can . . . and die on their feet if it comes to that."

"And leave their women alone? Leave them to die hidden away beneath the hills, like Greine and her sisters? I would never do such a thing to you. . . . Never would I leave you. . . ."

"And yet you would go with them if you could, when they set out to challenge the men of Dun Mor. You too would place your life in jeopardy for that which is important to you."

He closed his eyes. "So much of this has come about because of my presence. I must do what I can to put it right. I have no choice."

"Neither do they, Anlon. Neither do they." At last she turned to him, but he could not see her face in the cloudy darkness. "You are here because I called you here, and I do not regret it. You have done all you could. Now things must take a different course."

He covered her hand with his own and looked away. "If I cannot find a way to bring peace to both the worlds on Samhain Eve, it will be the last night you and I ever spend together. Both sides will despise me as a traitor. Both will want my blood. I shall be an outcast . . . or I shall be dead."

Scahta did not move. She hardly seemed to breathe for the space of several heartbeats. Then she ran her cool fingers in a feather-light movement down his cheek, and he kissed them, turned to her, and drew her close in a warm embrace.

As they had so many times before, they exchanged a gentle kiss. Anlon withdrew the pins from Scahta's cloak and slid the white wool from her shoulders, while she in turn reached for his fine leather belt and untied it. In a moment they wore only skin and twilight and embraced each other tenderly on the edge of the singing stream.

As always, their lovemaking was sweet and warm, a loving reinforcement of the bond between them; yet something was different this time. There was an urgency, an intensity, within Scahta that Anlon had not known before. She held him tightly, as if she were afraid he might slip away, and her body trembled as never before . . . almost as if she were weeping.

And when at last they lay quietly together on the soft bank, she continued to hold him closely, tightly, as though she would never let him go. He embraced her gently and stroked her back, her shoulder, her long shining hair, hoping to ease her tension and fear; but though her breathing slowed and steadied, he could still feel the tremors running through her.

After a long time she sat up and kissed him gently on the lips, and then she was gone. He could hear her getting dressed in the darkness, though he could see nothing but the faint white of her cloak and the occasional shine of the bronze pins. Then even those subtle signs faded and disappeared.

He quickly put on his own clothes, leaving his cloak and pin lying in the grass, then moved through the night in an effort to reach her. "Scahta," he called softly. "Scahta!"

There was no answer. She had vanished completely into the shadows of the silent forest.

Anlon strapped on his sword and tied the belt snugly. "Scahta!" he cried out. "I cannot see you. Where are you? Wait for me, please! I will walk with you back to our home, back to—"

He took a few steps, but found he could see nothing. There were no landmarks, only a wall of trees that all looked the same. He could hear the sound of the stream, but the wind began to blow and he could no longer determine where the stream was—behind him, in front of him, where?

He stopped and stood very still. What was happening here? He had never in his life gotten lost in a forest, not even an unfamiliar one. He had spent many days and nights in this place with Scahta. How could he possibly be lost?

Heart pounding, he forced himself to just stand and

listen. Somewhere, he could hear the stream running. Somewhere he could hear the wind in the trees. And somewhere—mostly within his own mind—he could hear Scahta talking to him.

"Go," her voice said. *"Go from here . . . go to your home."*

He shook his head violently, reaching out to steady himself against a tree. "My home is at Caher Idir," he said, and was shocked to discover that merely saying those words took all the determination he had.

"There is no Caher Idir," said Scahta's voice within his mind. *"Your home is where it has always been . . . with your family in their rath, among the men in their great fortress."*

He wrenched himself away from the tree, stumbling in the darkness. "Why are you doing this? Why are you trying to force me away? Why are you angry with me?"

"I am not angry." And he realized that she was telling the truth, for he could hear the sadness and despair even in that magical voice she was using against him, that voice which was carried only on the wind.

"Then why? Why would you drive me away?"

There came a long silence. Anlon continued to walk, difficult as it was, searching for Scahta in the confusion of wind and darkness.

After a few moments—or was it much longer?—he found that he could see a little more. He moved toward the glimmer of the stream. It looked strangely different now, much wider and faster, and there were large rocks along the bank he did not remember. Glancing about at the trees and the shrubs and the rise and fall of the terrain, he realized that he had never seen this place before. It was entirely new and strange to him.

"Go home, Anlon . . . go to your home. I will not watch you die. I love you too much. I have loved you since the day we first met. You will not die."

Anlon closed his eyes. "Scahta, Scahta . . . my home is with you at Caher Idir. And I am not going to die—not if I can do anything to stop it."

He turned and took a few steps forward, trying to keep the sound of the rushing stream directly behind him so he would not become lost again. "I will not watch your people die, either. I want to stop death, not add to it. I want to live, for I want to stay with you."

There was silence. Then the wind began to rise once more. *"You will live, Anlon. You will live among your own people. They are waiting for you. Go to them now."*

The wind rushed through the trees and became a roaring in his ears. He pressed his hands tightly over them. "I will not let you win!" he shouted. "I know what you are trying to do! I will not let you drive me away with your magic!"

"Forget the Sidhe . . . forget Caher Idir . . . forget me."

Shutting his eyes tightly, he struggled to walk against the wind, against the power Scahta was using to drive him away. "I will never forget you! You cannot make me forget you! I will find you, I will find Caher Idir, no matter what you do!"

"You are lost. . . . You are looking for the Fianna. . . . You are looking for the fortress of Dun Mor."

"Scahta . . . Scahta!" Anlon reached into the darkness, reaching for the woman he loved, but he could not see her, could not hear her, could not feel her. He saw nothing but blackness and trees, heard nothing but the roaring wind, felt nothing but a terrible agony of loneliness and loss.

"Scahta!" he cried out, one last time; but she was gone.

Chapter Twenty-one

After a long time, the wind began to die down.

It had been quite a strong storm, but around the time of Samhain, when the air was growing colder and more restless, it was not unusual to have such wild and windy weather. Anlon raised his head, brushing the dry leaves and dust from his hair, and got up from behind the tree where he had taken shelter.

He was alone in the forest. As the clouds flew overhead, allowing the light of the half-moon to shine down on him, he could see no sign of the Fianna or of the campsite he had worked so hard, as always, to build.

But, of course. He remembered now. They had sent him into the forest to get more wood for the fire. Or had it been to search for blackberries? He shook his head. Whatever he'd been looking for, he must have gone farther than he'd thought when the storm struck.

He was eager to get back to the camp. Tomorrow

morning he would ride out with the rest of the Fianna to Dun Mor, the king's own fortress, to spend the winter months. And he was more than a little uneasy about being out here alone in the woods so close to Samhain Eve. The Sidhe were likely to be abroad, and he certainly did not want them to find him out here alone. He was not sure all of them were as gentle and shy as the one he had seen near his home when he was a boy, so many years ago.

Scahta moved through the grounds of Caher Idir in silence. She held Anlon's folded cloak close to her chest and clutched his leaf-shaped pin inside her fist. Distantly she was aware that her feet took step after step across the damp earth, and that her heart still beat, and that her breath still came and went; but she felt strangely light, as if a great piece of her had been taken away and she was no longer complete.

Walking inside her home, she found Ean and Geal and Maidin waiting for her. Though a small fire crackled in the hearth, and all her fine bronze cups and plates hung from the walls, and her stack of soft furs covered the sleeping ledge, the house seemed empty and silent and cold. As she went to the ledge and ran her fingers through the beautiful white and grey furs lying there, she knew that from now on this house would always be empty for her—even if a hundred people should manage to crowd into it.

"Please sit down, my lady," Ean urged gently.

"We will bring you food and something to drink," said Geal.

"After that you must rest for a time," added Maidin.

Slowly Scahta sat on the furs. Geal walked over to her, glancing at the folded blue-and-grey cloak in Scahta's arms. "I must ask you, my lady—where is Anlon?"

"We know there was a duel between him and Mactire."

"Will Anlon return? Is he safe?"

Scahta closed her eyes and allowed her head to drop into her hands. "He is safe," was all she could tell them. "He is safe."

The forest seemed to go on forever.

The eastern sky began to turn to grey, but Anlon was finding it more and more difficult to make his way back to Dun Mor. Every path he took, every turn he tried, brought him only to yet another small clearing or thick stand of trees. There was no sign of any sort of campsite.

The men of the Fianna always took great pleasure in playing tricks on him. They loved to watch him work while they lounged about the comfortable camp that he had made, but this was the worst of their tricks so far. He wondered whose idea it had been to send him into the forest and then abandon him! Fehin's, most likely.

He paused yet again to get his bearings, and another thought came to him. Maybe this was a test—a test to see if he could find his way to Dun Mor even after being lost in an unfamiliar forest.

A test to see if he could still find his way home.

Anlon sighed and shook his head; then he smiled a little. No doubt it was the final test for any initiate of the Fianna. If he could not even find his way to his own home, how could he hope to be of any use to the king?

Though he had never been to Dun Mor, he knew the path that led from his family's home to the king's fortress—and he knew how to get to his family home from here.

Find the path and find Dun Mor. Anlon broke into a

run. If he kept a steady pace, he would be there well before sundown.

The sword and scabbard at his waist swung against his leg as he moved. All at once Anlon stopped and looked down at himself with something like surprise.

Gingerly he ran his fingers over the sword hilt. Somehow he did not recall ever having a sword. Before, his only weapons had been a sling and a blackthorn club. How had he come to have a sword?

The smooth leather of the tunic at his waist brushed against his bare arm. He realized that he wore a belt and a tunic and trousers and boots of fine deerskin—and wristbands made of gold. How had he come to have fine clothes of good leather and a sword in a heavy wooden scabbard, to say nothing of gold wristbands?

And such a beautiful sword, too, he marveled, cautiously raising it a little out of its scabbard. The hilt was of smooth bone and the blade of shining bronze. It looked like . . . it looked like something . . .

Like something the Sidhe would make.

The Sidhe. Slowly the memory formed in his mind. Last night he had made camp and prepared food for the Fianna as he always did. Then he had gone for a swim . . . and encountered a woman of the Sidhe looking down on him from the shadows of the trees. She had spoken to him, but it must not have been of any consequence; he remembered almost nothing of what she had said. Then he had been called back to the campsite and she had disappeared back into the forest.

The deerskin clothes, the fine bronze sword . . . these things could only have been made by the Sidhe. He wondered why they would leave such gifts for him. It was true that his own clothes had been in very bad condition, but the beautiful, mysterious woman he had met last night must have her own reasons for giving him such fine things. He could only wonder why she would be so kind to him when he had done nothing at all for her.

Perhaps it was her way of asking for help. The winter was nearly here; it could be that they were short of food. Once he reached Dun Mor he would go out and try to speak to the woman again, if he could find her.

He sighed. Again the Sidhe had given him a gift, just as they had given him the bronze pin—

He stopped. His hand flew to his right shoulder. His dark and ragged cloak was gone, and so was his cherished bronze pin. How could he have lost such a treasure?

Anlon shook his head, trying to remember. Why was it so difficult to recall exactly what had happened last night? The Sidhe did sometimes play tricks with one's memory, he had heard. He was absolutely sure that a woman of the Sidhe had come to him and spoken with him last night . . . but whatever happened after that had vanished from his mind like mist in the rising sun.

At last, after a lifetime of dreaming about it, Anlon approached the great circular fortress known as Dun Mor.

He walked across the open field in the windy cold of the late afternoon, and there before him rose the great curving walls and iron-faced gates. He felt pride in having found it on his own, at having made his way home and passing this last test which the Fianna had made for him. Now he was going to a new home and a new life, a life he had dreamt of for a very long time.

The gates began creaking open well before he reached them. Yet there was only a little space between them and he still could not see inside the fortress. All he could see was the frown of the watchman who had opened those gates and the suspicious glare of Fehin right behind him.

Anlon stopped, then smiled at them. "Good day to you, Fehin," he said. "I've found my way back, as you can see."

But Fehin only stared at him in silence, his eyes flicking over Anlon as if he could not believe what he was seeing. "Found your way back," he repeated. "Why have you come to us now? What do you want?"

"What—what do I want?" He paused, looking closely at Fehin, trying to understand what he meant. Then he straightened. Perhaps this, too, was part of the ritual. "I want to serve the king," he said solemnly, looking straight into Fehin's eyes.

But the other man's expression did not change. A few more of the king's warriors were beginning to gather behind him, looking equally wary and suspicious. "So, you have had a change of heart," Fehin said. "What brought this about?"

Anlon could only shake his head. "Nothing has changed," he said. "I am here to spend the winter and begin to serve the king, as do all the men of the Fianna."

Fehin's eyes widened. He reached for Anlon's arm and pulled him inside, and the rest of the men slammed the gate shut behind him.

They crowded around him and hurried him across the courtyard, pushing him so quickly that he barely got a look at the size of the yard or the buildings scattered across it. Anlon tried to look first one way and then the other, but could see little except the backs and shoulders of the men around him.

It was not the way he had envisioned his entry into Dun Mor.

They hustled him into the largest building he had ever seen. He hesitated at the darkened doorway, and he nearly tripped over the step going in. The sword in its bronze-tipped scabbard banged against the side of the door.

At last they were inside. He tried to get a look at the vastness of the great building, at the astonishing height of the roof, but his escorts were intent on pulling him to the far end of the structure.

Several men were already gathered there, sitting on furs thrown down on the rushes and listening as one of them spoke. Anlon recognized a few of the Fianna, and knew that the older men who carried no swords must be the king's druids. And the king himself—

The group of men quickly looked up as Anlon was half-walked, half-dragged in front of them. They got to their feet as Fehin stood him directly in front of the largest, a man with wide shoulders and a powerful build and colorful cloak so wide it was folded and pinned into pleats across his chest.

Fehin gave Anlon one last shove, which nearly sent him sprawling. "My king, he has returned," Fehin said. "He has returned to us from the Sidhe."

From the Sidhe . . . Anlon straightened, his humiliation momentarily forgotten. He turned to Fehin. "Why do you say that I have returned from the Sidhe?" he asked. "I did see one of them in the woods beside the lake last night, but only one. A woman came and spoke to me. She was the only one that I saw. She was there for a few moments, then went back into the forest."

Every one of the hall's occupants stood and stared at him. Silence filled the enormous room.

Anlon glanced at them all, his anxiety rising. "I do not understand," he finally said. He could feel his face growing hot with embarrassment. After years of dreaming about being here, the moment he set foot at Dun Mor the first thing he did was show them what an ignorant herdboy he really was. "What is wrong? Please tell me what it is that I have done wrong, so that I can try to make it right."

The king looked down at him. "You have done nothing wrong, Anlon. Go with Fehin. He will see that you are cared for."

Fehin stepped forward and the king leaned down to say something quietly in the man's ear. "Keep him close," he said. "He is not to leave again." Fehin gave him a quick nod and caught Anlon by the arm.

"Come with me," he said. "You're home to stay this time."

Fehin marched him across the seemingly endless grounds of Dun Mor, holding firmly to Anlon's arm as though he were afraid his charge might escape. Anlon was torn between wanting to drink in the sights and sounds of the king's great fortress and stopping to demand that Fehin tell him what was happening. Why was he being treated so oddly?

At last he did try to stop, but Fehin pushed on like a bull, and in a moment had him inside one of the round houses. The door slammed shut behind them.

It was not too different from his family's round house—just larger, with a fire smoldering in the hearth in the center and iron tools hanging everywhere on the walls. Yet there were plates with old scraps of bread and meat stuck to them still sitting on the hearth, and the rushes were dry and brown and scattered with apple cores and gnawed bits of bone. It had the look of a house where no women lived. But right now, Anlon had too many questions on his mind to notice even the long-thought-of home of a warrior of Dun Mor.

Fehin released him and then looked him up and down. "You can keep your wristbands, but get that tunic off and burn it," he ordered. "I will give you one to wear. And a cloak. The sword, too. Take it off and hide it in the rushes."

When Anlon simply stood and stared at him, Fehin's irritation grew. "The tunic! The sword! Get them off, and get them off now!" He began walking around the hearthfire toward the other side of the house.

Anlon had had enough. He grabbed Fehin's arm, forcing the man to stop and face him. "I do not understand what is happening here!" he said. "Nothing is as it should be! Everything has changed from the way it was yesterday!"

All he got was a cold glare. "You're right. You don't understand. It was not yesterday that you are talking about. It was one year ago."

"One year ago? How could it be a year ago? It was only yesterday!"

Fehin jerked his arm away, throwing off Anlon's grip. "We tried to tell you," he said. "We told you that those who are taken by the Sidhe are lost to us. And so you were."

"Lost to us . . ." Again Anlon looked down at himself, at his leather clothes and fine bronze sword. He looked up at Fehin again. "Tell me what happened," he whispered.

Still glaring at Anlon, his eyes filled with both pity and contempt, Fehin sat down on the edge of the hearth. "You recall the last morning you spent with the Fianna. You packed up the camp, as always, and we set out for Dun Mor expecting to arrive that afternoon."

Anlon looked closely at him, and then shook his head. "I remember last night," he said. "It was the last evening

265

that I spent with you and all the other men of the Fianna. I remember the last camp that I made, but I never packed it up."

"*So.* You do not remember packing up the camp the next morning. Tell me—just what *do* you remember of the last night you spent among the Fianna?"

Anlon paused, trying to think as coolly as possible. "The last thing I recall . . . I went for a swim, and I saw a woman of the Sidhe, and I spoke to her."

He struggled to remember. "After she left, I went into the forest for . . . for something. A storm came up. . . . I had trouble finding my way back. . . . I could not find the campsite. I thought all of you had tricked me, that you had left for Dun Mor while I was away. I thought it was simply a part of the initiation into the Fianna, a test to see whether I could find my way alone to the king's fortress—and so I did."

Fehin continued to scowl at him. Anlon straightened. "It was only last night that all of this happened," he insisted.

"*It was one year ago!*"

Anlon stared back at him. "How could it have been one year ago? I remember nothing—"

"That is exactly right! You remember nothing! You have been among the Sidhe for one year, and they have kept your memories!"

Anlon began to pace on the worn-out rushes. "How can that be? How could I live my life for a year and not know it? How could I remember nothing at all?"

"Tell me. Where did you get that sword?"

Anlon looked at the shining bronze-trimmed scabbard. "I don't—I—"

Fehin slid down from the hearthstones. "We tried to tell you when you went away with them—those who are lured away by the Sidhe are lost to us. We were amazed when you came back here at midsummer, but you refused to stay."

"Midsummer?" Anlon paused and tried to think. "You are saying that I left last Samhain to join the Sidhe, returned here last midsummer, and then left to live among the Sidhe again?"

"That is true. That is exactly what happened."

Anlon shook his head. The world seemed to be spinning. "Why would you tell me such a thing?" he whispered, though he already knew the answer.

"I tell you because it is the truth." It was plain that Fehin's limited patience was near its end. "You have been wearing deerskin and eating thistles for the past year as a prisoner of the Sidhe. Somehow you escaped—or they grew tired of you and pushed you out—and you found your way back to us. I suggest that you simply be grateful that you are here, and that you take off that ripped tunic and put away that brittle sword before it breaks."

With that, Fehin walked away, rummaged through a heap of furs and fabrics on one of the sleeping ledges, and tossed a dark wool shirt and cloak at Anlon. "You can sleep over there, against the bare wall. We will call you when the evening meal is ready." He shoved open the door, walked out, and slammed the door shut behind him.

Slowly Anlon unfastened his finely crafted leather belt, and then he wrapped it around the dark wooden scabbard that held his sword. He carried it to the spot against the wall that Fehin had indicated was his and hid it deep under the rushes. Moving to the hearth, he pulled the slashed leather tunic off over his head and then put on the familiar wool.

He held up the old ripped tunic. Gazing down at it,

and thinking of the strange bronze sword now buried beneath the rushes, he wondered at how such a thing could happen . . . at how he could live for an entire year and not remember a single moment of it.

Anlon tossed the leather tunic into the fire, realizing that all he could do now was to go forward with his life from here . . . and simply accept that he would never know how, or why, an entire year had been stolen from him.

Chapter Twenty-two

Anlon rose eagerly the next morning, throwing off his dark wool cloak and getting up out of the rushes in the corner. He was determined to start anew from this very moment, putting the shocking discoveries of yesterday far behind him. This was the day he had waited for since he was a young boy—the day he would begin serving the king as one of the men of Dun Mor.

He was alone in the house. There was no sign of Fehin or the other two men who lived there. Over his deerskin boots and breeches Anlon pulled on the dark wool tunic Fehin had given him and fastened the cloak at his shoulder with a piece of thorn left in the coarse fabric.

He looked down at himself and sighed. All summer he had thought of how it would be once he reached Dun Mor. At last he would be one of the king's own men, accepted and respected as a warrior charged with protecting the great fortress and all its people.

And like the other men of the warrior class, he would look the part. He would wear fine new tunics and cloaks made from beautifully dyed wool, woven from four or perhaps even five different colors. He would have an iron sword to wear at his hip. And best and most important of all, he would be given the same training and duties—and privileges—as the rest of the king's warriors.

Anlon glanced at the place near the wall where he had slept. He could just see the gleam of the bronze-tipped scabbard within the rushes. He thought of getting the sword and putting it on, but hesitated. He knew the bronze weapon of the Sidhe would only be sneered at by the other men. Quickly he heaped the rushes up over it, hiding it well, then walked out of the house into the cool grey morning.

Excitement rose in him again as he walked across the busy grounds of Dun Mor. After spending the summer with just twenty-six other men, it was strange to see so many new people—and so many women.

The men of the Fianna had seemed to think of nothing else but the women of Dun Mor, and now he could understand why. These women were tall and strong and as graceful as young willow trees. Some had red hair and some had gold, and they either wore it drawn back from their faces with pins or hanging to their knees in long plaits.

As one young woman walked past, Anlon tried to catch her eye and smile at her; but she only stared at him, then whispered something to the older woman at her side as the two hurried past.

Some of the chill he had felt last evening began to steal over him again. Yet he pushed on, making a circle of the grounds that he might see all of Dun Mor—the many round houses, the enormous hall at the center, the ar-

moring house, the metalsmiths' shed, the pens and low
sheds thrown up against the inner wall for the horses and
cattle and sheep that would be spared for the winter.

At last he saw Fehin and Donn standing near one of
the wooden fences, talking to a small group of other
young men. Anlon recognized most as being part of the
Fianna and hurried to join them.

"Good morning to you," he said, glad—and some-
what relieved—to see familiar faces. "Niall, Galvin! I am
very happy to be here with you at last. It was a long
summer—"

They all turned and stared at him, their eyes flicking
up and down as they looked him over. "Longer than you
know," Niall murmured.

Anlon looked at them and drew a deep breath. It was
so difficult to remember that for him, the summer had
ended yesterday—but for the others, that same summer
had ended one year ago.

He smiled at Fehin and tried to concentrate only on
the present. "I am here to work. What can I do?"

Fehin glanced away. Anlon saw that he was looking at
a group of servants carrying wooden buckets and headed
for the gates. "Go with them. Do whatever they do." The
warrior turned and walked off. The others followed,
glancing briefly over their shoulders as they went.

Anlon could only watch them go. Making himself as
tall as he could, aware of the curious eyes that stared at
him from every part of the *dun*, he broke into a jog and
caught up with the servants just as they walked through
the gates.

The sun moved slowly through the cold grey sky that
day. Anlon stayed with the servants, as Fehin had ordered
him to do, and did whatever they indicated he should.

271

He was quickly learning that hardly anyone here, whether servant or king, would make an effort to speak to him. The people of Dun Mor would only stare with both pity and suspicion in their eyes.

Despite that, he followed the servants all day, helping to carry buckets of water and pick up kindling wood in the forest and even throw hay to the animals in their pens. When darkness finally came, the servants all went into the great hall and pulled the doors closed behind them. Anlon was left alone to roam restlessly through the torchlit grounds of the *dun*.

Eventually he found himself walking toward the far end of the fortress, around the last of the houses, and stopped abruptly. Near the curving, grass-covered wall were Fehin and Donn and Niall and Galvin, sitting together on a group of boulders and talking quietly in the darkness.

Anlon was about to turn and leave, fearing they too would simply look at him and refuse to speak—but then he stopped. He had spent an entire day in virtual isolation and did not want to spend the evening in the same state.

If they thought him strange, so be it. He was here to stay, and they would have to get used to him sometime.

Anlon walked to the gathered men. "Good evening to you," he said.

There was indeed a long, staring silence, but then Fehin spoke. "Good evening. Sit down, if you wish."

With a feeling of some relief, Anlon settled himself on a rock. "It is a beautiful night."

"So it is."

"This is a magnificent fortress."

"Magnificent."

He did not have to see their eyes to feel them looking at him out of the darkness. "Fehin, please tell me. Will

I be required to work among the servants tomorrow?"

Fehin paused, then shifted on his rock. "Do you object to working among them?"

"I do not. But—I came here to continue to serve the king, as I did all summer long as one of the Fianna. I want to—"

"You want to walk through our gates after vanishing for a year, and go on as if nothing has happened!" Fehin shook his head. "You are fortunate to be here at all, fortunate that our king has allowed you to stay. If you are told to help the servants, I should think you would be happy to do it."

Anlon tried again, working very hard to keep his fear and anger in check. "I have told you that I remember nothing of the past year. For me, I was riding with the Fianna only yesterday."

"But it was not yesterday! You were held by the Sidhe for a year! You came back to us last summer and went straight back to them again. Now you have returned yet again and claim to remember nothing, yet you look just as you did last summer. You wear nothing of our world— only the clothes and weapons of the Sidhe."

Niall added his rough voice to the conversation. "They kept you and taught you and used you for a year, and now they have thrown you back. How did you think we would respond to you?"

Anlon's jaw tightened. "I hoped that you would remember the service I tried to give to the Fianna when I rode with them. I hoped I could do the same as a warrior of the king—"

"*You are not a warrior of the king!*"

Anlon held himself very still and gazed straight at Fehin, though his anger flared. "I am well aware of that.

273

Look at me! I wear the clothes of both servant and Sidhe. I have no sword. Even my horse is gone."

He slid down from the rock and began to walk slowly across the grass. "You should know that I am the last to complain about hard work. And if serving the king truly means being a servant, then a servant I will be."

He paused, standing for a moment, and then looked away. "I would welcome hard work and heavy responsibility. It is far more difficult to be given only simple tasks to do, as if I had not the wit to do anything more. It is far worse to see the women turn away from me, to see the silent stares of the people as I walk past, to see the pity and curiosity in their eyes when they look at me as though I were a crippled child.

"And it is as painful as a knife in the heart when I see more than pity in some of those eyes. I also see fear . . . fear of someone who disappeared into the hands of the Sidhe for an entire year and then returned without any memory at all of what had happened."

Slowly Anlon walked back to them and sat down again. For the first time he allowed his own fear and despair to enter his voice. "It seems I am living between two worlds—two worlds which are both unknown to me. This place, the world of Men, is the one I long to be a part of, though it is suddenly new and strange to me. But when the people here look at me, they see only a man who has been under the spell of the Sidhe for a year, his life forgotten during that time."

He sighed and looked down at the ground. "It is as if they believe I actually am one of the Sidhe . . . even though I have no memory, no knowledge, no thought, of what life among them is like.

"I know nothing of them. I am a stranger in the world of Men. I cannot help but wonder if I will ever find a

place anywhere. I have even thought of slipping away and
trying to return to my family, but I know in my heart
that it would be no different there. They, too, would find
me a stranger."

· Anlon looked up again. "It seems my only choice is to
find a place here, at Dun Mor, at the place where I have
wanted to be for so long. Somehow I must prove to all
of you that I am a Man, a servant of the king, no different
from any of you.

"The Sidhe have stolen more than just a year of my
life. They have also stolen my future. I can see that I will
be little more than a servant here for far longer than I
thought."

His mouth tightened. "I can understand now—I can
see why men despise them."

He looked at Fehin and the others again, trying to
meet their eyes. "But all that is over now. I must find a
way to convince you that whatever enchantment the
Sidhe placed upon me is gone and forgotten, and I am
truly one of your own."

Over the next few days Anlon threw himself into the daily
routines of the fortress, determined to make himself a
part of it. He would have liked nothing more than to be
rid of the deerskin breeches and boots he had apparently
gotten from the Sidhe, but Fehin did not offer him anything else to wear and Anlon could not bring himself to
ask. So he draped his dark wool cloak so that it hung low
over the leather garb and tried to forget he wore anything
associated with the fair folk.

The bronze sword and carved wooden scabbard remained buried below the heaps of old rushes in the
house.

One evening, just three nights before Samhain Eve,

Anlon returned from yet another day of working along-side the servants. There was no more work to do in the fields, for the first and second harvests were complete; and so he did his usual simple tasks of hauling water and feeding the animals. But his spirits rose when, late in the afternoon, he looked up from throwing hay to the cattle to see Donn approaching.

"We are going out to begin cutting wood for the bon-fire," Donn said. "Fehin said you might wish to go."

Anlon could not help grinning. "That I would," he answered. "You are sure no one will object?"

Donn shrugged. "We can always use another strong back to carry logs," he said, then turned and walked away.

A short time later, Anlon walked to the gates, and he looked happily at all the activity around him. This was what he had always pictured when he thought of life at Dun Mor. He stood with a small group of the other men, carrying a good iron axe on his shoulder and ready to help with an important task. He was one of these people now, one of the king's own men.

He glanced over his shoulder, still smiling—and saw three young women smiling back at him.

Like the other women of the *dun*, they were tall and fair. Two had blond hair, plaited and shining, while the third had long red tresses like a fall of flame. All three looked familiar—he thought he had seen them among the other people of the *dun*, over the last few days—but now they stood together at the gates and looked only at him. Anlon grinned back, then followed the group of men outside into the beautiful evening.

The men worked hard to fell as many dead and damaged trees as they could find in the winter-bare forest. Some chopped off the branches and dragged them out in great stacks, while others formed lines, hoisted the heavy logs to their shoulders, and carried them to the bare ashen circle at the center of the field in front of the *dun*.

Anlon labored harder and faster than he ever had in his life, welcoming the activity and throwing himself into it to the fullest. Once again he was in the company of other young men, just as he had been with the Fianna, doing hard and satisfying work and enjoying the crude and lively conversation that flew through the forest all around him. And in the back of his mind he kept the image of the three laughing young women who had watched him at the gate, and he worked even faster at the thought that they might still be there when he returned.

It was not long before a small mountain of wood sat waiting for the torches of Samhain Eve. It would grow even larger tomorrow, but the men had made a very good start this evening. A couple even slapped Anlon on the shoulders as they walked past—and he knew that at long last, longer than he even knew, he had come home.

Darkness had fallen by the time they walked back to the *dun* and pulled the gates closed. As Anlon had hoped, he saw the three women a short way from the path. They stood huddled together, seemingly just talking among themselves, but then all three glanced his way and began to smile and laugh.

Anlon went back to the house just long enough to put away the axe and wash the grime from his hands, and then he went out to search for three lovely young women of Dun Mor.

Scahta wandered alone in darkness.

She was surrounded by wet trees and faint mist and heavy black night, yet she was barely aware of her feet touching the damp earth as she walked. She moved through the forest because she could not sit still, could not lie down to sleep, could not bear to exist in the company of others.

Her mind whirled, for she must not think of him—yet she could think of nothing else. Anlon. He was gone, far from her and from Caher Idir. The wind and the glamyr had taken away all memory of his time among the Sidhe. He was safe among his own people, and there he would stay.

It was the only way she had of saving his life.

Yet she began to wonder whether perhaps, by saving his life, she might still lose her own. Never had there been such emptiness in the place where once she had felt the steady beat of her heart. Never had she known that loss and pain could flare with every breath she drew.

She wanted nothing more than to call out to him, to ask him to come back, even though he would be caught up in a battle to the death if he returned. She knew he would be willing to come to her and join the fight her people were determined to make. He would not hesitate to come to her side no matter what fate might await him ... and he would even forgive her for having used her magic to send him away.

But ...

Anlon walked hurriedly across the shadowy fortress grounds. His way was lit by scattered torches and the high white moon, rapidly approaching fullness, its light rising and falling as the clouds flew across it.

The three women from earlier were nowhere to be seen. Where had they gone? Were they only playing a trick on him, laughing at his expense as so many of the people here loved to do?

Then he spotted them standing near the grass-covered outer wall, not far from the fences of the horse paddock. A trio of tall and beautiful women, smiling, giggling, whispering to one another—but with eyes only for him.

Anlon took his time approaching the little group, as if he were merely out for an evening stroll and had just happened to see them. "Good evening to you all," he said politely, and gazed at their faces in the wan moonlight.

"Good evening to you, Anlon." the red-haired woman answered. All three turned to him and lit up the darkness with their bright smiles.

"Such a beautiful night," he said, and all three nodded in agreement. "May I know your names?" he asked, and all of them laughed again.

The red-haired woman looked him up and down. "So, you truly remember nothing of the past year?" asked the red-haired woman. "Or is it simply that you do not remember us?"

"I'm sure it's just us he does not remember," said the taller of the two blondes. "Every man has a short memory when it comes to women!"

"And he has probably had a woman of the Sidhe to help him forget," added the other. "Or perhaps several!" They laughed again.

Anlon bristled at the mention of the Sidhe, but moved on. "It is true that I recall nothing of the past year," he admitted. "The Sidhe kept me all that time and then let me go when they grew tired of me, releasing all but my memories of my time spent among them."

He glanced at each of the three and offered them his kindest smile. "At first I could hardly believe such a story, but now I do not doubt it—for only the most powerful of spells could have made me forget about you."

The three giggled again and moved closer, surrounding him. "My name is Morrin," said the taller of the two blond women.

"My name is Orla," said the shorter blonde.

"And I am Keavy," said the red-haired woman. "You may not remember us, but we remember you."

Chapter Twenty-three

Scahta halted for a moment, leaning against the rough wet bark of a great oak, and closed her eyes. Even now she could see Anlon's soft hazel eyes, his smooth fair skin, his young and noble face. She could feel his strong and gentle arms holding her close, the tenderness of his lips against her neck, his long hair falling down over her cheek as he rested his face ever so gently against her head. Just the memory made her feel warm and protected, even in the cold damp night.

Her breath grew ragged and her eyes began to burn, but she fought to control her emotions. She dared not call him. He must stay safe. That knowledge was the only thing that gave her the strength to rise from her bed each day.

The wind stirred her hair.

She dared not call him.

"Anlon," she whispered.

281

Anlon looked closely at their faces, glancing from one to the other to the other. "You remember me?" he asked, and felt a stab of both joy and apprehension. He tried to give them all his warmest smile. "I hope it is a happy memory."

"Oh, it is," said Keavy.

"But it is a short one," added Orla.

"Perhaps this time you will leave us with a new one," said Morrin, and placed her hand on his arm.

They must have seen the confusion on his face, for they all laughed and Keavy spoke again. "It was last Beltane Eve, near the bonfire. We saw you at the edge of the forest and thought you were one of the Sidhe."

"It seems we were right!" said Orla.

"Man or Sidhe, we knew that you were handsome and kind," Morrin said softly, stroking his arm with her fingertips. "And we were quite happy to know that you had come here to live among us."

"At Beltane," he whispered, and looked at each of them again, searching their faces for an answer. "Beltane. Please, tell me. Did we . . . I mean, were we . . ."

"You managed to escape us!" said Morrin, with a laugh.

"It seems we frightened you away."

"You will not run from us again, will you, Anlon?"

He smiled, though it was not without a feeling of relief. "I have always loved the Beltane ritual, but I would not want to go through it without even knowing what had happened. I am glad that experience—if it happens, of course—waits for a time when I am certain I can enjoy remembering it."

"Oh, you will remember it, I promise you," said Orla. She, too, took hold of his arm, standing warm and close against his side and smiling up at him with gleaming blue eyes.

Anlon looked back into those eyes and was prepared at that moment to go wherever these three might lead him—to a house, to the cow shed, even into the cold bare forest—but as he looked into Orla's eyes, a strange image began to form in his mind.

He saw not her blue eyes, but dark ones, deep brown and glistening, filled with wisdom and concern. He did not recognize those eyes at all, yet it seemed that somehow he should.

Anlon blinked and the vision was gone. Once again he was surrounded by three lovely, eager young women with nothing in their eyes but lusty affection for him.

He turned to Morrin, who also had blond hair like Orla—but as he gazed at her it seemed he was mistaken about her hair. Instead of blond plaits he saw a fall of golden-brown, soft and shining and as light and warm as the air.

And when he looked at Keavy, he saw the hair and eyes and delicate face of a woman he had never seen before—a woman who could only be a lady of the Sidhe.

Quickly he backed away from his companions. As they released him, the vision faded, and all he saw were three bewildered young women staring up at him.

Morrin shook her head, and laughed a little. "What must we do to gain your affection, Anlon?" she asked. "You are a handsome young man. Any one of us would be happy to go with you . . . yet always you turn away from us. What is it about us that you do not like?"

"Oh," he breathed, looking at all of them. "There is nothing about any of you that I do not find attractive. It is just . . . it is just—" He closed his eyes tightly and pressed one hand against his forehead, trying to drive away the vision of the Sidhe woman that insisted upon appearing to him.

"The Sidhe have done more to me than I know," he whispered, his voice edged with bitterness. "I thought they had merely stolen my memories—but it seems that they have left me with something in return." He turned and moved away from them, half-walking, half-stumbling, for he kept his eyes closed against the vision of that beautiful, mysterious face.

Anlon found himself in the shadows, up against the curving outer wall. He opened his eyes and saw only darkness, faintly lit by the flickering torchlights among the houses and by the moon casting its glow behind the fast-moving clouds. And within his mind he continued to envision that face, that ethereal face that gazed at him and would not go away.

"What have you done to me?" he cried, his anger rising. "You have stolen a year of my life! And now, when I am drawn to the beautiful women of Dun Mor, you force me to see only the face of a Sidhe woman!

"Is this a curse you have placed upon me? Why would you do such a thing?"

In anger and despair, he struck at the grass-covered wall with his fists. And as he did he saw the vision of the dark-haired woman again. This time she turned to him and seemed to look straight into his eyes . . . and her face softened into a gentle smile.

Anlon stopped. As he looked at that face a sense of love and warmth settled over him, a feeling stronger than any he had ever known . . . one that made him forget all about the three young women who had flirted with him so briefly. He looked into the dark eyes of the lady of the Sidhe and forgot his anger and pain, and knew only a deep sense of love, longing, and loss.

Anlon woke suddenly, jarred back to consciousness by
Fehin slamming the wooden handle of an axe against the
hearthstones. "Let's go!" he shouted, as Anlon and the
other two men stirred and sat up. "We've got more wood
to gather for the blaze! Let's go!"

Only the faintest grey light filled the house; the sun
had not yet risen. Anlon got up from his bed of rushes
and took a few moments to ready himself to leave. There
was still bread and beef from last night's meal lying out
on the hearth, and he caught up what was left. The other
men were already out the door, and he started to follow
them—but then he glanced back at the rushes where he
had slept.

A sword rested there. A beautiful sword and scabbard,
made of bronze and bone and dark polished wood. A
sword he should be wearing, not hiding.

In that moment, he realized he no longer cared what
the other men might think if he wore a weapon of the
Sidhe. Pushing the rushes aside, he lifted out the sword
and strapped it on. Then he walked out into the soft grey
mist that preceded the dawn.

This day Anlon kept himself apart from the others as they
walked across the field to the forest, past the mountain
of wood they had started building the day before. The
others paid him little attention, for they were anxious to
be done with their work and return to the warmth and
safety of their great fortress.

This was Samhain Eve.

He had not brought an axe, for none had been left to
take by the time he had left . . . and he found that he had
no wish to carry the cold implement on his shoulder anyway. Anlon walked into the woods and began picking up

fallen sticks and twigs, and breaking off any dead and broken branches he could find. Once he had an armload of kindling, he carried it back to the waiting bonfire and dropped it there, then started back across the open field.

He was nearly to the edge of the treeline. The other men were working in the woods some distance away and paid him no attention at all.

He looked to the east, up over the treetops to the hills that rose behind them. In a moment, the sun would climb over those hills and touch the field and the *dun* with light.

His hand fell to the bone hilt of the sword. There was something warm and familiar about the bronze weapon. As soon as he touched it, a single word seemed to fill his mind.

Home.

He must get home. It was calling him. This was no time to be out alone, for tonight was Samhain Eve. The eastern sky was beginning to lighten and the dawn would help show him the way.

But—where was home?

Anlon took a few more steps toward the east, then stopped again. Why was it so hard to think? Home was at Dun Mor, with the Fianna and the king.

Yet somehow that was not right. He had only just arrived at the great earthen fortress and he was still a stranger there. Home was where it had always been, with his mother and father, brothers and sisters, and cousins in the *rath*.

But that was not right, either. He had left that place for another. He must find his home, but where was it? If not at the *rath* or Dun Mor, where was it?

Rays of light were beginning to show above the hills. Slowly, carefully, Anlon pulled the bronze sword out of the scabbard and held it in front of him.

There was a brilliant flash as it caught the first light of sun, the bronze so bright and gleaming that he was nearly blinded. Quickly he lowered it, turning the weapon so its light no longer shone directly in his eyes—and then he heard it.

It seemed the wind sang along the blade, whispering a single word to him in a voice that was beautiful, feminine, and familiar.

Home.

Scahta lay back on the furs and closed her eyes against the dawn. She had to rest, just for a little while, for she would need all her strength for the long night to come. She tried to still the clamor in her mind, which was filled with images of war and danger and death . . . and with memories of Anlon.

That was the most difficult, the most painful of all, and she knew she must find a place in her heart for those memories, or else the pain of her loss would simply overwhelm her.

He was safe. It was the only source of comfort on this day that might very well be the last for the Sidhe. Even if any did survive, even if she lived to see another morning, she knew that after this night nothing would ever be the same again.

Anlon stared at the gleaming sword.

Home, said the voice in his mind again.

He looked into the distance toward the east, toward the hills and the dawn.

Home.

This was the way. Whatever he searched for lay to the east. Gently he replaced the sword in the scabbard and turned his face to the rising sun.

With every step he took it seemed the sky grew brighter. Anlon experienced the strange sensation of not knowing where he was going, yet being absolutely sure this was the right way. He kept his hand on the hilt of his sword and walked on as fast as he could, for it was important he get there quickly. Someone was waiting for him.

A woman waited for him. And not just any woman. She was like no woman he had ever known before— beautiful, magical, ethereal, but real, real enough to touch and to hold and to love. She had dark shining eyes and golden-brown hair and a lovely, delicate face. She was a woman of the Sidhe . . . and her name was Scahta.

All of it came back to him now. He had lived with the queen of the Sidhe since last Samhain Eve at her beautiful home called Caher Idir. They had loved and trusted and married each other, but she could not make him her king because her people would not accept him. They despised and feared him because he was of the world of Men, not the Sidhe . . . yet he had learned he too carried the blood of the Sidhe, because his grand-sire had been one of their kings.

His heart beat faster. He remembered everything, even how Scahta had tried to send him away forever and make him forget her. She had done it because there would be a battle this night between Men and the Sidhe, a battle the Men would surely win . . . and she had chosen to never see him again if it meant that he would stay alive.

But his love for her had been stronger than her spell, and now he was going home to her, home to Scahta, home to face whatever awaited them together.

All day Anlon ran across the countryside and made his way through the woods. He let his heart tell him where the hidden stone fortress called Caher Idir rested beneath the trees. Soon now, he would be there, another turn, one more path, he was sure of it. . . .

Finally, as he reached the summit of yet another hill, he had to stop to rest. He was almost surprised to look up and see the sun had moved low in the west. He stood breathing deeply of the cold damp air, looking around at the sky.

To the west was the enormous red disc of the sun, hanging just above the horizon. To the east was the equally large yellow moon, sitting just above the hills.

It seemed he stood in perfect balance between the two great bodies. Facing the north, he closed his eyes and held out one hand to the moon and one hand to the sun, wishing he could halt their journeys across the sky and maintain the balance that existed at just this moment . . . maintain the peace, maintain Caher Idir, maintain Sidhe and Man side by side forever . . . but he did not know how to do that, and after a time he lowered his arms and opened his eyes.

Anlon turned eastward to face the moon. It rose higher and higher and in moments drove the sun from the sky.

The darkness had come.

"Samhain," he whispered.

Anlon struggled to find his way in the dark forest. All day he had felt certain he knew exactly where he was going, but his confidence had faded with the setting of the sun. Since then he had wandered in the darkness, suddenly unable to remember the way or find any trace of where he wished to go. So thick were the clouds that the stars and full moon were hidden, and he could see almost nothing.

He stopped, peering into the gloom and clenching his

fists in frustration. Which way was the path? Was there even a path at all? Perhaps he had only imagined there was. Perhaps he had imagined all of it—his life among the Sidhe, their magical hidden fortress, the beautiful lady who had loved him and made him her husband and even wanted to make him her king.

How could such things be real? How could he have believed them? Now he was lost in the night on Samhain Eve, led here by visions given to him by the Sidhe, visions no more real than the shadows cast by the racing moon.

Scahta sat alone in the newly fallen darkness, beneath an ancient oak a little distance from the gates of Caher Idir. She faced the black forest, her back turned to the stone walls, for she could hardly bear to look at the place that had always been her home.

The fortress was like a boiling cauldron on this night. It blazed with light from the fire leaping in the pit at the center, sending up showers of sparks. Clouds of black smoke, lit orange from below by the glare of the flames, hovered over the trees. Flaring torches moved and bobbed throughout the interior, carried by women circling and dancing around the warriors as they armed themselves for the battle to come.

And the sound, the terrible ominous sound from within the high stone walls, had started at sunset and continued to build. There was the crying and shouting and hissing voices, the roaring and snapping flames, and the rattle of the wind in the dry bare branches overhead. It set her heart to pounding with dread, and she had sought refuge in the forest in an effort to shut it out.

Her people had given her the chance to save them. She had failed.

Now she was alone, with only the black clouds and the

dark and windy night for company. She did not even have the one for whom she had risked everything, the one she had come to love, for she had sent him away and he would never return.

"Anlon," she whispered.

There was no path at all that he could see. He was lost in the night with no idea which way to go, just as he had been lost on the morning of this day—until he had drawn the sword.

Anlon's hand fell upon the bone hilt. It was the only chance he had. Slowly, deliberately, he drew the bronze blade, holding it high in front of him in the darkness.

At first he could see nothing. Then the wind stirred and the treetops clattered. The heavy clouds moved overhead and seemed to grow thinner; then silvery lines appeared among them as they broke apart and allowed the full white moon to shine down upon him.

The sword flashed and gleamed as the moonlight struck it. All around him the forest was lit by its glow—and there, directly ahead, he saw a faint mossy path.

Anlon lowered the sword and headed down the trail. He was almost home.

There was a soft sound from somewhere in the blackness of the forest.

Scahta looked up. Instantly she tensed. Everyone else at Caher Idir was within its walls, frantically preparing for the battle to come. None of her people were out in the forest on this night.

Yet there were footsteps walking toward her on the path.

Scahta stood and quickly moved into the darkest of the shadows. Her mind whirled with a hundred questions—

291

who could be coming here now? Had Men managed to find their hidden fortress? Were they bringing the battle here? Did they plan to attack the Sidhe in their own home, catching them by surprise and finishing them before they even knew what had happened?

She began to creep through the darkness. If she hurried, she could circle around to the back of the fortress—go inside through the horse enclosure—warn the people—

She stopped and listened again. There was only one set of footsteps on the path. This was no army.

Scahta turned and peered through the bare branches. Moving through the forest toward Caher Idir was a faint gleam of light, like a reflection of the moon on polished metal. And as she watched, her heart pounding and her breath catching in her throat, she saw Anlon step from the darkness of the forest, his sword held in front of him and casting a radiant light to show him the way.

He knew this fortress. He had seen it before, he had lived here for a year—yet tonight it was a strange and frightening place, blazing with fire and ringing with shouts and cries.

"Death to Men," chanted the voices within the walls. *"Death! Death! Death!"*

Anlon started toward the gates, but then stopped. They would kill him the instant they saw him, for to them he was a Man—an enemy. It would not matter to the warriors of the Sidhe that he had lived among them, that he knew their ways, that he carried their blood . . . not even that he had been the chosen consort of their queen.

They would kill him where he stood.

Scahta. He must find Scahta, but how? He dared not go inside. She would have no reason to come out. Perhaps when the army of the Sidhe marched this night, leaving the women and the children and the aged men in the fortress, he could slip in through the gates and—

There was a small movement off in the forest. Both hands on the hilt of his sword, he turned to get a better look.

He was prepared for an attack, but instead he saw a flash of bronze and gold . . . a fall of white . . . the glow of warm golden skin and then a pair of shining brown eyes gazing up at him.

Anlon put his sword away and went to her. After days of emptiness and nights filled with longing, at long last he held his true love in his arms.

Chapter Twenty-four

Scahta drew him close to her, deep into the sheltering blackness of the forest. For a long time they simply stood together in a powerful embrace, holding each other in a way that said more than any words ever could.

He held her close and stroked her hair, listening to her ragged breathing and feeling the swift beating of her heart against his chest. "You are real," Anlon whispered at last, resting his face gently against the top of her head. "Real, and standing here with me now. I was afraid I had only imagined you, that it was all just a dream or a glamyr. . . ."

Scahta looked up at him, her eyes bright and wet. "Do you doubt me any longer?" she asked. "I used all my strength, all the power I possess, to send you away from here and make you forget me . . . but you overcame even that to find your way back. If you are here, Anlon, it is only because you wanted nothing more in life than to be here."

"To be with you," he told her in return; then his throat tightened, and he could say no more. He could only hold her close, as if tomorrow would never come, as if they would never be separated again.

After a time Scahta raised her head and faced the stone fortress. "You see what is happening," she said. "You understand what they intend to do."

Anlon, too, looked at the glare of flame and smoke and sparks rising from the center of Caher Idir. "They mean to make war on the men of Dun Mor," he said. "Is there nothing we can do to stop this?"

"Nothing can stop them on this night. They are determined to survive . . . to make war on Men before they destroy us entirely. And I cannot argue with that."

"If they attack Dun Mor, they will lose all chance of surviving," he said quietly. "All of them will die. All."

He moved away from her and sat beneath the oak, closing his eyes as the weariness of the long, long day caught up to him. "Their king should be able to stop them. You hoped I would be a king, a king who could help your people to survive. It should be clear to you now that I am nothing of the kind. And for that I am sorry. . . . I am so sorry."

She took a step toward him and folded her hands. "Their queen was not able to prevent it, either. There are some things my people are determined to do for themselves—and not even their king or queen can stop them."

Scahta moved close enough to rest her hand on his shoulder. "You have done all you could, and more. No one alive, Man or Sidhe, could make a better king than you."

He reached up and covered her hand with his own. "Your people think differently. Even though I feel my home is here, and my love for you could never be matched . . . even though I carry the blood of a king of the Sidhe . . . your people look at me and see only a Man. They see an enemy.

"I am the enemy of both these people and of neither, and I do not know how to convince either one to trust me. Perhaps it is no longer possible. Perhaps it never was."

Her hand tightened on his shoulder. "I have struggled against reaching that conclusion—but I know in my heart that it is true."

Scahta moved away, pacing slowly in the darkness. "I am their queen, but I cannot stop my warriors from what they are determined to do. I cannot prevent what will happen on this night. I hoped to bring strength and survival to my people, but instead, I have brought them to this.

"Instead of new life, nothing awaits the Sidhe but oblivion. Instead of seeking warmth and safety inside their fortress on Samhain Eve, they prepare for the battle that will destroy them all."

He could feel her gaze, even in the darkness. "Yet I still clung to the hope that I might find a way to stop this, even in the face of certain destruction . . . and now that you are here, I will tell you I dare to hope again." She stepped toward him. "It has not ended yet. There is a long night yet to come. Perhaps—"

Anlon stopped her with his hand on her wrist. "It does not matter how it goes for your warriors tonight. The best the Sidhe can hope for is a truce of some kind with

Men, and how long could it last? I tried to persuade the men of Dun Mor to do just such a thing, and they simply laughed.

"The Sidhe have no chance, no chance, to defeat the Fianna in combat. The men of Dun Mor are larger, stronger, have more powerful weapons. . . . Your folk are like the bronze they wield—beautiful, but too easily destroyed. In this war, they will not prevail."

"I know this, Anlon." She glanced at the ominous light radiating from the fortress. "But they feel that they must go; they feel they have no choice but to defend their own as best they can . . . and die on their feet, if it comes to that. And you will go with them. I don't believe you would ever simply stay here, in the safety of the forest, and watch them as they go to meet their doom."

He closed his eyes, sighed. "Perhaps you are right. You know as well as I that I could not simply sit and watch them go." He sighed again and was surprised at the pain he felt even though he was once again with Scahta. "This is all my fault. My presence has caused such grief. . . . I must do what I can to put it right. I have no choice."

"Neither of us do, Anlon. Neither of us do." She looked up at him in the darkness, and it seemed to him that she smiled. "You are here because the two of us desire nothing more in life than for you to be here. First, I called you to my side . . . and then, when you should have forgotten everything and stayed to live a comfortable life with your people, you still found your way back to me."

His voice dropped to a whisper. "I hope you do not regret it, Queen Scahta. You have every reason to wish that you had never known me."

She looked up at him. "I do not regret it. You have done all you could to help my people, just as I have. And we shall continue to do so. But now things will take their own course . . . and you and I will face them together, for that is all that we can do."

He bowed his head, unable to face her. "If I cannot find a way to bring peace to both the worlds on this night, it will be our last together. Your folk and mine will see me as a traitor . . . and both will want my blood. I shall be an outcast, or I shall be dead." As he said them, his words sounded familiar—as if he'd said them before—but they were none the less true for it.

Scahta did not move. She hardly seemed to breathe for the space of several heartbeats. Then she ran her cool fingers feather-light over his cheek, and down his back. He kissed her and drew her close in a warm embrace.

And then the gates of Caher Idir were flung violently open.

Twenty-one men of the Sidhe stood gathered at the gate, surrounded by women with flaming, smoking torches. Gleaming and flashing in the torchlight were their great round shields of polished bronze, with concentric circles etched into them in the same design as Scahta's pins. The circles gave the shields the look of huge, staring, malevolent eyes. Each man wore a torque and a pin and a wristband of bronze, and at each man's belt was a sword in a finely wrought scabbard.

As the warriors marched out, they grabbed the torches from the women and began an ominous chant.

"*Slua Sidhe* . . ."

"*Slua Sidhe* . . ."

"Slua Sidhe," Scahta whispered, as they passed by. "The Trooping Spirits. They have become an army with a single purpose. They mean to attack, and nothing will stop them—nothing."

Anlon released her and looked down into her eyes. "I

told you that I would find a way to put this right. I will find a way to stop them, or I will die in their company."

He kissed her, then started to go after them—but Scahta caught his arm. "I will not let you suffer this alone," she said. "We will do this together."

Anlon shook his head, hardly believing what he heard. "You cannot mean that! Please—you are the queen! We cannot risk losing you, too. Your people who remain will need you, if there are any. You must stay here where it is safe—"

"I know what it is like to stay behind the walls and wait for the outcome of a battle. It was part of the story Greine showed to me. I will not go through that again." She held firmly to his arm. "We will do this together. If we fail, there will be nothing left to return to anyway."

He gazed down at her and knew in his heart she was right. "We will do this together," he whispered. Together he and Scahta walked into the darkness, following the glaring flames and hissing, malevolent voices of the Slua Sidhe.

Steadily, unswervingly, the Sidhe army moved through the woods on its way to the fortress of Dun Mor. A short distance behind them, taking care not to be seen or heard, Anlon and Scahta paused atop a rise and looked down into the valley below. All they could see were flickering pinpoints of flame and intermittent gleams of yellowish metal in the moonlight. Over it all rose the hissing, endless chant of the bloodthirsty warriors of Caher Idir.

It was an eerie sight combined with a frightening sound.

The white moon was high overhead when at last they reached the fortress. Anlon's heart pounded as he walked with Scahta to the edge of the surrounding woods. The Slua Sidhe put out their torches and gathered together close by.

Scahta caught hold of Anlon's arm. "Look," she whispered. And he, too, caught his breath as he looked out at the great fortress.

An enormous bonfire burned outside the gates, but aside from that, Dun Mor did not look the way it had on Samhain Eve last year. On this night the walls were bare and clean, as they were on any other night. There was no sign of the gruesome severed heads that had met them last year. The slaughtering of the animals seemed to have been completed earlier in the day, for the field was littered with new scraps of hide and fresh pieces of bone.

But something very strange rested near the center of the field, almost directly in front of the spot where the Slua Sidhe had gathered. There, just at the edge of the light cast by the bonfire, was a large stack of what looked like well-filled leather bags. They seemed to have been abandoned in the shadowy, windy field.

Anlon stared at the puzzling sight. It did not look like a mere pile of rubbish. The bags had been neatly and carefully stacked. And to his amazement, he realized that there was a neatly tied sheaf of ripened wheat atop the stack, surrounded by generous heaps of small green apples.

He caught his breath. "Scahta—earlier on this night, you said that you still dared to hope, in spite of everything. Now it looks as if you have reason to hope—and so do I."

Eagerly he pointed to the stack. "Look at that! Grain, and apples, and bags filled with food," he whispered, struggling to keep his voice down in his excitement.

"Stacks of food! And it must be meant for us—for the Sidhe. Why else would they leave it out here?"

Scahta could only shake her head, and Anlon could see the fear and suspicion in her eyes. "It may be a trap. It is still near to the walls, still close enough for a sling or a javelin to find its mark."

But Anlon allowed his hope to build until he fairly shook with excitement. "I asked the king of Dun Mor to do just such a thing as this, when I spoke to him on that day last summer! I did not dare to hope that he might listen to me—but perhaps he has! What else could it be? What else could it be?"

"A trap," Scahta whispered. But Anlon only unbuckled his belt and slid the sword and scabbard off of it. "I will go first," he said, handing the sword to Scahta and re-fastening his belt. "If anything is wrong, I will discover it before anyone else. But I don't think it's a trap! I think this is a new beginning."

He turned and faced the field. But before he could walk out, he saw three Sidhe men had already left the woods and were moving toward the stack.

Hardly daring to breathe, Anlon and Scahta hid and watched as the three small shadows crept over the field. Careful to keep the stacked goods between themselves and the fortress, the trio began to examine the leather bags. In a moment they returned. Each carried a heavy bag over his shoulder.

Anlon and Scahta crept closer to the other Sidhe. "Look at this!" the first warrior said, swinging the bag to the ground. "Wheat, dried and clean!"

"This one's got fresh pork, ready for salt and smoke," said the second man.

"And this," said the third, hefting the bag high where they could all see it, "is blackberry wine!"

The Sidhe crowded around, their excitement growing. To Anlon's great relief they began to lay down their shields, and then nine or ten started back out to the field to collect the rest of the leather bags.

He turned to Scahta, who held his bronze sword and scabbard tight against her chest, and placed his hands on her shoulders. "It has happened," he said, almost trembling with relief. "The king did listen to me. The men have chosen peace. They have chosen to live in peace with the Sidhe. Now no one will die . . . not Man, not Sidhe."

Scahta looked up at him, searching his eyes. "I want to believe that," she whispered urgently. Her glance moved toward the fortress walls sitting behind the bonfire. "Yet surely you cannot think that it would be so simple."

"It is over, Queen Scahta," he said to her. "Now we can hope. Now we can—"

Above the field came a rushing sound Anlon knew only too well. He and Scahta turned just in time to see a rain of javelins thudding into the earth and into the leather sacks.

The Sidhe scattered. They abandoned the food and wine and raced back to the safety of the forest. Only two lagged behind, pierced by the thrown missiles—one limping, one holding his shoulder. But those two were enough.

Instantly the woods filled with shimmering light as the Slua Sidhe drew their shining swords and raised their shields. Gleaming and silent, they moved out onto the field and faced the great fortress.

Anlon pushed Scahta behind him just as the gates of Dun Mor swung open.

Sixty, seventy warrior men moved on foot out onto the

field, dark shadows with heavy wool cloaks and dull iron swords and thick wooden shields. The king's men, the invaders, with their brute strength and sheer power and weight, had come to do battle against their elusive and ethereal enemy . . . had come to destroy a foe that had not even a third of their number, whose fragile bronze armor and weapons shone in the light of the fire and the moon, who had nothing on their side but desperation.

The king's men stopped just short of the bonfire. "Now begins the fourth harvest!" one of them shouted. "Now we take the blood of the thieving Sidhe for the very last time!" Some readied another volley of the cold iron javelins. The rest began beating their wooden shields with their iron swords, shattering the night with a terrifying, deafening clamor.

The Slua Sidhe were not intimidated. They halted on the far side of the fire and began to form a line, hidden behind shields that stared at their foes with glowering eyes. Some raised their swords and others pulled out deadly slings.

"It is over," Scahta said. "This is the end. It is death for the Sidhe." She seemed to melt away into the darkness behind him.

Anlon took a deep and ragged breath. "Not while I live," he said. In an instant he ripped off his tunic and raced out to the center of the field, where he stood beside the blazing bonfire plainly visible for all to see—directly between the determined Sidhe and the angry, murderous men of Dun Mor.

He feared he had as much chance of stopping them as he'd had of stopping the sun and moon, but as he stood in the light of the fire he realized the pounding had stopped. Both the king's men and the Slua Sidhe stood motionless. No doubt both sides were surprised to see a bare-chested Man—or was he one of the Sidhe?—standing alone and unarmed between them.

"Listen to me!" Anlon cried, turning to face first one army and then the other. "This cannot be settled with yet another battle. I have come here to offer you a single life. My life."

Both sides stood in silence. He rushed on while he still had their attention. "I offer it to whichever one of you wants it, to whoever will make peace by taking it!"

"You, the men of Dun Mor—will you kill me as the consort of the queen of the Sidhe, thereby ending their best chance for survival? You can then attack an outnumbered army, one that you have ruined and starved.

"And you, the Sidhe of Caher Idir—will you kill me as a Man, as one of those who has caused the death and destruction of your own? You can strike me down, I who am unarmed and ask you for nothing but peace.

"My life is offered up to whichever of you wants to take it. Let the bards sing of that through the ages. Let the poets glorify such bravery forever! The poets of both your people!"

The entire world seemed to hold its breath. The only sounds were the snapping of the bonfire and the sound of Anlon's own heartbeat in his ears. . . . *one . . . two . . . three . . .*

From the ranks of the men of Dun Mor flew a single deadly javelin.

Anlon could not bring himself to move. He had offered his life and he would not turn away now. With eyes wide open, he turned his face to the dark night sky and watched as the iron missile flew straight for him.

How slowly the world seemed to move, as he stood there waiting for death. It seemed he could hear the voice of Scahta, who stood now at the edge of the open field . . .

hear it on the wind as she spoke words he did not understand, words aimed at the airborne weapon, words that caused it to move slower and slower through the night until at last it hovered like a bird.

Suddenly the javelin dropped to earth—knocked away by the iron sword of a man, a huge bearded man with a heavy gold torque around his neck and a great wool cloak of purple and red and blue hanging from his broad shoulders.

A man who was the king of Dun Mor.

"Perhaps you are right," the monarch said, approaching Anlon with his iron sword in his hand. "Perhaps this is not a battle for armies. Perhaps this is a battle for champions."

Anlon could only stare at him, breathing deeply of the cold night air. "Send out your champion," he said at last. "I will stand for the Sidhe."

The king's glance flicked over him. Anlon drew himself up straighter, well aware that he was half-naked and unarmed. "Get your weapon," the king said, as he turned and walked back toward his waiting Men. "I will send out my own."

Anlon turned to face the Sidhe and found Scahta right beside him with his bronze sword resting across her open palms. He took it from her without a word; then she moved away, and Anlon stepped out onto the dark and shadowed field to face the king's champion.

Chapter Twenty-five

Shouldering his way through the crowd of men, raising his long iron sword and heavy wooden shield and striding out onto the dark field, was no other than Fehin. He struck his wooden shield hard with his sword and laughed aloud.

"Anlon! You have come back to us for a third time. Put down that child's toy you call a sword and come inside where you belong!"

Anlon shook his head. Gazing steadily at the man he had once served in the Fianna, he held out his Sidhe weapon with both hands on its hilt. "I will fight you if I must, Fehin. I will fight every man in Dun Mor if I must."

Fehin laughed again. "You don't even have a shield!"

"I have never used a shield."

"Well, then—let no one say I took unfair advantage of you." Fehin pulled his left arm from his shield's leather straps, held the shield up for all to see, and then threw it back at the feet of his companions-in-arms. He walked toward Anlon, his voice low and serious. "Last chance, boy. Yield now, or never."

"I fight for the Sidhe," Anlon whispered, through clenched teeth.

"Fight then!" shouted Fehin, and raised his sword. He charged straight at Anlon.

Anlon leaped out of the way of Fehin's first attack and found himself with his back to the army of men—and they would let him retreat no further. He raised his sword and used it to ward off Fehin's next attack, falling back as the bronze took blow after blow from the mortal's cold and heavy iron.

"Too easy, Anlon!" cried Fehin. "I don't even have to attack you—only your weak and worthless weapon!" Anlon swung hard and forced the warrior to jump back, but Fehin only laughed again. "Now, that will be something for the poets to make a satire about! The Man who was not a man, defeated by his own weapon!"

Anlon swung again and so did Fehin. This time their swords crashed together with all the force their wielders possessed—and this time Anlon felt his bronze weapon weaken and give way.

He stepped back, trying to adjust his grip and turn the bent blade—but as he did, Fehin struck a final blow that sent the sword flying from his hands.

It landed near the line of Sidhe. Fehin pushed the tip of his iron sword against Anlon's throat. "Yield now," Fehin growled. "This was never a match. You are no champion. Come with us now, or we will let loose our forces against this pitiful gathering you have chosen as your people."

Anlon clenched his fists. "If it will save them, even for

today," he said, "then I am yours to do with as you wish."

"Call it what you like," Fehin said. "This time you are here to stay." The ranks of his fellows began to open as Fehin turned his back and walked toward them, iron sword still in hand. He began to call out to them, asking if he should spare Anlon's life—or if he should strike him down as an enemy to mankind.

There was a touch on Anlon's arm. He looked down to see Scahta beside him, holding his sword. As he watched, she ran her hand down the bent and dented blade, and he saw it become as clean and straight as the day it had been forged.

He reached for it and gripped the bone hilt. Fehin continued to stride carelessly away from him, calling to the men of Dun Mor. In an instant Anlon was on him, flying onto his shoulders and pulling him hard to the ground, kicking away the man's iron sword as he fell and pinning the man to the earth with all of his weight.

Fehin struggled for breath and started to raise his head—but the sword at his throat held him still. "Shall I kill you?" Anlon said, his voice tight with anger. "Is such the only way to save a dying people? More death?"

"It is," Fehin hissed, glaring up at Anlon. "I will never yield as you did. Kill me now, champion of the Sidhe, or watch the king's warriors slaughter the last of your kind."

Anlon glared back at him . . . then pushed himself away, standing up and turning his back on his rival. He was aware of Fehin getting slowly to his feet but did not bother to look at him again.

Scahta stood waiting, fearless and noble, and Anlon got down on one knee before her. "Walk with me, Queen Scahta, if you will, for one last time." She nodded, and gave him her hand as he rose, and together they moved toward the lines of Men. Anlon held up the sword before them like a gleaming torch of bronze.

Baffled, curious, the men allowed them to pass, until Anlon and Scahta stood before the king of Dun Mor. Then the ranks of the mortals closed around them and the two stood surrounded by a cage of cold iron swords.

Anlon faced the king. "I could have killed your man," he said. "I had Fehin down at the point of my sword, and he would be dead at this moment if I had so chosen. But he is not."

"You are a Man after all, Anlon," said the king. "The battle must have brought you to your senses. You saw no reason to kill one of your own."

Anlon raised his head to look the king straight in the eye. "You are wrong when you say I am a Man. And you are right. I carry the blood of both Man and Sidhe. I am neither, and I am both."

He lowered his sword, turned it so the hilt was aimed at the king, and held it out. "If you still wish to take my life, if doing so will save this dying people, I ask only that you use this. Use the bronze of the ancients and not the cold iron of your making."

"And if you kill him," said Scahta, in a voice as cool and soft as the night air, "I myself will fall upon that same bronze sword. I, too, am both Man and Sidhe."

Carefully the king took the sword, holding it out to see it gleam in the firelight. He stared hard at Scahta, and after a moment he turned to Anlon.

"What is this hold they have over you?" the king asked. "Have they promised you wealth? Power? What?" He shook his head. "You seem to have nothing. But they must have offered you something of great value to earn such loyalty."

Anlon smiled, and turned to glance at Scahta. "So they

did." He looked up at the king once more. "When I came to Dun Mor one day last summer, your men believed the Sidhe had cast a glamyr to force me to stay with them. I told the men they were right—but the only glamyr placed over me was one of love.

"Oh, how they laughed at that! Not one took my answer seriously, not for a moment. But I can tell you there is no glamyr anywhere, among Man or Sidhe, that is more powerful than that.

"It is for love of this woman, this queen of the Sidhe, and the place I have found by her side, that I do not fear to stand before you now, no matter what you may choose to do with me.

"That love is what gives me hope that you, and all your men, will know at last that the Sidhe are not your enemy, but your brothers and sisters; not your competitors, but your ancestors, a simple people who ask for nothing more than to live unmolested in the shelter of the forest."

Shifting his grip on the bronze sword, the king turned to Scahta. With one hand he reached out to touch her shining brown hair. "It would be difficult to use this weapon—or any other—on beauty such as this. On one who could, indeed, be a sister to the best who live at Dun Mor."

He spent a long moment in thought; then he turned the sword around and offered the hilt back to Scahta. "Perhaps you will keep this instead . . . keep it safe within the shelter of the forest."

"I *will* keep it." Scahta took the bronze sword from the king's hands. "And we will return home."

The king of Dun Mor did not speak. The ranks of his Men parted once more, allowing Anlon and Scahta to pass. Anlon looked up as they walked out onto the empty section of the field and was nearly blinded by a shimmering line of light.

The Sidhe, carrying their polished bronze shields before them, surrounded their queen and her husband. Anlon looked back, saw the awed faces of Fehin and the others, then he and Scahta walked together within that shining protective circle. Inside of it, they reached the shelter of the forest, then vanished from the sight of men forever.

A gentle dawn had come to Caher Idir by the time the Sidhe returned home. The wounded were taken in to rest and heal, while the others gathered around Scahta and placed the overstuffed leather bags they'd taken at her feet.

The women and children and aged men all came out of their homes to join the warriors. Scahta stepped back against Anlon, thinking to allow her people to get at the sacks of meat and grain and wine. But to her surprise they did not even look at the food. They formed a circle around her and Anlon, and then Liath stepped forward.

"My lady queen," he began. "Once you brought before us one whom you said should be our king. Yet we were uncertain and demanded proof. I am here to say to you now that we have seen that proof. We believe Anlon is your true husband, and if you wish it, lady, I will have Anlon as my king."

And each and every one of the Sidhe who stood in the circle said the same.

"I will have Anlon as my king."

"I will have Anlon as my king."

"I will have Anlon as my king."

Scahta looked out at them, at her people, and could

311

not find the words to say, and so she turned and looked up into Anlon's eyes, and spoke to him.

"Anlon," she began, "once I told you that I would make you a king . . . if I found you worthy. Now, after all that you have done, I find that I cannot do that."

He stood very still, watching her, as did all of her people. All the world seemed to be holding its breath. "I cannot make you a king," she went on, "because you are already a king. You have shown that to us many times over in this past year, and you have proved it beyond a doubt on this night."

She smiled, gently, sincerely, and her voice rose so that all could hear her. "I would ask you instead if you would take your place among us as our king. I would ask you instead if you would make me a queen."

He went to her and gently took her hand, then got down on one knee before her. "Ah, Scahta, you have always been my queen, and always will be. And if you wish to call me a king, then a king I shall be . . . as long as I am your husband forever." He got to his feet as she raised him up, and the two drew each other close.

All around them the Sidhe knelt, quiet and at peace in the soft light of the dawn, watching as their king and queen embraced.

Epilogue

The seasons passed, as they always did, as the Wheel of the Year made its turn. But this year was not the same as any other.

The winter passed in silence and in peace, and the Sidhe had no fears of starvation. The food the men of Dun Mor had shared with them on Samhain Eve, supplemented by fish from the streams and trapped animals from the forest, would be enough to see them through.

When the trees above Caher Idir began to show the green tips of new leaves, the men of the Sidhe went to their hidden fields—but this year they dared to clear a few more trees, and make their fields a little larger, and plant a bit of wheat along with the barley.

Nealta and her bay companion both dropped their foals, two sturdy black fillies whose sooty coats would lighten over the years into grey. The Sidhe now had a herd of five horses, and to their daily work was added the task of driving the two mares, the two fillies, and the yearling colt out to graze each morning and bringing them back at night.

None of the Sidhe were heard to complain.

When the air softened and warmed, and the trees and flowers bloomed, the Sidhe walked without fear on the dappled forest paths. At first harvest, they had more grain to store in the souterrain pit than ever before, as well as a good store of hay for their horses. And when they found a little left for them in the fields of the Men, they cut the extra wheat quickly and cleanly.

The second harvest yielded several untouched stands of nuts and apples. The Sidhe collected it all and carefully stored it away against the coming winter. And when the skies turned cold and grey, and the trees went bare and the Samhain moon rose full, the Sidhe gathered together at the gates of Caher Idir and set out on the path that led to the fortress of Men.

They carried the leather sacks brought back from Dun Mor the year before—but the sacks were not quite empty. Each rattled a bit with small heavy objects that had been placed inside.

Near the back of the group, Anlon and Scahta walked together. In the soft woolen sling tied over her shoulder, Scahta held her infant son close to her heart and smiled up at Anlon in the moonlight.

In the darkness they approached the fortress. Its walls were clean and bare. The bonfire at the center of the field burned low, and beside it, again, were bulging leather sacks, all filled with fresh beef and pork and good blackberry wine.

The Sidhe placed their own leather sacks neatly beside the fire before lifting the new ones to their shoulders. As they walked back into the quiet darkness of the forest,

Anlon and Scahta glanced back at the stack they had left. One sack had fallen open, and in the fire's light was the bright gleam of golden wristbands and sun-discs and half-rings spilling out onto the field.

You cannot eat gold, Scahta had said. *It cannot give you children. It cannot give you love. But I believe we have found a use for it.*

The king and queen of the Sidhe smiled at each other. They might have asked for the gifts they had received, but had not neglected to leave something in return . . . just as an old and lonely woman of the Sidhe had once left something in return for a young boy's kindness.

On this day last year they had had nothing but hope, but now they had far more. A measure of peace existed between the two worlds and now the Sidhe-folk would never entirely disappear. They may be hidden in their beautiful fortress, but they would still live on, kept safe by Scahta, their queen, and Anlon, their king. Forever.

Janeen O'Kerry
QUEEN of The SUN

Riding along the Irish countryside, Teresa MacEgan is swept into a magical Midsummer's Eve that lands her in ancient Eire. There the dark-haired beauty encounters the quietly seductive King Conaire of Dun Cath. Tall and regal, he kindles a fiery need within her, and she longs to yield to his request to become his queen but can relinquish her independence to no one. But when an enemy endangers Dun Cath's survival, Terri finds herself facing a fearsome choice: desert the only man she'd ever loved, or join her king of the moon and become the queen of the sun.

___52269-1 $5.99 US/$7.99 CAN

Dorchester Publishing Co., Inc.
P.O. Box 6640
Wayne, PA 19087-8640   50

Please add $2.50 for shipping and handling for the first book and $.75 for each book thereafter. NY, NYC, and PA residents, please add appropriate sales tax. No cash, stamps, or C.O.D.s. All orders shipped within 6 weeks via postal service book rate. Canadian orders require $2.00 extra postage and must be paid in U.S. dollars through a U.S. banking facility.

Name_____
Address_____
City_____State_____Zip_____
I have enclosed $_____ in payment for the checked book(s).
Payment <u>must</u> accompany all orders. ❏ Please send a free catalog.
    CHECK OUT OUR WEBSITE! www.dorchesterpub.com

CELTIC FIRE
JOY NASH

In the wilds of Britannia, a fierce battle rages. Rhiannon, rightful ruler of the Celts, longs to see the invading Romans driven from her land. But when she is taken by the enemy, she can't deny her reaction to their compelling leader.

Having to look upon the ghost of his murdered brother every day is torture for Commander Lucius Aquila. But the strangely fascinating woman he captured has the power to make the visions disappear, and Lucius knows she can help him solve the mystery of Aulus's death. Even as he questions her loyalty, her courage and beauty hold him spellbound, and Lucius can only dream of the day he might succumb to her *CELTIC FIRE*.

- -

Highland Magic

Tess Mallory

The only thing more heated than Dr. Samantha Riley's arguments with time-traveler Duncan Campbell is the one passionate night they shared, a night Sam longs to forget. But when lightning strikes the time crystals at Jacob's Well, she ends up trapped in ancient Scotland with the irritating—and irresistible—Scotsman.

Mistaken for the Queen of the Fairies, Sam claims Duncan as her consort, and delights in ordering him around...until she learns he is there to save a Scottish princess. If he is, why does he take Sam in his arms nightly, stealing kisses and caresses, before turning away with a groan? The whole tangle makes her head—and heart—ache.

TRAVELER
MELANIE JACKSON

Evil forces are on the rise, and Io is part of a secret association dedicated to stopping them. Lutins are replacing society's bigwigs—no one is safe. The only solution is to travel beneath the Motor City into the hordes thronging Goblin Town, rendezvous with Jack Frost and uncover the plot.

The quest will force Io through labyrinths of vice and challenge every aspect of her incomplete training. And if enemies aren't enough, her ally will imperil her heart. Jack Frost is much more than a simple sorceror: He rules the realms of love and death. Yet in Jack's hands, a little death could be a very, very good thing.